Beginner's Guide to

Quintessence

Beginner's Guide to Quintessence

Copyright © 2015 J.C. Nusbaum

For more, visit www.eltaninpublishing.com

ISBN 978-0692340820 (paperback)

Cover art and design by Hermes Mercurius Trismegistus

Beginner's Guide to

Quintessence

J.C. Nusbaum & Nicholas Flamel

Blessed is the lion which the man eats, and the lion will become man; and cursed is the man whom the lion eats, and the lion will become man.

Thomas 2:7

Contents Page

Introduction by Sir Isaac Newton

The nature of things is more securely & naturally deduced from their operacions one upon another than upon our senses. And when by the former Experiments we have found the nature of bodys, by the latter we may more clearely find the nature of our senses. But so long as we are ignorant of the nature of both soule & body we cannot clearely distinguish how far an act of sensation proceeds from the soule & how far from the body &c.

The action of the soule and of resurrection is continued either by the aire or by force imprest. Or by the naturall gravity in the body moved. For it is certain we preferre to continue through aire. Indeed Quintessence may only be achieved by such a Conjuntio of opposites.

Why are coles black and ashes white.

No colour will arise out of the mixture of pure black & white for then pictures drawne with inke would be coloured or printed would seeme coloured at a distance & the verges of shadows would be coloured. & lamb black & spanish whiteing would produce colours whence they cannot arise from more or lesse reflection of light or shadows mixed with light.

Of touching, a man hath beene deprived of his feeling.

Things out of mind are remembred sometimes by meeting with other things of like nature: as dreames never thought upon in that morning at the time of awakeing are remembred by some actions of the like nature met withall in the day time.

Forgetfullnesse ariseth sometimes out of the want of thinking of things. Things seene & words heard at the same distance are distinctly remembred. So are distance & widenes or extension & bignesse. So are things which enter not the sences as meditations, thoughts, dreames, & that a man hath remembred.

Meditations reminde a man of actions, & actions of meditatio. Colours, actions, sounds loud softly, high & low, Time as that things were done together or so long after one another reconing how long since such a thing done by counting the time from one action to another untill the present time.

A man cannot remember what hee never thought uppon as a blow or prick or noise in his sleepe the things & sounds which hee heares & sees but minds not.

Objects from either eye or eare affect the memory alike. The same thing seene or heard from divers places or distances acte alike on the memory.

Things done in the same time helpe the memory of one another If memory bee done by characters in the braine yet the soule remembers too, for shee must remember those characters.

And yet we can fancie the thing we see in a right posture with the heeles upward. Phantasie is helped by good aire fasting moderate wine. But spoiled by drunkenesse, Gluttony, too much study, (whence &

from extreame passion cometh madnesse), of the spirits.

Meditation heates the brain in some to distraction in others to an akeing & dizzinesse.

The boyling blood of youth puts the spirits upon too much motion or else causeth too many spirits. but could age make the brain either too dry to move roundly through or else is defective of Spirits yet theire memory is bad.

A man by heitning his fansie & immagination may bind anothers to thinke what hee thinks as in the story of the Oxfordscollar in Glanvill Van of Dogmatizing.

When I had looked upon the Sun all light coloured bodys appeared red & darke coloured bodys appeared blew. If I lookedon white paper with my bare eye it looked red, but if I looked on it through a very little hole so that but a little light could come to my eye from the paper it looked greene. Hence the orderred colour of truths.

Whither this guide finds our soule, it is a call to Quintessence that may rightly be met. Still fewe will follow either by Some corporeall efflux or incorporeall one or nothing.

Quintessence of the soule is for each to Sublimate.

Sir Isaac Newton

Montpelier
January 2015

TO OUR READERS

Curiously enough, the events that have taken place in the last few years in the great outside world have brought forth both the need and the possibility of the ready guide you now hold in your hands. You are invited to explore with this guide and embark on a marvelous journey that began eons ago at the advent of your soul's arrival.

However, this guide is really more strange and unusual than anything you have likely read or heard about. The order to follow will be unique to you, and you must puzzle out many of the passages to experience many others described herein.

We hope it appeals to your love of adventure and transcendence. Quintessence is to be taken lightly. Be curious and playful, and allow yourself to falter and set in again.

Yours faithfully,

Jos. Nusbaum & Nich. Flamel

"Three Chimneys"
  at Charlotte
  in Vermont
  2015

Four Causes

I.   Material Cause: that out of which something is made

II.   Efficient Cause: that by which something is made

III.   Formal Cause: that into which something is made

IV.   Final Cause: that for the sake of which something is made

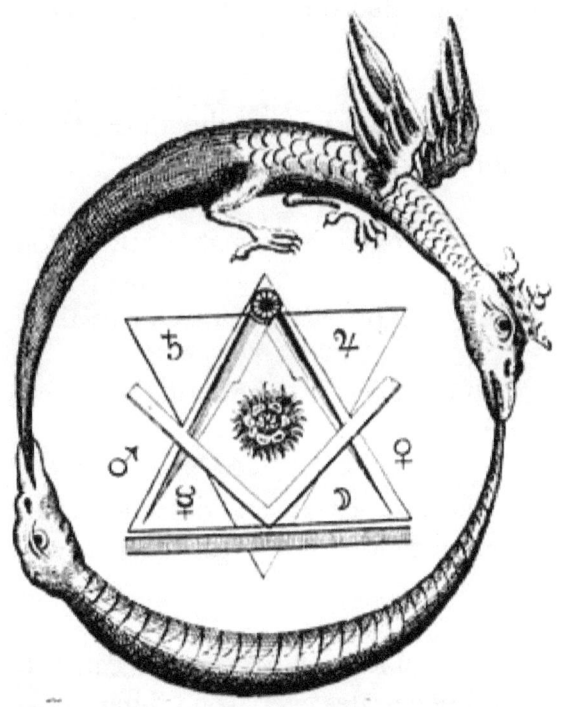

Fire is the original Cause; the Sun is that; so is Air; so is the Moon; such, too, is that pure Brahm, and those waters, and that Lord of creatures. Moments and other measures of time proceeded from that effulgent Person, whom none can apprehend as an object of Perception, above, around, or in the midst.

The Emerald Tablet

∞ I speak not fiction, but what is certain and most true.

∞ What is below is like that which is above, and what is above is like that which is below for performing the miracle of one thing.

∞ And as all things were produced from One by the Mediation of One, so all things are produced from this One thing by adaptation.

∞ Its father is the Sun, its mother was the Moon, the wind carried it in its belly, its nurse is the Earth.

∞ It is the cause of all perfection throughout the whole world.

∞ Its power is perfect if it be changed into the earth.

∞ Separate the earth from the fire, the subtle from the gross, gently and with judgment.

∞ It ascends from earth to heaven, and descends again to earth, thus you will possess the glory of the whole World and all obscurity will fly away.

∞ This thing is the fortitude of all fortitude, because it overcomes all subtle things, and penetrates every solid thing.

∞ Thus were all things created.

∞ Thence proceed wonderful adaptations which are produced in this way.

∞ Therefore am I possessing the three parts of the philosophy of the whole World.

☉   What I had to say concerning the operation of the Sun is complete.

ΜΥΣΤΕΣ (MYSTES)

In Greek: to close the lips.

The experience is ineffable.

It is beyond words.

In the original Greek practices, you do not speak of this. It remains in *mystery*. Mysticism can be an exploration of consciousness. This is not evident today, but remains in Interspirituality (movement away from segregation, divisions of sex, etc.).

The spiritual impulse is as strong as the need for sexual passion.

The Self is the inner divine core (the omniscient pleroma).

Love = Attraction (Gravity)

"The divine is the love that moves the stars."

~Dante

Your Quintessential Experience Entails:

1. Being Present in the now
2. Vacatio (emptying)
3. Paradox
4. Obliterate/intensify time & sensation
5. Heightened awareness
6. Panentheistic connectedness
7. Change in ethical behavior
8. Bliss & Ecstasy
9. π

1. Separatio

Never forget that the key to the situation lies in the will and not in the imagination.

Evelyn Underhill

The most highly developed branches of the human family have in common one peculiar characteristic. They tend to produce—sporadically it is true, and often in the teeth of adverse external circumstances—a curious and definite type of personality; a type which refuses to be satisfied with that which other men call experience, and is inclined, in the words of its enemies, to "deny the world in order that it may find reality." We meet these persons in the east and the west; in the ancient, mediaeval, and modern worlds. Their one passion appears to be the prosecution of a certain spiritual and intangible quest: the finding of a "way out" or a "way back" to some desirable state in which alone they can satisfy their craving for absolute truth. This quest, for them, has constituted the whole meaning of life. They have made for it without effort sacrifices which have appeared enormous to other men: and it is an indirect testimony to its objective actuality, that whatever the place or period in which they have arisen, their aims, doctrines and methods have been substantially the same. Their experience, therefore, forms a body of evidence, curiously self-consistent and often mutually explanatory, which must be taken into account before we can add up the sum of the energies and potentialities of the human spirit, or reasonably speculate on its relations to the unknown world which lies outside the boundaries of sense.

All men, at one time or another, have fallen in love with the veiled Isis whom they call Truth. With most, this has been a passing passion: they have early seen its hopelessness and turned to more practical things. But others remain all their lives the devout lovers of reality: though the manner of their love, the vision which they make to themselves of the beloved object varies enormously. Some see Truth as Dante saw Beatrice: an adorable yet intangible figure, found in this world yet revealing the next. To others she seems rather an evil but an irresistible enchantress: enticing, demanding payment and betraying her lover at the last. Some have seen her in a test tube, and some in a poet's dream: some before the altar, others in the slime. The extreme pragmatists have even sought her in the kitchen; declaring that she may best be recognized by her utility. Last stage of all, the philosophic skeptic has comforted an unsuccessful courtship by assuring himself that his mistress is not really there.

Under whatsoever symbols they have objectified their quest, none of these seekers have ever been able to assure the world that they have found, seen face to face, the Reality behind the veil. But if we may trust the reports of the mystics—and they are reports given with a strange accent of certainty and good faith—they have succeeded where all these others have failed, in establishing immediate communication between the spirit of man, entangled as they declare amongst material things, and that "only Reality," that immaterial and final Being, which some philosophers call the Absolute, and most theologians call God. This, they say—and here many who are not mystics agree with them—is the hidden Truth which is the object of man's craving; the only satisfying goal of his quest. Hence, they should claim from us the same attention that we give to other explorers of countries in which we are not competent to adventure ourselves; for the mystics are the pioneers of the spiritual world, and we have no right to deny validity to their discoveries, merely because we lack the opportunity or the courage necessary to those who would prosecute such explorations for themselves.

It is the object of this book to attempt a description, and also—though this is needless for those who read that description in good faith—a justification of these experiences and the conclusions which have been drawn from them. So remote, however, are these matters from our ordinary habits of thought, that their investigation entails, in those who would attempt to understand them, a definite preparation: a purging of the intellect. As with those who came of old to the Mysteries, purification is here the gate of knowledge. We must come to this encounter with minds cleared of prejudice and convention, must deliberately break with our inveterate habit of taking the "visible world" for granted; our lazy assumption that somehow science is "real" and metaphysics is not. We must pull down our own card houses—descend, as the mystics say, "into our nothingness"—and examine for ourselves the foundations of all possible human experience, before we are in a position to criticize the buildings of the visionaries, the poets, and the saints. We must not begin to talk of the unreal world of these dreamers until we have discovered—if we can—a real world with which it may be compared.

Such a criticism of reality is of course the business of philosophy. I need hardly say that this book is not written by a philosopher, nor is it addressed to students of that imperial science. Nevertheless, amateurs though we be, we cannot reach our starting-point without trespassing to some extent on philosophic ground. That ground covers the whole area of first principles: and it is to first principles that we must go, if we would understand the true significance of the mystic type.

Let us then begin at the beginning: and remind ourselves of a few of the trite and primary facts which all practical persons agree to ignore. That beginning, for human thought, is of course the I, the Ego, the self-conscious subject which is writing this book, or the other self-conscious subject which is reading it; and which declares, in the teeth of all arguments, I AM. Here is a point as to which we all feel quite sure. No metaphysician has yet shaken the ordinary individual's belief in his own existence. The uncertainties only begin for most of us when we ask what else is .

To this I, this conscious self "imprisoned in the body like an oyster in his shell," come, as we know, a constant stream of messages and experiences. Chief amongst these are the stimulation of the tactile nerves whose result we call touch, the vibrations taken up by the optic nerve which we call light, and those taken up by the ear and perceived as sound.

What do these experiences mean? The first answer of the unsophisticated Self is, that they indicate the nature of the external world: it is to the "evidence of her senses" that she turns, when she is asked what the world is like. From the messages received through those senses, which pour in on her whether she will or no, battering upon her gateways at every instant and from every side, she constructs that "sense-world" which is the "real and solid world" of normal men. As the impressions come in—or rather those interpretations of the original impressions which her nervous system supplies—she pounces on them, much as players in the spelling game pounce on the separate letters dealt out to them. She sorts, accepts, rejects, combines: and then triumphantly produces from them a "concept" which is, she says, the external world. With an enviable and amazing simplicity she attributes her own sensations to the unknown universe. The stars, she says, are bright; the grass is green. For her, as for the philosopher Hume, "reality consists in impressions and ideas."

It is immediately apparent, however, that this sense-world, this seemingly real external universe—though it may be useful and valid in other respects—cannot be the external world, but only the Self's projected picture of it. It is a work of art, not a scientific fact; and, whilst it may well possess the profound significance proper to great works of art, is dangerous if treated as a subject of analysis. Very slight investigation shows that it is a picture whose relation to reality is at best symbolic and approximate, and which would have no meaning for selves whose senses, or channels of communication, happened to be arranged upon a different plan. The evidence of the senses, then, cannot be accepted as evidence of the nature of ultimate reality: useful servants, they are dangerous guides. Nor can their testimony disconcert those seekers whose reports they appear to contradict.

The conscious self sits, so to speak, at the receiving end of a telegraph wire. On any other theory than that of mysticism, it is her one channel of communication with the hypothetical "external world." The receiving instrument registers certain messages. She does not know, and—so long as she remains dependent on that instrument—never can know, the object, the reality at the other end of the wire, by which those messages are sent; neither can the messages truly disclose the nature of that object. But she is justified on the whole in accepting them as evidence that something exists beyond herself and her receiving instrument. It is obvious that the structural peculiarities of the telegraphic instrument will have exerted a modifying effect upon the message. That which is conveyed as dash and dot, colour and shape, may have been received in a very different form. Therefore this message, though it may in a partial sense be relevant to the supposed reality at the other end, can never be adequate to it. There will be fine vibrations which it fails to take up, others which it confuses together. Hence a portion of the message is always lost; or, in other language, there are aspects of the world which we can never know.

The sphere of our possible intellectual knowledge is thus strictly conditioned by the limits of our own personality. On this basis, not the ends of the earth, but the external termini of our own sensory nerves, are the termini of our explorations: and to "know oneself" is really to know one's universe. We are locked up with our receiving instruments: we cannot get up and walk away in the hope of seeing whither the lines lead. Eckhart's words are still final for us: "the soul can only approach created things by the voluntary reception of images." Did some mischievous Demiurge choose to tickle our sensory apparatus in a new way, we should receive by this act a new universe.

William James once suggested as a useful exercise for young idealists, a consideration of the changes which would be worked in our ordinary world if the various branches of our receiving instruments exchanged duties; if, for instance, we heard all colours and saw all sounds. Such a remark throws a sudden light on the strange and apparently insane statement of the visionary Saint-Martin, "I heard flowers that sounded, and saw notes that shone"; and on the reports of other mystics concerning a rare moment of consciousness in which the senses are fused into a single and ineffable act of perception, and colour and sound are known as aspects of one thing.

Since music is but an interpretation of certain vibrations undertaken by the ear, and colour an interpretation of other vibrations performed by the eye, this is less mad than it sounds and may yet be brought within the radius of physical science. Did such an alteration of our senses take place the world would still send us the same messages—that strange unknown world from which, on this hypothesis, we are hermetically sealed—but we should interpret them differently. Beauty would still be ours, though speaking another tongue. The bird's song would then strike our retina as a pageant of colour: we should see the magical tones of the wind, hear as a great fugue the repeated and harmonized greens of the forest, the cadences of stormy skies. Did we realize how slight an adjustment of our organs is needed to initiate us into such a world, we should perhaps be less contemptuous of those mystics who tell us that they apprehended the Absolute as "heavenly music" or "Uncreated Light": less fanatical in our determination to make the solid "world of common sense" the only standard of reality. This "world of common sense" is a conceptual world. It may represent an external universe: it certainly does represent the activity of the human mind. Within that mind it is built up: and there most of us are content "at ease for aye to dwell," like the soul in the Palace of Art.

A direct encounter with absolute truth, then, appears to be impossible for normal non-mystical consciousness. We cannot know the reality, or even prove the existence, of the simplest object: though this is a limitation which few people realize acutely and most would deny. But there persists in the race a type of personality which does realize this limitation: and cannot be content with the sham realities that furnish the universe of normal men. It is necessary, as it seems, to the comfort of persons of this type to form for themselves some image of the Something or Nothing which is at the end of their telegraph lines: some "conception of being," some "theory of knowledge." They are tormented by the Unknowable, ache for first principles, demand some background to the shadow show of things. In so far as man possesses this temperament, he hungers for reality, and must satisfy that hunger as best he can: staving off starvation, though he many not be filled.

It is doubtful whether any two selves have offered themselves exactly the same image of the truth outside their gates: for a living metaphysic, like a living religion, is at bottom a strictly personal affair—a matter, as William James reminded us, of vision rather than of argument. Nevertheless such a living metaphysic may—and if sound generally does—escape the stigma of subjectivism by outwardly attaching itself to a traditional School; as personal religion may and should outwardly attach itself to a traditional church. Let us then consider shortly the results arrived at by these traditional schools—the great classic theories concerning the nature of reality. In them we see crystallized the best that the human intellect, left to itself, has been able to achieve.

The most obvious and generally accepted explanation of the world is of course that of Naturalism, or naive Realism: the point of view of the plain man. Naturalism states simply that we see the real world, though we may not see it very well. What seems to normal healthy people to be there, is approximately there. It congratulates itself on resting in the concrete; it accepts material things as real. In other words, our corrected and correlated sense impressions, raised to their highest point of efficiency, form for it the only valid material of knowledge: knowledge itself being the classified results of exact observation.

Such an attitude as this may be a counsel of prudence, in view of our ignorance of all that lies beyond: but it can never satisfy our hunger for reality. It says in effect, "The room in which we find ourselves is fairly comfortable. Draw the curtains, for the night is dark: and let us devote ourselves to describing the furniture." Unfortunately, however, even the furniture refuses to accommodate itself to the naturalistic view of things. Once we begin to examine it attentively, we find that it abounds in hints of wonder and mystery: declares aloud that even chairs and tables are not what they seem.

We have seen that the most elementary criticism, applied to any ordinary object of perception, tends to invalidate the simple and comfortable creed of "common sense"; that not merely faith but gross credulity, is needed by the mind which would accept the apparent as the real. I say, for instance, that I "see" a house. I can only mean by this that the part of my receiving instrument which undertakes the duty called vision is affected in a certain way, and arouses in my mind the idea "house." The idea "house" is now treated by me as a real house, and my further observations will be an unfolding, enriching, and defining of this image. But what the external reality is which evoked the image that I call "house," I do not know and never can know. It is as mysterious, as far beyond my apprehension, as the constitution of the angelic choirs. Consciousness shrinks in terror from contact with the mighty verb "to be." I may of course call in one sense to "corroborate," as we trustfully say, the evidence of the other; may approach the house, and touch it. Then the nerves of my hand will be affected by a sensation which I translate as hardness and solidity; the eye by a peculiar and wholly incomprehensible sensation called redness; and from these purely personal changes my mind constructs and externalizes an idea which it calls red bricks. Science herself, however, if she be asked to verify the reality of these perceptions, at once declares that though the material world be real, the ideas of solidity and colour are but hallucination. They belong to the human animal, not to the physical universe: pertain to accident not substance, as scholastic philosophy would say.

"The red brick," says Science, "is a mere convention. In reality that bit, like all other bits of the universe, consists, so far as I know at present, of innumerable atoms whirling and dancing one about the other. It is no more solid than a snowstorm. Were you to eat of Alice-in-Wonderland's mushroom and shrink to the dimensions of the infra-world, each atom with its electrons might seem to you a solar system and the red brick itself a universe. Moreover, these atoms themselves elude me as I try to grasp them. They are only manifestations of something else. Could I track matter to its lair, I might conceivably discover that it has no extension, and become an idealist in spite of myself. As for redness, as you call it, that is a question of the relation between your optic nerve and the light waves which it is unable to absorb. This evening, when the sun slopes, your brick will probably be purple, a very little deviation from normal vision on your part would make it green. Even the sense that the object of perception is outside yourself may be fancy; since you as easily attribute this external quality to images seen in dreams, and to waking hallucinations, as you do to those objects which, as you absurdly say, are 'really there.'"

Further, there is no trustworthy standard by which we can separate the "real" from the "unreal" aspects of phenomena. Such standards as exist are conventional: and correspond to convenience, not to truth. It is no argument to say that most men see the world in much the same way, and that this "way" is the true standard of reality: though for practical purposes we have agreed that sanity consists in sharing the hallucinations of our neighbours. Those who are honest with themselves know that this "sharing" is at best incomplete. By the voluntary adoption of a new conception of the universe, the fitting of a new alphabet to the old Morse code—a proceeding which we call the acquirement of knowledge—we can and do change to a marked extent our way of seeing things: building up new worlds from old sense impressions, and transmuting objects more easily and thoroughly than any magician. "Eyes and ears," said Heracleitus, "are bad witnesses to those who have barbarian souls": and even those whose souls are civilized tend to see and hear all things through a temperament. In one and the same sky the poet may discover the habitation of angels, whilst the sailor sees only a promise of dirty weather ahead. Hence, artist and surgeon, Christian and rationalist, pessimist and optimist, do actually and truly live in different and mutually exclusive worlds, not only of thought but also of perception. Only the happy circumstance that our ordinary speech is conventional, not realistic, permits us to conceal from one another the unique and lonely world in which each lives. Now and then an artist is born, terribly articulate, foolishly truthful, who insists on "Speaking as he saw." Then other men, lapped warmly in their artificial universe, agree that he is mad: or, at the very best, an "extraordinarily imaginative fellow."

Moreover, even this unique world of the individual is not permanent. Each of us, as we grow and change, works incessantly and involuntarily at the re-making of our sensual universe. We behold at any specific moment not "that which is," but "that which we are", and personality undergoes many readjustments in the course of its passage from birth through maturity to death. The mind which seeks the Real, then, in this shifting and subjective "natural" world is of necessity thrown back on itself: on images and concepts which owe more to the "seer" than to the "seen." But Reality must be real for all, once they have found it: must exist "in itself" upon a plane of being unconditioned by the perceiving mind. Only thus can it satisfy that mind's most vital instinct, most sacred passion—its "instinct for the Absolute," its passion for truth.

You are not asked, as a result of these antique and elementary propositions, to wipe clean the slate of normal human experience, and cast in your lot with intellectual nihilism. You are only asked to acknowledge that it is but a slate, and that the white scratches upon it which the ordinary man calls facts, and the Scientific Realist calls knowledge, are at best relative and conventionalized symbols of that aspect of the unknowable reality at which they hint. This being so, whilst we must all draw a picture of some kind on our slate and act in relation therewith, we cannot deny the validity—though we may deny the usefulness—of the pictures which others produce, however abnormal and impossible they may seem; since these are sketching an aspect of reality which has not come within our sensual field, and so does not and cannot form part of our world. Yet as the theologian claims that the doctrine of the Trinity veils and reveals not Three but One, so the varied aspects under which the universe appears to the perceiving consciousness hint at a final reality, or in Kantian language, a Transcendental Object, which shall be, not any one, yet all of its manifestations; transcending yet including the innumerable fragmentary worlds of individual conception. We begin, then, to ask what can be the nature of this One; and whence comes the persistent instinct which—receiving no encouragement from sense experience—apprehends and desires this unknown unity, this all-inclusive Absolute, as the only possible satisfaction of its thirst for truth.

The second great conception of Being—Idealism—has arrived by a process of elimination at a tentative answer to this question. It whisks us far from the material universe, with its interesting array of "things," its machinery, its law, into the pure, if thin, air of a metaphysical world. Whilst the naturalist's world is constructed from an observation of the evidence offered by the senses, the Idealist's world is constructed from an observation of the processes of thought. There are but two things, he says in effect, about which we are sure: the existence of a thinking subject, a conscious Self, and of an object, an Idea, with which that subject deals. We know, that is to say, both Mind and Thought. What we call the universe is really a collection of such thoughts; and these, we agree, have been more or less distorted by the subject, the individual thinker, in the process of assimilation. Obviously, we do not think all that there is to be thought, conceive all that there is to be conceived; neither do we necessarily combine in right order and proportion those ideas which we are capable of grasping. Reality, says Objective Idealism, is the complete, undistorted Object, the big thought, of which we pick up these fragmentary hints: the world of phenomena which we treat as real being merely its shadow show or "manifestation in space and time."

According to the form of Objective Idealism here chosen from amongst many as typical—for almost every Idealist has his own scheme of metaphysical salvation—we live in a universe which is, in popular language, the Idea, or Dream of its Creator. We, as Tweedledum explained to Alice in the most philosophic of all fairy tales, are "just part of the dream." All life, all phenomena, are the endless modifications and expressions of the one transcendent Object, the mighty and dynamic Thought of one Absolute Thinker, in which we are bathed. This Object, or certain aspects of it—and the place of each individual consciousness within the Cosmic Thought, or, as we say, our position in life, largely determines which these aspects shall be—is interpreted by the senses and conceived by the mind, under limitations which we are accustomed to call matter, space and time. But we have no reason to suppose that matter, space, and time are necessarily parts of reality; of the ultimate Idea. Probability points rather to their being the pencil and paper with which we sketch it. As our vision, our idea of things, tends to approximate more and more to that of the Eternal Idea, so we get nearer and nearer to reality: for the idealist's reality is simply the Idea, or Thought of God. This, he says, is the supreme unity at which all the illusory appearances that make up the widely differing worlds of "common sense," of science, of metaphysics, and of art dimly hint. This is the sense in which it can truly be said that only the supernatural possesses reality; for that world of appearance which we call natural is certainly largely made up of preconception and illusion, of the hints offered by the eternal real world of Idea outside our gates, and the quaint concepts which we at our receiving instrument manufacture from them.

There is this to be said for the argument of Idealism: that in the last resort, the destinies of mankind are invariably guided, not by the concrete "facts" of the sense world, but by concepts which are acknowledged by every one to exist only on the mental plane. In the great moments of existence, when he rises to spiritual freedom, these are the things which every man feels to be real. It is by these and for these that he is found willing to live, work suffer, and die. Love, patriotism, religion, altruism, fame, all belong to the transcendental world. Hence, they partake more of the nature of reality than any "fact" could do; and man, dimly recognizing this, has ever bowed to them as to immortal centres of energy. Religions as a rule are steeped in idealism: Christianity in particular is a trumpet call to an idealistic conception of life, Buddhism is little less. Over and over again, their Scriptures tell us that only materialists will be damned.

In Idealism we have perhaps the most sublime theory of Being which has ever been constructed by the human intellect: a theory so sublime, in fact, that it can hardly have been produced by the exercise of "pure reason" alone, but must be looked upon as a manifestation of that natural mysticism, that instinct for the Absolute, which is latent in man. But, when we ask the idealist how we are to attain communion with the reality which he describes to us as "certainly there," his system suddenly breaks down; and discloses itself as a diagram of the heavens, not a ladder to the stars. This failure of Idealism to find in practice the reality of which it thinks so much is due, in the opinion of the mystics, to a cause which finds epigrammatic expression in the celebrated phrase by which St. Jerome marked the distinction between religion and philosophy. "Plato located the soul of man in the head; Christ located it in the heart." That is to say, Idealism, though just in its premises, and often daring and honest in their application, is stultified by the exclusive intellectualism of its own methods: by its fatal trust in the squirrel-work of the industrious brain instead of the piercing vision of the desirous heart. It interests man, but does not involve him in its processes: does not catch him up to the new and more real life which it describes. Hence the thing that matters, the living thing, has somehow escaped it; and its observations bear the same relation to reality as the art of the anatomist does to the mystery of birth.

But there is yet another Theory of Being to be considered: that which may be loosely defined as Philosophic Scepticism. This is the attitude of those who refuse to accept either the realistic or the idealistic answer to the eternal question: and, confronted in their turn with the riddle of reality, reply that there is no riddle to solve. We of course assume for the ordinary purposes of life that for every sequence a: b: present in our consciousness there exists a mental or material A: B: in the external universe, and that the first is a strictly relevant, though probably wholly inadequate, expression of the second. The bundle of visual and auditory sensations, for instance, whose sum total I am accustomed to call Mrs. Smith, corresponds with something that exists in the actual as well as in my phenomenal world. Behind my Mrs. Smith, behind the very different Mrs. Smith which the X rays would exhibit, there is, contends the Objective Idealist, a transcendental, or in the Platonic sense an ideal Mrs. Smith, at whose qualities I cannot even guess; but whose existence is quite independent of my apprehension of it. But though we do and must act on this hypothesis, it remains only a hypothesis; and it is one which philosophic scepticism will not let pass.

The external world, say the sceptical schools, is—so far as I know it—a concept present in my mind. If my mind ceased to exist, so far as I know the concept which I call the world would cease to exist too. The one thing which for me indubitably is, the self's experience, its whole consciousness. Outside this circle of consciousness I have no authority to indulge in guesses as to what may or may not Be. Hence, for me, the Absolute is a meaningless diagram, a superfluous complication of thought: since the mind, wholly cut off from contact with external reality, has no reason to suppose that such a reality exists except in its own ideas. Every effort made by philosophy to go forth in search of it is merely the metaphysical squirrel running round the conceptual cage. In the completion and perfect unfolding of the set of ideas with which our consciousness is furnished, lies the only reality which we can ever hope to know. Far better to stay here and make ourselves at home: only this, for us, truly is.

This purely subjective conception of Being has found representatives in every school of thought: even including by a curious paradox, that of mystical philosophy—its one effective antagonist. Thus Delacroix, after an exhaustive and even sympathetic analysis of St. Teresa's progress towards union with the Absolute, ends upon the assumption that the God with whom she was united was the content of her own subconscious mind. Such a mysticism is that of a kitten running after its own tail: a different path indeed from that which the great seekers for reality have pursued. The reductio ad absurdum of this doctrine is found in the so-called "philosophy" of New Thought, which begs its disciples to "try quietly to realize that the Infinite is really You." By its utter denial not merely of a knowable, but of a logically conceivable Transcendent, it drives us in the end to the conclusion of extreme pragmatism; that Truth, for us, is not an immutable reality, but merely that idea which happens to work out as true and useful in any given experience. There is no reality behind appearance; therefore all faiths, all figments with which we people that nothingness are equally true, provided they be comfortable and good to live by.

Logically carried out, this conception of Being would permit each man to regard other men as non-existent except within his own consciousness: the only place where a strict scepticism will allow that anything exists. Even the mind which conceives consciousness exists for us only in our own conception of it; we no more know what we are than we know what we shall be. Man is left a conscious Something in the midst, so far as he knows, of Nothing: with no resources save the exploring of his own consciousness.

Philosophic scepticism is particularly interesting to our present inquiry, because it shows us the position in which "pure reason," if left to itself, is bound to end. It is utterly logical; and though we may feel it to be absurd, we can never prove it to be so. Those who are temperamentally inclined to credulity may become naturalists, and persuade themselves to believe in the reality of the sense world. Those with a certain instinct for the Absolute may adopt the more reasonable faith of idealism. But the true intellectualist, who concedes nothing to instinct or emotion, is obliged in the end to adopt some form of sceptical philosophy. The horrors of nihilism, in fact, can only be escaped by the exercise of faith, by a trust in man's innate but strictly irrational instinct for that Real "above all reason, beyond all thought" towards which at its best moments his spirit tends. If the metaphysician be true to his own postulates, he must acknowledge in the end that we are all forced to live, to think, and at last to die, in an unknown and unknowable world: fed arbitrarily and diligently, yet how we know not, by ideas and suggestions whose truth we cannot test but whose pressure we cannot resist. It is not by sight but by faith—faith in a supposed external order which we can never prove to exist, and in the approximate truthfulness and constancy of the vague messages which we receive from it—that ordinary men must live and move. We must put our trust in "laws of nature" which have been devised by the human mind as a convenient epitome of its own observations of phenomena, must, for the purposes of daily life, accept these phenomena at their face value: an act of faith beside which the grossest superstitions of the Neapolitan peasant are hardly noticeable.

The intellectual quest of Reality, then, leads us down one of three blind alleys: (1) To an acceptance of the symbolic world of appearance as the real; (2) to the elaboration of a theory also of necessity symbolic—which, beautiful in itself, cannot help us to attain the Absolute which it describes; (3) to a hopeless but strictly logical skepticism.

In answer to the "Why? Why?" of the bewildered and eternal child in us, philosophy, though always ready to postulate the unknown if she can, is bound to reply only,"Nescio! Nescio!" In spite of all her busy map-making, she cannot reach the goal which she points out to us, cannot explain the curious conditions under which we imagine that we know; cannot even divide with a sure hand the subject and object of thought. Science, whose business is with phenomena and our knowledge of them, though she too is an idealist at heart, has been accustomed to explain that all our ideas and instincts, the pictured world that we take so seriously, the oddly limited and illusory nature of our experience, appear to minister to one great end: the preservation of life, and consequent fulfilment of that highly mystical hypothesis, the Cosmic Idea. Each perception, she assures us, serves a useful purpose in this evolutionary scheme: a scheme, by the way, which has been invented—we know not why—by the human mind, and imposed upon an obedient universe.

By vision, hearing, smell, and touch, says Science, we find our way about, are warned of danger, obtain our food. The male perceives beauty in the female in order that the species may be propagated. It is true that this primitive instinct has given birth to higher and purer emotions; but these too fulfil a social purpose and are not so useless as they seem. Man must eat to live, therefore many foods give us agreeable sensations. If he overeats, he dies; therefore indigestion is an unpleasant pain. Certain facts of which too keen a perception would act detrimentally to the life-force are, for most men, impossible of realization: i.e., the uncertainty of life, the decay of the body, the vanity of all things under the sun. When we are in good health, we all feel very real, solid, and permanent; and this is of all our illusions the most ridiculous, and also the most obviously useful from the point of view of the efficiency and preservation of the race.

But when we look closer, we see that this brisk generalization does not cover all the ground—not even that little tract of ground of which our senses make us free; indeed, that it is more remarkable for its omissions than for its inclusions. Récéjac has well said that "from the moment in which man is no longer content to devise things useful for his existence under the exclusive action of the will-to-live, the principle of (physical) evolution has been violated." Nothing can be more certain than that man is not so content. He has been called by utilitarian philosophers a tool-making animal—the highest praise they knew how to bestow. More surely he is a vision-making animal; a creature of perverse and unpractical ideals, dominated by dreams no less than by appetites— dreams which can only be justified upon the theory that he moves towards some other goal than that of physical perfection or intellectual supremacy, is controlled by some higher and more vital reality than that of the determinists. We are driven to the conclusion that if the theory of evolution is to include or explain the facts of artistic and spiritual experience—and it cannot be accepted by any serious thinker if these great tracts of consciousness remain outside its range—it must be rebuilt on a mental rather than a physical basis.

Even the most ordinary human life includes in its range fundamental experiences—violent and unforgettable sensations—forced on us as it were against our will, for which science finds it hard to account. These experiences and sensations, and the hours of exalted emotion which they bring with them—often recognized by us as the greatest, most significant hours of our lives—fulfill no office in relation to her pet "functions of nutrition and reproduction." It is true that they are far-reaching in their effects on character; but they do little or nothing to assist that character in its struggle for physical life. To the unprejudiced eye many of them seem hopelessly out of place in a universe constructed on strictly physico-chemical lines—look almost as though nature, left to herself, tended to contradict her own beautifully logical laws. Their presence, more, the large place which they fill in the human world of appearance, is a puzzling circumstance for deterministic philosophers; who can only escape from the dilemma here presented to them by calling these things illusions, and dignifying their own more manageable illusions with the title of facts.

Amongst the more intractable of these groups of perceptions and experiences are those which we connect with religion, with pain and with beauty. All three, for those selves which are capable of receiving their messages, possess a mysterious authority far in excess of those feelings, arguments, or appearances which they may happen to contradict. All three, were the universe of the naturalists true, would be absurd; all three have ever been treated with the reverence due to vital matters by the best minds of the race.

I need not point out the hopelessly irrational character of all great religions: which rest, one and all, on a primary assumption that can never be intellectually demonstrated, much less proved—the assumption that the supra-sensible is somehow important and real, and is intimately connected with the life of man. This fact has been incessantly dwelt upon by their critics, and has provoked many a misplaced exercise of ingenuity on the part of their intelligent friends. Yet religion—emphasizing and pushing to extremes that general dependence on faith which we saw to be an inevitable condition of our lives—is one of the most universal and ineradicable functions of man, and this although it constantly acts detrimentally to the interests of his merely physical existence, opposes "the exclusive action of the will-to-live," except in so far as that will aspires to eternal life. Strictly utilitarian, almost logical in the savage, religion becomes more and more transcendental with the upward progress of the race.

Separatio

It begins as black magic; it ends as Pure Love. Why did the Cosmic Idea elaborate this religious instinct, if the construction put upon its intentions by the determinists be true?

Consider again the whole group of phenomena which are known as "the problem of suffering": the mental anguish and physical pain which appear to be the inevitable result of the steady operation of "natural law" and its voluntary assistants, the cruelty, greed, and injustice of man. Here, it is true, the naturalist seems at first sight to make a little headway, and can point to some amongst the cruder forms of suffering which are clearly useful to the race: punishing us for past follies, spurring to new efforts, warning against future infringements of "law." But he forgets the many others which refuse to be resumed under this simple formula: forgets to explain how it is that the Cosmic Idea involves the long torments of the incurable, the tortures of the innocent, the deep anguish of the bereaved, the existence of so many gratuitously agonizing forms of death. He forgets, too, the strange fact that man's capacity for suffering tends to increase in depth and subtlety with the increase of culture and civilization; ignores the still more mysterious, perhaps most significant circumstance that the highest types have accepted it eagerly and willingly, have found in Pain the grave but kindly teacher of immortal secrets, the conferrer of liberty, even the initiator into amazing joys.

Those who "explain" suffering as the result of nature's immense fecundity—a by-product of that overcrowding and stress through which the fittest tend to survive—forget that even were this demonstration valid and complete it would leave the real problem untouched. The question is not, whence come those conditions which provoke in the self the experiences called sorrow, anxiety, pain: but, why do these conditions hurt the self? The pain is mental; a little chloroform, and though the conditions continue unabated the suffering is gone. Why does full consciousness always include the mysterious capacity for misery as well as for happiness—a capacity which seems at first sight to invalidate any conception of the Absolute as Beautiful and Good? Why does evolution, as we ascend the ladder of life, foster instead of diminishing the capacity for useless mental anguish, for long, dull torment, bitter grief? Why, when so much lies outside our limited powers of perception, when so many of our own most vital functions are unperceived by consciousness, does suffering of some sort form an integral part of the experience of man? For utilitarian purposes acute discomfort would be quite enough; the Cosmic Idea, as the determinists explain it, did not really need an apparatus which felt all the throes of cancer, the horrors of neurasthenia, the pangs of birth. Still less did it need the torments of impotent sympathy for other people's irremediable pain the dreadful power of feeling the world's woe. We are hopelessly over-sensitized for the part science calls us to play.

Pain, however we may look at it, indicates a profound disharmony between the sense-world and the human self. If it is to be vanquished, either the disharmony must be resolved by a deliberate and careful adjustment of the self to the world of sense, or, that self must turn from the sense-world to some other with which it is in tune. Pessimist and optimist here join hands. But whilst the pessimist, resting in appearance, only sees "nature red in tooth and claw" offering him little hope of escape, the optimist thinks that pain and anguish—which may in their lower forms be life's harsh guides on the path of physical evolution—in their higher and apparently "useless" developments are her leaders and teachers in the upper school of Supra-sensible Reality. He believes that they press the self towards another world, still "natural" for him, though "supernatural" for his antagonist, in which it will be more at home. Watching life, he sees in Pain the complement of Love: and is inclined to call these the wings on which man's spirit can best take flight towards the Absolute. Hence he can say with A Kempis, "Gloriari in tribulatione non est grave amanti," and needs not to speak of morbid folly when he sees the Christian saints run eagerly and merrily to the Cross.

He calls suffering the "gymnastic of eternity," the "terrible initiative caress of God"; recognizing in it a quality for which the disagreeable rearrangement of nerve molecules cannot account. Sometimes, in the excess of his optimism, he puts to the test of practice this theory with all its implications. Refusing to be deluded by the pleasures of the sense world, he accepts instead of avoiding pain, and becomes an ascetic; a puzzling type for the convinced naturalist, who, falling back upon contempt—that favourite resource of the frustrated reason—can only regard him as diseased.

Pain, then, which plunges like a sword through creation, leaving on the one side cringing and degraded animals and on the other side heroes and saints, is one of those facts of universal experience which are peculiarly intractable from the point of view of a merely materialistic philosophy.

From this same point of view the existence of music and poetry, the qualities of beauty and of rhythm, the evoked sensations of awe, reverence, and rapture, are almost as difficult to account for. The question why an apparent corrugation of the Earth's surface, called for convenience' sake an Alp, coated with congealed water, and perceived by us as a snowy peak, should produce in certain natures acute sensations of ecstasy and adoration, why the skylark's song should catch us up to heaven, and wonder and mystery speak to us alike in "the little speedwell's darling blue" and in the cadence of the wind, is a problem that seems to be merely absurd, until it is seen to be insoluble. Here Madam How and Lady Why alike are silent. With all our busy seeking, we have not found the sorting house where loveliness is extracted from the flux of things. We know not why "great" poetry should move us to unspeakable emotion, or a stream of notes, arranged in a peculiar sequence, catch us up to heightened levels of vitality: nor can we guess how a passionate admiration for that which we call "best" in art or letters can possibly contribute to the physical evolution of the race. In spite of many lengthy disquisitions on Esthetics, Beauty's secret is still her own. A shadowy companion, half seen, half guessed at, she keeps step with the upward march of life: and we receive her message and respond to it, not because we understand it but because we must.

Here it is that we approach that attitude of the self, that point of view, which is loosely and generally called mystical. Here, instead of those broad blind alleys which philosophy showed us, a certain type of mind has always discerned three strait and narrow ways going out towards the Absolute. In religion, in pain, and in beauty—and not only in these, but in many other apparently useless peculiarities of the empirical world and of the perceiving consciousness—these persons insist that they recognize at least the fringe of the real. Down these three paths, as well as by many another secret way, they claim that news comes to the self concerning levels of reality which in their wholeness are inaccessible to the senses: worlds wondrous and immortal, whose existence is not conditioned by the "given" world which those senses report. "Beauty," said Hegel, who, though he was no mystic, had a touch of that mystical intuition which no philosopher can afford to be without, "is merely the Spiritual making itself known sensuously." In the good, the beautiful, the true," says Rudolph Eucken, "we see Reality revealing its personal character. They are parts of a coherent and substantial spiritual world." Here, some of the veils of that substantial world are stripped off: Reality peeps through and is recognized, dimly or acutely, by the imprisoned self.

Récéjac only develops this idea when he says, "If the mind penetrates deeply into the facts of aesthetics, it will find more and more, that these facts are based upon an ideal identity between the mind itself and things. At a certain point the harmony becomes so complete, and the finality so close that it gives us actual emotion. The Beautiful then becomes the sublime; brief apparition, by which the soul is caught up into the true mystic state, and touches the Absolute. It is scarcely possible to persist in this Esthetic perception without feeling lifted up by it above things and above ourselves, in an ontological vision which closely resembles the Absolute of the Mystics." It was of this underlying reality—this truth of things—that St. Augustine cried in a moment of lucid vision, "Oh, Beauty so old and so new, too late have I loved thee!" It is in this sense also that "beauty is truth, truth beauty": and as regards the knowledge of ultimate things which is possible to ordinary men, it may well be that

"That is all

Ye know on earth, and all ye need to know."

"Of Beauty," says Plato in an immortal passage, "I repeat again that we saw her there shining in company with the celestial forms; and coming to earth we find her here too, shining in clearness through the clearest aperture of sense. For sight is the most piercing of our bodily senses: though not by that is wisdom seen; her loveliness would have been transporting if there had been a visible image of her, and the other ideas, if they had visible counterparts, would be equally lovely. But this is the privilege of Beauty, that being the loveliest she is also the most palpable to sight. Now he who is not newly initiated, or who has been corrupted, does not easily rise out of this world to the sight of true beauty in the other. . . . But he whose initiation is recent, and who has been the spectator of many glories in the other world, is amazed when he sees anyone having a godlike face or form, which is the expression of Divine Beauty; and at first a shudder runs through him, and again the old awe steals over him. . ."

Most men in the course of their lives have known such Platonic hours of initiation, when the sense of beauty has risen from a pleasant feeling to a passion, and an element of strangeness and terror has been mingled with their joy. In those hours the world has seemed charged with a new vitality; with a splendour which does not belong to it but is poured through it, as light through a coloured window, grace through a sacrament, from that Perfect Beauty which "shines in company with the celestial forms" beyond the pale of appearance. In such moods of heightened consciousness each blade of grass seems fierce with meaning, and becomes a well of wondrous light: a "little emerald set in the City of God." The seeing self is indeed an initiate thrust suddenly into the sanctuary of the mysteries: and feels the "old awe and amazement" with which man encounters the Real. In such experiences, a new factor of the eternal calculus appears to be thrust in on us, a factor which no honest seeker for truth can afford to neglect; since, if it be dangerous to say that any two systems of knowledge are mutually exclusive, it is still more dangerous to give uncritical priority to any one system. We are bound, then, to examine this path to reality as closely and seriously as we should investigate the most neatly finished safety-ladder of solid ash which offered a salita alle stelle.

Why, after all, take as our standard a material world whose existence is affirmed by nothing more trustworthy than the sense-impressions of "normal men"; those imperfect and easily cheated channels of communication? The mystics, those adventurers of whom we spoke upon the first page of this book, have always declared, implicitly or explicitly, their distrust in these channels of communication. They have never been deceived by phenomena, nor by the careful logic of the industrious intellect. One after another, with extraordinary unanimity, they have rejected that appeal to the unreal world of appearance which is the standard of sensible men: affirming that there is another way, another secret, by which the conscious self may reach the actuality which it seeks. More complete in their grasp of experience than the votaries of intellect or of sense, they accept as central for life those spiritual messages which are mediated by religion, by beauty, and by pain. More reasonable than the rationalists, they find in that very hunger for reality which is the mother of all metaphysics, an implicit proof that such reality exists; that there is something else, some final satisfaction, beyond the ceaseless stream of sensation which besieges consciousness. "In that thou hast sought me, thou hast already found me," says the voice of Absolute Truth in their ears. This is the first doctrine of mysticism. Its next is that only in so far as the self is real can it hope to know Reality: like to like: Cot ad cot loquitur. Upon the propositions implicit in these two laws the whole claim and practice of the mystic life depends.

"Finite as we are," they say—and here they speak not for themselves, but for the race—"lost though we seem to be in the woods or in the wide air's wilderness, in this world of time and of chance, we have still, like the strayed animals or like the migrating birds, our homing instinct. . . . We seek. That is a fact. We seek a city still out of sight. In the contrast with this goal, we live. But if this be so, then already we possess something of Being even in our finite seeking. For the readiness to seek is already something of an attainment, even if a poor one."

Further, in this seeking we are not wholly dependent on that homing instinct. For some, who have climbed to the hill-tops, that city is not really out of sight. The mystics see it and report to us concerning it. Science and metaphysics may do their best and their worst: but these pathfinders of the spirit never falter in their statements concerning that independent spiritual world which is the only goal of "pilgrim man." They say that messages come to him from that spiritual world, that complete reality which we call Absolute: that we are not, after all, hermetically sealed from it. To all who will receive it, news comes of a world of Absolute Life, Absolute Beauty, Absolute Truth, beyond the bourne of time and place: news that most of us translate—and inevitably distort in the process—into the language of religion, of beauty, of love, or of pain.

Of all those forms of life and thought with which humanity has fed its craving for truth, mysticism alone postulates, and in the persons of its great initiates proves, not only the existence of the Absolute, but also this link: this possibility first of knowing, finally of attaining it. It denies that possible knowledge is to be limited (a) to sense impressions, (b) to any process of intellection, (c) to the unfolding of the content of normal consciousness. Such diagrams of experience, it says, are hopelessly incomplete. The mystics find the basis of their method not in logic but in life: in the existence of a discoverable "real," a spark of true being, within the seeking subject, which can, in that ineffable experience which they call the "act of union," fuse itself with and thus apprehend the reality of the sought Object. In theological language, their theory of knowledge is that the spirit of man, itself essentially divine, is capable of immediate communion with God, the One Reality.

In mysticism that love of truth which we saw as the beginning of all philosophy leaves the merely intellectual sphere, and takes on the assured aspect of a personal passion. Where the philosopher guesses and argues, the mystic lives and looks; and speaks, consequently, the disconcerting language of first-hand experience, not the neat dialectic of the schools. Hence whilst the Absolute of the metaphysicians remains a diagram—impersonal and unattainable—the Absolute of the mystics is lovable, attainable, alive.

"Oh, taste and see!" they cry, in accents of astounding certainty and joy. "Ours is an experimental science. We can but communicate our system, never its result. We come to you not as thinkers, but as doers. Leave your deep and absurd trust in the senses, with their language of dot and dash, which may possibly report fact but can never communicate personality. If philosophy has taught you anything, she has surely taught you the length of her tether, and the impossibility of attaining to the doubtless admirable grazing land which lies beyond it. One after another, idealists have arisen who, straining frantically at the rope, have announced to the world their approaching liberty; only to be flung back at last into the little circle of sensation. But here we are, a small family, it is true, yet one that refuses to die out, assuring you that we have slipped the knot and are free of those grazing grounds. This is evidence which you are bound to bring into account before you can add up the sum total of possible knowledge; for you will find it impossible to prove that the world as seen by the mystics, 'unimaginable, formless, dark with excess of bright,' is less real than that which is expounded by the youngest and most promising demonstrator of a physicochemical universe. We will be quite candid with you. Examine us as much as you like: our machinery, our veracity, our results. We cannot promise that you shall see **what** we have seen, for here each man must adventure for himself; but we defy you to stigmatize our experiences as impossible or invalid. Is your world of experience so well and logically founded that you dare make of it a standard? Philosophy tells you that it is founded on nothing better than the reports of your sensory apparatus and the traditional concepts of the race. Certainly it is imperfect, probably it is illusion in any event, it never touches the foundation of things. Whereas 'what the world, which truly knows nothing, calls "mysticism" is the science of ultimates, . . . the science of self-evident Reality, which cannot be "reasoned about," because it is the object of pure reason or perception.

Okay. Let's begin.

2. Calcinatio

Light is the alchemical key! The words 'Let there be light' are the first fiat of the creation and the first step in proper precipitation.

SAINT GERMAIN

Hard by a great forest dwelt a poor wood-cutter with his wife and his two children. He had little to bite and to break, and once, when great dearth fell on the land, he could no longer procure even daily bread.

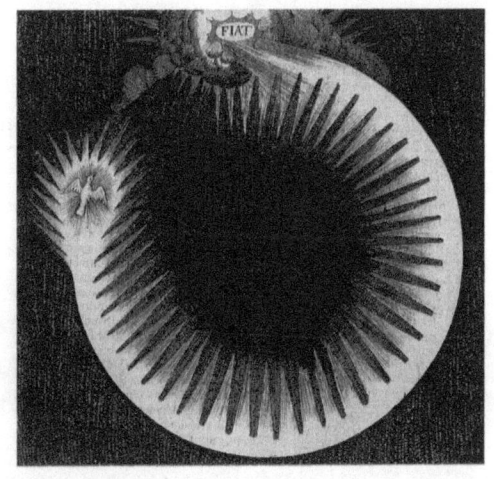

Now when he thought over this by night in his bed, and tossed about in his anxiety. He groaned and said to his wife, "What is to become of us? How are we to feed our poor children, when we no longer have anything even for ourselves?"

"I'll tell you what, husband," answered the woman, "early tomorrow morning we will take the children out into the forest to where it is the thickest. There we will light a fire for them, and give each of them one more piece of bread, and then we will go to our work and leave them alone. They will not find the way home again, and we shall be rid of them."

"No, wife," said the man, "I will not do that. How can I bear to leave my children alone in the forest? The wild animals would soon come and tear them to pieces."

"Oh! you fool," said she, "then we must all four die of hunger, you may as well plane the planks for our coffins," and she left him no peace until he consented.

"But I feel very sorry for the poor children, all the same," said the man.

The two children had also not been able to sleep for hunger, and had heard what their step-mother had said to their father. Gretel wept bitter tears, and said to Hansel, "Now all is over with us."

"Be quiet, Gretel," said Hansel, "do not distress yourself, I will soon find a way to help us." And when the old folks had fallen asleep, he got up, put on his little coat, opened the door below, and crept outside.

The moon shone brightly, and the white pebbles which lay in front of the house glittered like real silver pennies. Hansel stooped and stuffed the little pocket of his coat with as many as he could get in. Then he went back and said to Gretel, "Be comforted, dear little sister, and sleep in peace, God will not forsake us," and he lay down again in his bed.

When day dawned, but before the sun had risen, the woman came and awoke the two children, saying, "Get up, you sluggards.

We are going into the forest to fetch wood." She gave each a little piece of bread, and said, "There is something for your dinner, but do not eat it up before then, for you will get nothing else."

Gretel took the bread under her apron, as Hansel had the pebbles in his pocket. Then they all set out together on the way to the forest.

When they had walked a short time, Hansel stood still and peeped back at the house, and did so again and again. His father said, "Hansel, what are you looking at there and staying behind for? Pay attention, and do not forget how to use your legs."

"Ah, father," said Hansel, "I am looking at my little white cat, which is sitting up on the roof, and wants to say good-bye to me."

The wife said, "Fool, that is not your little cat, that is the morning sun which is shining on the chimneys."

Hansel, however, had not been looking back at the cat, but had been constantly throwing one of the white pebble-stones out of his pocket on the road.

When they had reached the middle of the forest, the father said, "Now, children, pile up some wood, and I will light a fire that you may not be cold."

Hansel and Gretel gathered brushwood together, as high as a little hill. The brushwood was lighted, and when the flames were burning very high, the woman said, "Now, children, lay yourselves down by the fire and rest, we will go into the forest and cut some wood. When we have done, we will come back and fetch you away."

Hansel and Gretel sat by the fire, and when noon came, each ate a little piece of bread, and as they heard the strokes of the wood-axe they believed that their father was near. It was not the axe, however, but a branch which he had fastened to a withered tree which the wind was blowing backwards and forwards. And as they had been sitting such a long time, their eyes closed with fatigue, and they fell fast asleep.

When at last they awoke, it was already dark night. Gretel began to cry and said, "How are we to get out of the forest now?"

But Hansel comforted her and said, "Just wait a little, until the moon has risen, and then we will soon find the way." And when the full moon had risen, Hansel took his little sister by the hand, and followed the pebbles which shone like newly-coined silver pieces, and showed them the way.

They walked the whole night long, and by break of day came once more to their father's house. They knocked at the door, and when the woman opened it and saw that it was Hansel and Gretel, she said, "You naughty children, why have you slept so long in the forest? We thought you were never coming back at all."

The father, however, rejoiced, for it had cut him to the heart to leave them behind alone.

Not long afterwards, there was once more great dearth throughout the land, and the children heard their mother saying at night to their father:

"Everything is eaten again, we have one half loaf left, and that is the end. The children must go, we will take them farther into the wood, so that they will not find their way out again. There is no other means of saving ourselves."

The man's heart was heavy, and he thought, "It would be better for you to share the last mouthful with your children." The woman, however, would listen to nothing that he had to say, but scolded and reproached him. He who says a must say, likewise, and as he had yielded the first time, he had to do so a second time also.

The children, however, were still awake and had heard the conversation. When the old folks were asleep, Hansel again got up, and wanted to go out and pick up pebbles as he had done before, but the woman had locked the door, and Hansel could not get out. Nevertheless he comforted his little sister, and said, "Do not cry, Gretel, go to sleep quietly, the good God will help us."

Early in the morning came the woman, and took the children out of their beds. Their piece of bread was given to them, but it was still smaller than the time before. On the way into the forest Hansel crumbled his in his pocket, and often stood still and threw a morsel on the ground.

"Hansel, why do you stop and look round?" Said the father. "Go on."

"I am looking back at my little pigeon which is sitting on the roof, and wants to say good-bye to me, answered Hansel.

"Fool." Said the woman,

"That is not your little pigeon, that is the morning sun that is shining on the chimney."

Hansel, however, little by little, threw all the crumbs on the path. The woman led the children still deeper into the forest, where they had never in their lives been before.

Then a great fire was again made, and the mother said, "Just sit there, you children, and when you are tired you may sleep a little. We are going into the forest to cut wood, and in the evening when we are done, we will come and fetch you away."

When it was noon, Gretel shared her piece of bread with Hansel, who had scattered his by the way. Then they fell asleep and evening passed, but no one came to the poor children.

They did not awake until it was dark night, and Hansel comforted his little sister and said, "Just wait, Gretel, until the moon rises, and then we shall see the crumbs of bread which I have strewn about, they will show us our way home again."

When the moon came they set out, but they found no crumbs, for the many thousands of birds which fly about in the woods and fields had picked them all up. Hansel said to Gretel, "We shall soon find the way."

But they did not find it. They walked the whole night and all the next day too from morning till evening, but they did not get out of the forest, and were very hungry, for they had nothing to eat but two or three berries, which grew on the ground. And as they were so weary that their legs would carry them no longer, they lay down beneath a tree and fell asleep.

It was now three mornings since they had left their father's house. They began to walk again, but they always came deeper into the forest, and if help did not come soon, they must die of hunger and weariness. When it was mid-day, they saw a beautiful snow-white bird sitting on a bough, which sang so delightfully that they stood still and listened to it. And when its song was over, it spread its wings and flew away before them, and they followed it until they reached a little house, on the roof of which it alighted. And when they approached the little house they saw that it was built of bread and covered with cakes, but that the windows were of clear sugar.

"We will set to work on that," said Hansel, "and have a good meal. I will eat a bit of the roof, and you Gretel, can eat some of the window, it will taste sweet."

Hansel reached up above, and broke off a little of the roof to try how it tasted, and Gretel leant against the window and nibbled at the panes. Then a soft voice cried from the parlor -

"Nibble, nibble, gnaw

who is nibbling at my little house?"

The children answered -

"The wind, the wind,

the heaven-born wind,"

and went on eating without disturbing themselves. Hansel, who liked the taste of the roof, tore down a great piece of it, and

Gretel pushed out the whole of one round window-pane, sat down, and enjoyed herself with it.

Suddenly the door opened, and a woman as old as the hills, who supported herself on crutches, came creeping out. Hansel and Gretel were so terribly frightened that they let fall what they had in their hands.

The old woman, however, nodded her head, and said, "Oh, you dear children, who has brought you here? Do come in, and stay with me. No harm shall happen to you."

She took them both by the hand, and led them into her little house. Then good food was set before them, milk and pancakes, with sugar, apples, and nuts. Afterwards two pretty little beds were covered with clean white linen, and Hansel and Gretel lay down in them, and thought they were in heaven.

The old woman had only pretended to be so kind. She was in reality a wicked witch, who lay in wait for children, and had only built the little house of bread in order to entice them there. When a child fell into her power, she killed it, cooked and ate it, and that was a feast day with her. Witches have red eyes, and cannot see far, but they have a keen scent like the beasts, and are aware when human beings draw near. When Hansel and Gretel came into her neighborhood, she laughed with malice, and said mockingly, "I have them, they shall not escape me again."

Early in the morning before the children were awake, she was already up, and when she saw both of them sleeping and looking so pretty, with their plump and rosy cheeks, she muttered to herself, that will be a dainty mouthful.

Then she seized Hansel with her shriveled hand, carried him into a little stable, and locked him in behind a grated door. Scream as he might, it would not help him. Then she went to Gretel, shook her till she awoke, and cried, "Get up, lazy thing, fetch some water, and cook something good for your brother, he is in the stable outside, and is to be made fat. When he is fat, I will eat him."

Gretel began to weep bitterly, but it was all in vain, for she was forced to do what the wicked witch commanded. And now the best food was cooked for poor Hansel, but Gretel got nothing but crab-shells. Every morning the woman crept to the little stable, and cried, "Hansel, stretch out your finger that I may feel if you will soon be fat."

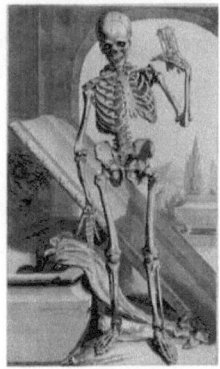

Hansel, however, stretched out a little bone to her, and the old woman, who had dim eyes, could not see it, and thought it was Hansel's finger, and was astonished that there was no way of fattening him. When four weeks had gone by, and Hansel still remained thin, she was seized with impatience and would not wait any longer.

"Now, then, Gretel," she cried to the girl, "stir yourself, and bring some water. Let Hansel be fat or lean, to-morrow I will kill him, and cook him."

Ah, how the poor little sister did lament when she had to fetch the water, and how her tears did flow down her cheeks. "Dear God, do help us," she cried. "If the wild beasts in the forest had but devoured us, we should at any rate have died together."

"Just keep your noise to yourself," said the old woman, "it won't help you at all."

Early in the morning, Gretel had to go out and hang up the cauldron with the water, and light the fire.

"We will bake first," said the old woman, "I have already heated the oven, and kneaded the dough." She pushed poor Gretel out to the oven, from which flames of fire were already darting. "Creep in," said the witch, "and see if it properly heated, so that we can put the bread in." And once Gretel was inside, she intended to shut the oven and let her bake in it, and then she would eat her, too.

But Gretel saw what she had in mind, and said, "I do not know how I am to do it. How do I get in?"

"Silly goose," said the old woman, "the door is big enough. Just look, I can get in myself." And she crept up and thrust her head into the oven.

Then Gretel gave her a push that drove her far into it, and shut the iron door, and fastened the bolt. Oh. Then she began to howl quite horribly, but Gretel ran away, and the godless witch was miserably burnt to death. Gretel, however, ran like lightning to Hansel, opened his little stable, and cried, "Hansel, we are saved. The old witch is dead."

Then Hansel sprang like a bird from its cage when the door is opened. How they did rejoice and embrace each other, and dance about and kiss each other. And as they had no longer any need to fear her, they went into the witch's house, and in every corner there stood chests full of pearls and jewels.

"These are far better than pebbles." Said Hansel, and thrust into his pockets whatever could be got in.

And Gretel said, "I, too, will take something home with me," and filled her pinafore full.

"But now we must be off," said Hansel, "that we may get out of the witch's forest."

When they had walked for two hours, they came to a great stretch of water.

"We cannot cross," said Hansel, "I see no foot-plank, and no bridge.

"And there is also no ferry," answered Gretel, "but a white duck is swimming there. If I ask her, she will help us over." Then she cried -

"Little duck, little duck, dost thou see,

Hansel and Gretel are waiting for thee.

There's never a plank, or bridge in sight,

take us across on thy back so white."

The duck came to them, and Hansel seated himself on its back, and told his sister to sit by him.

"No," replied Gretel, "that will be too heavy for the little duck. She shall take us across, one after the other."

The good little duck did so, and when they were once safely across and had walked for a short time, the forest seemed to be more and more familiar to them, and at length they saw from afar their father's house. Then they began to run, rushed into the parlor, and threw themselves round their father's neck. The man had not known one happy hour since he had left the children in the forest. The woman, however, was dead. Gretel emptied her pinafore until pearls and precious stones ran about the room, and Hansel threw one handful after another out of his pocket to add to them. Then all anxiety was at an end, and they lived together in perfect happiness.

My tale is done, there runs a mouse, whosoever catches it, may make himself a big fur cap out of it.

3. Sublimatio

Out of the One comes Two, out of Two comes Three,
and from the Third comes the One as the Fourth.

MARIA PROPHETISSA

My son, after having imparted to thee a knowledge of all things, and after having taught thee how to live, after what manner to regulate thy conduct by the maxims of a most excellent wisdom, and after having also enlightened thee in that which concerns the order and the nature of the monarchy of the universe, it only remains for me to communicate those Keys of Nature which hitherto I have so carefully held back.

Among all these Keys, that which is most closely allied to the highest spirits of the universe deserves to take the first rank, and there is no one who questions that it is very specially endowed with an altogether divine property. When one is in possession of this Key, the rich become miserable in our eyes, inasmuch as there is no treasure which can possibly be compared to it. In effect, what is the use of wealth, when one is liable to be afflicted

with human infirmities? Where is the advantage of treasures, when death is about to destroy us? There is no earthly abundance which we are not bound to abandon upon the threshold of the tomb. But it is no longer thus when I am possessed of this Key, for then I behold death from afar, and I am convinced that I have within my hands a secret which extinguishes all fear of misfortunes in this life. Wealth is ever at my command, and I no longer want for treasures; weakness flees away from me; and I can ward off the approach of the destroyer while I own this Golden Key of the Grand Work.

My son, it is of this Key that I propose to make thee the inheritor; but I conjure thee, by the name of God, and by the Holy Place wherein He dwelleth, to lock it up in the cabinet of thy heart, under the seal of silence. If thou knowest how to make use of it, it will overwhelm thee with good things, and when thou shalt be old or ill, it will rejuvenate, console, and cure thee; for it has the special virtue of curing all diseases, of transfigurating metals, and of making happy those who possess it. It is that Key to which our fathers have often exhorted us under the bond of an inviolable oath. Learn, then, to know it, cease not to do good to the poor, to the widow, to the orphan, and learn its seal of me, and its true character.

Know that all beings which are under heaven, each after its own kind, derives origin from the same principle, and it is, as a fact, unto Air that all owe their birth as to a common principle.

The nourishment of each existence makes evident the nature of its principle, for that which sustains the life is that which gives the being. The fish joys in the water; the child sucks from its mother. The tree no longer bears fruit when its trunk is deprived of humidity. It is by the life that we discern the principle of things; the life of things is the Air, and by consequence Air is their principle. It is for this reason that Air corrupts all things, and even as it gives life, so also it takes it away. Wood, iron, stones, are consumed by fire, and fire cannot subsist but by Air. Now, that which is the cause of corruption is also the cause of generation. When, by reason of divers corruptions, it comes to pass that creatures fall sick and do suffer, either through length of days or by mischance, the Air coming to their succour cures them, whether they be imperfect or languishing. The earth, the tree, the herb languish under the heat of excessive drought;  but all things are recuperated by the dew of the Air. But, nevertheless, as no creature can be restored and re-established except by its own nature, Air being the fountain and original source of all things, it is in like manner the universal source. It is manifestly certain that the seed, the death, the sickness, and the remedy of all things are all alike in the Air. There has Nature stored up all her treasures, establishing therein the principles of the generation and corruption of all things, and concealing them as behind special and secret doors. To know how to open these doors with sufficient facility so as to draw upon the radical Air of the Air, is to possess in truth the golden Keys, and to be in ignorance thereof precludes all possibility of acquiring that which cures all maladies and recreates or preserves the life of men.

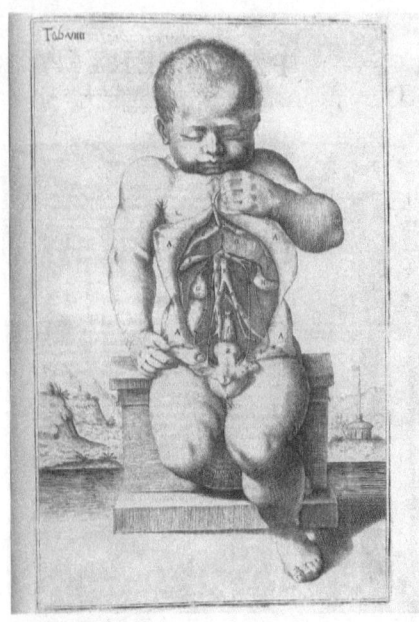

If thou desirest then, O my Son, to chase away all thine infirmities, thou must seek the means in the primal and universal source. Nature produces like from like alone, and that only which is in correspondence or conformity with Nature can effect good to her. Learn then, my Son, to make use of Air, learn to conserve the Key of Nature. It is truly a secret which transcends the possibilities of the vulgar man, but not those of the sage, this knowledge of the Extraction of Air, the Celestial Aerial Substance, from Air; for Air may be familiar to all beings, but he who would truly avail himself thereof must possess the secret Key of Nature.

It is a great secret to understand the virtue which Nature has imprinted in substances. For natures are attracted by their like; a fish is attracted by a fish - a bird by a bird - and air by another air, as with a gentle allurement. Snow and ice are an air that has been congealed by cold; Nature has endowed them with the qualities which are requisite to attract air.

Place thou, therefore, one of these two things in an earthen or metallic vessel, well closed, well sealed, and take thou the Air which congeals round this vessel when it is warm. Receive that which is distilled in a deep vessel with a narrow neck, neat and strong, so that thou canst use it at thy pleasure, and adapt to the rays of the Sun and Moon - that is, Silver and Gold. When thou

hast filled a vessel cork it well, so that the heavenly scintillation concentrated therein shall not escape into the air. Fill as many vases as thou wilt with liquid; then hearken to thy next task, and keep silent. Build a furnace, place a small vessel therein, half full of the Liquid Air which thou hast collected ; seal and lute the said vessel effectually. Light thy fire in such a manner that the thinner portion of the smoke may rise frequently above. Thus shall Nature perform that which is continually accomplished by the central fire in the bowels of the earth, where it agitates the vapours of the air by an unceasing circulation. The fire must be light, mild, and moist, like that of a hen brooding over her eggs, and it must be sustained in such a manner that it will cook without burning the aerial fruits, which, having been for a long time agitated by a movement, shall rest at the bottom of the vessel in a state of perfect coction.

Add next unto this Cocted Air a fresh air, not in great quantity, but as much as may be necessary; that is to say, a little less than on the first occasion. Continue this process until there shall be no more than half a bowl of Liquid Air uncooked. Proceed in such wise that the cooked portion shall gently liquefy by fermentation in a warm dunghill, and shall in like manner blacken, harden, amalgamate, become fixed, and grow red. Finally, the pure part being separated from the impure by means of a legitimate fire, and by a wholly divine artifice, thou shalt take one part of pure crude Air and one part of pure hardened Air, taking care that the whole is dissolved and united together till it becomes moderately black, more white, and finally perfectly red. Here is the end of the work, and then hast thou composed that elixir which produces all the wonders that our Sages aforetime have with reason held so precious; and thou dost possess in this wise the Golden Key of the most inestimable secret of Nature -

the true Potable Gold and the Universal Medicine. I bequeathe unto thee a small sample, the quality and virtues of which are attested by the perfect health which I enjoy, being aged over one hundred and eight years.

Allá vá eso.

Do thou work, and thou shalt achieve as I have done. So be it in the name and by the power of the great Architect of the Aniverse. Such skilful artists of the Great Work as have pondered deeply on the principles confided to the son of Aristeus, have concluded that it would be no vain operation to make an Amalgam with the veritable Balm of Mercury, and this is the way in which they claim to produce this Balm: Take one pound of the best Mercury that can be obtained; purge it three times through a skin, and once by calcined Montpellier Tartar. Place it in a glass horn, which shall be strong enough to resist a fierce heat. With it combine Vitriol, Salt of Nitre, Rock Alum, and eight ounces of good Spirit of Wine. Having hermetically sealed the horn, so that nothing can evaporate, place it for digestion in a warm dung-hill during a space of fifteen days. At the end of this time the composition will be transformed into a phlegmatic grease; it must then be exposed to a sand fire, and the fire must be raised gradually to an extreme point, till a white, milky humour exudes from the substance and falls into the recipient. Let it then be replaced in the horn to be rectified, and for the consumption of the phlegm. This second distillation will cause a sweet, white oil to exude; this oil will be devoid of corrosive qualities; it will surpass all other metallic oils in excellence; and there is no doubt that, combined with the Elixir of Aristeus, it will be possible to perform such marvels as might be expected from so admirable an experiment.

4. Solutio

Full many a glorious morning have I seen

Flatter the mountain-tops with sovereign eye,

Kissing with golden face the meadows green,

Gilding pale streams with heavenly alchemy.

ADAM was the first inventor of arts, because he had knowledge of all things as well after the Fall as before. Thence he predicted the world's destruction by water. From this cause, too, it came about that his successors erected two tables of stone, on which they engraved all natural arts in hieroglyphical characters, in order that their posterity might also become acquainted with this prediction, that so it might be heeded, and provision made in the time of danger. Subsequently, Noah found one of these tables under Mount Araroth, after the Deluge. In this table were described the courses of the upper firmament and of the lower globe, and also of the planets. At length this universal knowledge was divided into several parts, and lessened in its vigour and power. By means of this separation, one man became an astronomer, another a magician, another a cabalist, and a fourth an alchemist.

When a son of Noah possessed the third part of the world after the Flood, this Art broke into Chaldaea and Persia, and thence spread into Egypt. The Art having been found out by the superstitious and idolatrous Greeks, some of them who were wiser than the rest betook themselves to the Chaldeans and Egyptians, so that they might draw the same wisdom from their schools. Since, however, the theological study of the law of Moses did not satisfy them, they trusted to their own peculiar genius, and fell away from the right foundation of those natural secrets and arts. This is evident from their fabulous conceptions, and from their errors respecting the doctrine of Moses. It was the custom of the Egyptians to put forward the traditions of that surpassing wisdom only in enigmatical figures and abstruse histories and terms. This was afterwards followed by Homer with marvellous poetical skill; and Pythagoras was also acquainted with it, seeing that he comprised in his writings many things out of the law of Moses and the Old Testament. In like manner, Hippocrates, Thales of Miletus, Anaxagoras, Democritus, and others, did not scruple to fix their minds on the same subject. And yet none of them were practised in the true Astrology, Geometry, Arithmetic, or Medicine, because their pride prevented this, since they would not admit disciples belonging to other nations than their own. Even when they had got some insight from the Chaldeans and Egyptians, they became more arrogant still than they were before by Nature, and without any diffidence propounded the subject substantially indeed, but mixed with subtle fictions or falsehoods; and then they attempted to elaborate a certain kind of philosophy which descended from them to the Latins. These in their turn, being educated herewith, adorned it with their own doctrines, and by these the philosophy was spread over Europe. Many academies were founded for the propagation of their dogmas and rules, so that the young might be instructed; and this system flourishes with the Germans, and other nations, right down to the present day.

The Magi in their wisdom asserted that all creatures might be brought to one unified substance, which substance they affirm may, by purifications and purgations, attain to so high a degree of subtlety, such divine nature and occult property, as to work wonderful results. For they considered that by returning to the earth, and by a supreme magical separation, a certain perfect substance would come forth, which is at length, by many industrious and prolonged preparations, exalted and raised up above the range of vegetable substances into mineral, above mineral into metallic, and above perfect

Man was regarded by Paracelsus as himself in a special manner the true Quintessence. The Creator extracted the essence out of the four elements into one mass; He extracted also the essence of wisdom, art, and reason out of the stars, and this twofold essence He congested into one mass: which mass Scripture calls the slime of the earth. From that mass two bodies were made – the sidereal and the elementary. These, according to the light of Nature, are called the *quintum esse*. The mass was extracted, and therein the firmament and the elements were condensed. What was extracted from the four after this manner constituted a fifth. The Quintessence is the nucleus and the place of the essences and properties of all things in the universal world. All nature came into the hand of God – all potency, all property, all essence of the superior and inferior globe. All these had God joined in His hand, and from these He formed man according to His image.
– *Philosophia Sagax*, Lib. I., c. 2.

metallic substances into a perpetual and divine Quintessence[*], including in itself the essence of all celestial and terrestrial 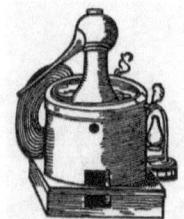 creatures. The Arabs and Greeks, by the occult characters and hieroglyphic descriptions of the Persians and the Egyptians, attained to secret and abstruse mysteries. When these were obtained and partially understood they saw with their own eyes, in the course of experimenting, many wonderful and strange effects. But since the supercelestial operations lay more deeply hidden than their capacity could penetrate, they did not call this a supercelestial arcanum according to the institution of the Magi, but the arcanum of the Philosophers' Stone according to the counsel and judgment of Pythagoras. Whoever obtained this Stone overshadowed it with various enigmatical figures, deceptive resemblances, comparisons, and fictitious titles, so that its matter might remain occult. Very little or no knowledge of it therefore can be had from them.

Philosophers have laboured greatly in the art of ferments and of fermentations, which seems important above all others. With reference thereto some have made a vow to God and to the

---

[*] For an insightful exploration of the perpetual and divine Quintessence, see *The Book of Dust* (Charlotte, VT: Eltanin Publishing. 2015).

philosophers that they would never divulge its arcanum by similitudes or by parables.

Nevertheless, Hermes, the father of all philosophers, in the "Book of the Seven Treatises", most clearly discloses the secret of ferments, saying that they consist only of their own paste; and  more at length he says that the ferment whitens the confection, hinders combustion, altogether retards the flux of the tincture, consoles bodies, and amplifies unions. He says, also, that this is the key and the end of the work, concluding that the ferment is nothing but paste, as that of the sun is nothing but sun, and that of the moon nothing but moon. Others affirm that the ferment is the soul, and if this be not rightly prepared from the magistery, it effects nothing. Some zealots of this Art seek the Art in common sulphur, arsenic, tutia, auripigment, vitriol, etc., but in vain; since the substance which is sought is the same as that from which it has to be drawn forth. It should be remarked, therefore, that fermentations of this kind do not succeed according to the wishes of the zealots in the way they desire, but, as is clear from what has been said above, simply in the way of natural successes.

But, to come at length to the weight; this must be noted in two ways. The first is natural, the second artificial. The natural attains its result in the earth by Nature and concordance. Of this, Arnold says: If more or less earth than Nature requires be added, the soul is suffocated, and no result is perceived, nor any fixation. It is the same with the water. If more or less of this be taken it will bring a corresponding loss. A superfluity renders the matter unduly moist, and a deficiency makes it too dry and too hard. If there be over much air present, it is too strongly impressed on the tincture; if there be too little, the body will turn out pallid. In the same way, if the fire be too strong, the matter is burnt up; if it be too slack, it has not the power of drying, nor of dissolving or heating the other elements. In these things elemental heat consists.

Artificial weight is quite occult. It is comprised in the magical art of ponderations. Between the spirit, soul, and body, say the philosophers, weight consists of Sulphur as the director of the work; for the soul strongly desires Sulphur, and necessarily observes it by reason of its weight.

You can understand it thus: Our matter is united to a red fixed Sulphur, to which a third part of the regimen has been entrusted, even to the ultimate degree, so that it may perfect to infinity the operation of the Stone, may remain therewith together with its fire, and may consist of a weight equal to the matter itself, in and through all, without variation of any degree. Therefore, after the matter has been adapted and mixed in its proportionate weight, it should be closely shut up with its seal in the vessel of the philosophers, and committed to the secret fire. In this the Philsophic Sun will rise and surge up, and will illuminate all things that have been looking for his light, expecting it with highest hope.

In these few words we will conclude the arcanum of the Stone, an arcanum which is in no way maimed or defective, for which we give God undying thanks. Now have we opened to you our treasure, which is not to be paid for by the riches of the whole world.

5. Mortificatio & Putrificatio

A fish that leaves the water has this relief:

the dying it endures ends at last in death.

SAINT JOHN OF THE CROSS

Dark Night of the Soul

On a dark night,
Kindled in love with yearnings—oh, happy chance!—
I went forth without being observed,
My house being now at rest.

In darkness and secure,
By the secret ladder, disguised—oh, happy chance!—
In darkness and in concealment,
My house being now at rest.

Mortificatio & Putrificatio

In the happy night,
In secret, when none saw me,
Nor I beheld aught,
Without light or guide, save that which burned in my
heart.

This light guided me
More surely than the light of noonday
To the place where he (well I knew who!) was awaiting me—
A place where none appeared.

Oh, night that guided me,
Oh, night more lovely than the dawn,
Oh, night that joined Beloved with lover,
Lover transformed in the Beloved!

Upon my flowery breast,
Kept wholly for himself alone,
There he stayed sleeping, and I caressed him,
And the fanning of the cedars made a breeze.

The breeze blew from the turret
As I parted his locks;
With his gentle hand he wounded my neck
And caused all my senses to be suspended.

I remained, lost in oblivion;
My face I reclined on the Beloved.
All ceased and I abandoned myself,
Leaving my cares forgotten among the lilies.

6. Coagulatio

The Star which guided them is that same Blazing Star, the image whereof we find in all initiations. To the Alchemists it is the sign of the Quintessence.

M de L

Coagulatio

∴ξπξζαζ∴ξπξζαζ∴ξπξζαζ∴ξπξ∴ξπξ∴ξπξζαζζαζ∴ξπξζαζ∴ξπξ∴ξπξ∴ξπξ
∴ξπξζαζζαζ∴ξπξ∴ξπξζαζ∴ξπξζαζ∴ξπξ∴ξπξζαζ∴ξπξ∴ξπξ∴ξπξ∴ξπξ∴ξπξ
∴ξπξζαζζαζζαζ∴ξπξ∴ξπξ∴ξπξ∴ξπξ∴ξπξζαζζαζζαζ∴ξπξζαζ∴ξπξζαζ
∴ξπξζαζζαζζαζ∴ξπξ∴ξπξζαζ∴ξπξ∴ξπξζαζζαζζαζ∴ξπξ∴ξπξ∴ξπξ∴ξπξ
∴ξπξζαζζαζ∴ξπξζαζζαζζαζζαζ∴ξπξζαζζαζζαζ∴ξπξ∴ξπξζαζζαζ
∴ξπξζαζζαζ∴ξπξ∴ξπξζαζ∴ξπξζαζ∴ξπξ∴ξπξζαζ∴ξπξ∴ξπξ∴ξπξ∴ξπξ∴ξπξ
∴ξπξζαζζαζ∴ξπξζαζζαζζαζ∴ξπξζαζζαζ∴ξπξ∴ξπξζαζζαζ∴ξπξ
∴ξπξ∴ξπξζαζ∴ξπξ∴ξπξ∴ξπξ∴ξπξ∴ξπξ∴ξπξζαζζαζζαζ∴ξπξζαζ∴ξπξ∴ξπξ
∴ξπξζαζζαζ∴ξπξζαζ∴ξπξ∴ξπξ∴ξπξ∴ξπξζαζζαζ∴ξπξ∴ξπξζαζ∴ξπξζαζ
∴ξπξ∴ξπξζαζ∴ξπξ∴ξπξ∴ξπξ∴ξπξ∴ξπξ∴ξπξζαζζαζζαζ∴ξπξ∴ξπξζαζζαζ
∴ξπξζαζζαζ∴ξπξζαζζαζζαζζαζ∴ξπξζαζζαζζαζ∴ξπξζαζ∴ξπξζαζ
∴ξπξζαζζαζ∴ξπξζαζζαζ∴ξπξ∴ξπξ∴ξπξ∴ξπξζαζ∴ξπξ∴ξπξ∴ξπξ∴ξπξ∴ξπξ
∴ξπξζαζζαζ∴ξπξ∴ξπξζαζ∴ξπξζαζ∴ξπξζαζζαζ∴ξπξζαζζαζζαζ∴ξπξ
∴ξπξζαζζαζζαζ∴ξπξζαζ∴ξπξ∴ξπξ∴ξπξζαζζαζ∴ξπξ∴ξπξζαζ∴ξπξζαζ
∴ξπξζαζζαζζαζ∴ξπξ∴ξπξζαζ∴ξπξ∴ξπξζαζζαζ∴ξπξζαζ∴ξπξ∴ξπξζαζ
∴ξπξζαζζαζ∴ξπξζαζζαζζαζ∴ξπξ∴ξπξζαζζαζ∴ξπξ∴ξπξζαζζαζζαζ
∴ξπξ∴ξπξζαζ∴ξπξ∴ξπξ∴ξπξ∴ξπξ∴ξπξ∴ξπξζαζζαζζαζ∴ξπξζαζ∴ξπξ∴ξπξ
∴ξπξζαζζαζ∴ξπξζαζ∴ξπξ∴ξπξ∴ξπξ∴ξπξζαζζαζ∴ξπξ∴ξπξζαζ∴ξπξζαζ
∴ξπξ∴ξπξζαζ∴ξπξ∴ξπξ∴ξπξ∴ξπξ∴ξπξ∴ξπξζαζζαζ∴ξπξ∴ξπξ∴ξπξζαζ∴ξπξ
∴ξπξζαζζαζ∴ξπξζαζζαζζαζ∴ξπξζαζζαζ∴ξπξ∴ξπξζαζ∴ξπξ∴ξπξ
∴ξπξζαζζαζζαζ∴ξπξ∴ξπξζαζ∴ξπξ∴ξπξζαζ∴ξπξ∴ξπξ∴ξπξ∴ξπξ∴ξπξ
∴ξπξζαζζαζ∴ξπξζαζ∴ξπξ∴ξπξζαζ∴ξπξζαζζαζζαζ∴ξπξ∴ξπξζαζζαζ
∴ξπξ∴ξπξζαζ∴ξπξ∴ξπξ∴ξπξ∴ξπξ∴ξπξ∴ξπξζαζζαζζαζ∴ξπξζαζ∴ξπξ∴ξπξ
∴ξπξζαζζαζ∴ξπξζαζζαζζαζζαζ∴ξπξ∴ξπξζαζ∴ξπξ∴ξπξ∴ξπξ∴ξπξ∴ξπξ
∴ξπξζαζζαζ∴ξπξ∴ξπξζαζ∴ξπξ∴ξπξ∴ξπξζαζζαζ∴ξπξζαζ∴ξπξ∴ξπξζαζ
∴ξπξζαζζαζζαζ∴ξπξ∴ξπξζαζζαζ∴ξπξζαζζαζζαζ∴ξπξ∴ξπξ∴ξπξ∴ξπξ
∴ξπξζαζζαζ∴ξπξζαζζαζ∴ξπξ∴ξπξ∴ξπξζαζζαζ∴ξπξ∴ξπξ∴ξπξ∴ξπξζαζ
∴ξπξζαζζαζζαζζαζ∴ξπξ∴ξπξζαζ∴ξπξ∴ξπξζαζ∴ξπξ∴ξπξ∴ξπξ∴ξπξ∴ξπξ
∴ξπξζαζζαζ∴ξπξζαζ∴ξπξ∴ξπξ∴ξπξ∴ξπξζαζζαζ∴ξπξ∴ξπξζαζ∴ξπξζαζ
∴ξπξζαζζαζζαζ∴ξπξ∴ξπξζαζ∴ξπξ∴ξπξ∴ξπξζαζ∴ξπξ∴ξπξ∴ξπξ∴ξπξ∴ξπξ
∴ξπξζαζζαζζαζ∴ξπξ∴ξπξ∴ξπξ∴ξπξ∴ξπξζαζζαζ∴ξπξζαζζαζζαζζαζ

∴ξπξζαζζαζζαζ∴ξπξζαζζαζζαζ ∴ξπξζαζζαζ∴ξπξ∴ξπξζαζ∴ξπξζαζ
∴ξπξζαζζαζζαζ∴ξπξ∴ξπξζαζ∴ξπξ ∴ξπξζαζζαζζαζ∴ξπξ∴ξπξζαζζαζ
∴ξπξ∴ξπξζαζ∴ξπξ∴ξπξ∴ξπξ∴ξπξ∴ξπξ ∴ξπξζαζζαζ∴ξπξ∴ξπξ∴ξπξ∴ξπξζαζ
∴ξπξζαζζαζ∴ξπξζαζζαζζαζ∴ξπξ ∴ξπξζαζζαζ∴ξπξ∴ξπξζαζ∴ξπξ∴ξπξ
∴ξπξ∴ξπξζαζ∴ξπξ∴ξπξ∴ξπξ∴ξπξ∴ξπξ ∴ξπξζαζζαζ∴ξπξ∴ξπξ∴ξπξ∴ξπξζαζ
∴ξπξζαζζαζ∴ξπξ∴ξπξ∴ξπξζαζζαζ ∴ξπξζαζζαζζαζ∴ξπξζαζ∴ξπξ∴ξπξ

∴ξπξζαζζαζ∴ξπξζαζ∴ξπξ∴ξπξζαζ ∴ξπξζαζζαζ∴ξπξζαζζαζζαζζαζ
∴ξπξζαζζαζ∴ξπξζαζζαζζαζ∴ξπξ ∴ξπξζαζζαζζαζ∴ξπξ∴ξπξζαζζαζ
∴ξπξ∴ξπξζαζ∴ξπξ∴ξπξ∴ξπξ∴ξπξ∴ξπξ ∴ξπξζαζζαζ∴ξπξζαζ∴ξπξ∴ξπξζαζ
∴ξπξζαζζαζ∴ξπξζαζζαζζαζ∴ξπξ ∴ξπξ∴ξπξζαζ∴ξπξ∴ξπξ∴ξπξ∴ξπξ∴ξπξ
∴ξπξζαζζαζζαζ∴ξπξζαζ∴ξπξ∴ξπξ ∴ξπξζαζζαζ∴ξπξζαζ∴ξπξ∴ξπξ∴ξπξ

Coagulatio

∴ξπξζαζζαζ∴ξπξζαζ∴ξπξ∴ξπξζαζ ∴ξπξζαζζαζζαζ∴ξπξ∴ξπξζαζζαζ
∴ξπξ∴ξπξζαζ∴ξπξ∴ξπξ∴ξπξ∴ξπξ∴ξπξ ∴ξπξζαζζαζζαζ∴ξπξζαζζαζζαζ
∴ξπξζαζζαζ∴ξπξζαζζαζζαζζαζ ∴ξπξζαζζαζζαζ∴ξπξ∴ξπξζαζ∴ξπξ
∴ξπξζαζζαζ∴ξπξζαζζαζ∴ξπξ∴ξπξ ∴ξπξζαζζαζ∴ξπξ∴ξπξζαζ∴ξπξ∴ξπξ
∴ξπξ∴ξπξζαζ∴ξπξζαζζαζ∴ξπξ∴ξπξ ∴ξπξ∴ξπξζαζ∴ξπξ∴ξπξ∴ξπξ∴ξπξ∴ξπξ
∴ξπξζαζζαζ∴ξπξ∴ξπξζαζζαζ∴ξπξ ∴ξπξζαζζαζ∴ξπξζαζζαζζαζζαζ
∴ξπξζαζζαζζαζ∴ξπξ∴ξπξζαζ∴ξπξ ∴ξπξ∴ξπξζαζ∴ξπξ∴ξπξ∴ξπξ∴ξπξ∴ξπξ
∴ξπξζαζζαζζαζ∴ξπξ∴ξπξζαζζαζ ∴ξπξζαζζαζ∴ξπξζαζ∴ξπξ∴ξπξ∴ξπξ
∴ξπξζαζζαζ∴ξπξ∴ξπξζαζ∴ξπξζαζ ∴ξπξ∴ξπξζαζ∴ξπξ∴ξπξ∴ξπξ∴ξπξ∴ξπξ
∴ξπξζαζζαζ∴ξπξζαζζαζζαζ∴ξπξ ∴ξπξζαζζαζ∴ξπξ∴ξπξζαζ∴ξπξζαζ
∴ξπξζαζζαζ∴ξπξ∴ξπξζαζ∴ξπξζαζ ∴ξπξζαζζαζ∴ξπξ∴ξπξζαζ∴ξπξ∴ξπξ
∴ξπξζαζζαζζαζ∴ξπξ∴ξπξζαζζαζ ∴ξπξ∴ξπξζαζ∴ξπξ∴ξπξ∴ξπξ∴ξπξ∴ξπξ
∴ξπξζαζζαζ∴ξπξ∴ξπξ∴ξπξ∴ξπξζαζ ∴ξπξζαζζαζ∴ξπξζαζζαζζαζ∴ξπξ
∴ξπξ∴ξπξζαζ∴ξπξ∴ξπξ∴ξπξ∴ξπξ∴ξπξ ∴ξπξζαζζαζ∴ξπξζαζ∴ξπξ∴ξπξζαζ
∴ξπξζαζζαζ∴ξπξζαζζαζζαζ∴ξπξ ∴ξπξζαζζαζζαζ∴ξπξ∴ξπξζαζζαζ
∴ξπξζαζζαζ∴ξπξζαζ∴ξπξ∴ξπξ ∴ξπξζαζζαζζαζ∴ξπξ∴ξπξζαζ∴ξπξ
∴ξπξζαζζαζζαζ∴ξπξζαζ∴ξπξζαζ ∴ξπξζαζζαζ∴ξπξζαζζαζ∴ξπξζαζ
∴ξπξζαζζαζ∴ξπξ∴ξπξζαζ∴ξπξζαζ ∴ξπξζαζζαζ∴ξπξζαζζαζζαζ∴ξπξ
∴ξπξζαζζαζζαζ∴ξπξζαζ∴ξπξ∴ξπξ ∴ξπξ∴ξπξζαζ∴ξπξζαζζαζζαζ∴ξπξ
∴ξπξ∴ξπξζαζ∴ξπξ∴ξπξ∴ξπξ∴ξπξ∴ξπξ
∴ξπξζαζ∴ξπξ∴ξπξ∴ξπξ∴ξπξζαζ∴ξπξ ∴ξπξζαζζαζζαζζαζ∴ξπξ∴ξπξζαζ
∴ξπξ∴ξπξζαζ∴ξπξ∴ξπξ∴ξπξ∴ξπξ∴ξπξ ∴ξπξζαζζαζ∴ξπξ∴ξπξζαζ∴ξπξ∴ξπξ
∴ξπξζαζζαζ∴ξπξ∴ξπξζαζ∴ξπξζαζ ∴ξπξζαζζαζζαζ∴ξπξ∴ξπξζαζζαζ
∴ξπξζαζζαζ∴ξπξ∴ξπξ∴ξπξζαζζαζ ∴ξπξζαζζαζ∴ξπξ∴ξπξζαζ∴ξπξζαζ
∴ξπξζαζζαζ∴ξπξζαζζαζζαζ∴ξπξ ∴ξπξζαζζαζ∴ξπξ∴ξπξζαζ∴ξπξ∴ξπξ
∴ξπξζαζζαζ∴ξπξζαζ∴ξπξ∴ξπξζαζ ∴ξπξζαζζαζ∴ξπξζαζζαζζαζ∴ξπξ
∴ξπξζαζζαζ∴ξπξ∴ξπξζαζζαζζαζ ∴ξπξ∴ξπξζαζ∴ξπξ∴ξπξ∴ξπξ∴ξπξ∴ξπξ
∴ξπξζαζζαζζαζ∴ξπξζαζ∴ξπξ∴ξπξ ∴ξπξζαζζαζ∴ξπξζαζζαζζαζζαζ
∴ξπξ∴ξπξζαζ∴ξπξ∴ξπξ∴ξπξ∴ξπξ∴ξπξ ∴ξπξζαζζαζζαζ∴ξπξζαζ∴ξπξ∴ξπξ
∴ξπξζαζζαζ∴ξπξζαζ∴ξπξ∴ξπξ∴ξπξ ∴ξπξζαζζαζ∴ξπξζαζ∴ξπξ∴ξπξζαζ
∴ξπξζαζζαζζαζ∴ξπξ∴ξπξζαζζαζ ∴ξπξ∴ξπξζαζ∴ξπξ∴ξπξ∴ξπξ∴ξπξ∴ξπξ

∴ξπξζαζζαζζαζζαζ∴ξπξζαζζαζζαζ∴ξπξζαζζαζ∴ξπξζαζζαζζαζζαζ
∴ξπξζαζζαζζαζ∴ξπξ∴ξπξζαζ∴ξπξ∴ξπξζαζζαζ∴ξπξζαζζαζ∴ξπξ∴ξπξ
∴ξπξζαζζαζ∴ξπξ∴ξπξζαζ∴ξπξ∴ξπξ∴ξπξ∴ξπξζαζ∴ξπξζαζζαζ∴ξπξ∴ξπξ
∴ξπξ∴ξπξζαζ∴ξπξ∴ξπξ∴ξπξ∴ξπξ∴ξπξ∴ξπξζαζζαζζαζ∴ξπξ∴ξπξζαζζαζ
∴ξπξζαζζαζ∴ξπξζαζ∴ξπξ∴ξπξ∴ξπξ∴ξπξζαζζαζ∴ξπξ∴ξπξζαζ∴ξπξζαζ
∴ξπξ∴ξπξζαζ∴ξπξ∴ξπξ∴ξπξ∴ξπξ∴ξπξ∴ξπξζαζζαζ∴ξπξζαζ∴ξπξ∴ξπξζαζ
∴ξπξζαζζαζ∴ξπξζαζζαζζαζ∴ξπξ∴ξπξζαζζαζ∴ξπξ∴ξπξ∴ξπξζαζζαζ
∴ξπξζαζζαζζαζ∴ξπξ∴ξπξζαζ∴ξπξ∴ξπξζαζζαζ∴ξπξ∴ξπξζαζ∴ξπξζαζ
∴ξπξζαζζαζ∴ξπξ∴ξπξ∴ξπξ∴ξπξζαζ∴ξπξζαζζαζζαζ∴ξπξ∴ξπξζαζζαζ
∴ξπξζαζζαζ∴ξπξ∴ξπξζαζ∴ξπξζαζ∴ξπξζαζζαζζαζ∴ξπξ∴ξπξζαζζαζ
∴ξπξ∴ξπξζαζ∴ξπξ∴ξπξ∴ξπξ∴ξπξ∴ξπξ∴ξπξζαζζαζ∴ξπξζαζ∴ξπξ∴ξπξ∴ξπξ
∴ξπξζαζζαζ∴ξπξ∴ξπξζαζ∴ξπξζαζ∴ξπξ∴ξπξζαζ∴ξπξ∴ξπξ∴ξπξ∴ξπξ∴ξπξ
∴ξπξζαζζαζ∴ξπξ∴ξπξζαζζαζ∴ξπξ∴ξπξζαζζαζ∴ξπξζαζζαζ∴ξπξ∴ξπξ
∴ξπξζαζζαζ∴ξπξζαζζαζζαζζαζ∴ξπξζαζζαζζαζ∴ξπξζαζζαζζαζ
∴ξπξ∴ξπξζαζ∴ξπξ∴ξπξ∴ξπξ∴ξπξ∴ξπξ∴ξπξζαζζαζ∴ξπξζαζζαζζαζζαζ
∴ξπξζαζζαζ∴ξπξ∴ξπξζαζζαζ∴ξπξ∴ξπξ∴ξπξζαζ∴ξπξ∴ξπξ∴ξπξ∴ξπξ∴ξπξ
∴ξπξζαζζαζ∴ξπξζαζ∴ξπξ∴ξπξ∴ξπξ∴ξπξζαζζαζ∴ξπξ∴ξπξζαζ∴ξπξζαζ
∴ξπξζαζζαζζαζ∴ξπξ∴ξπξζαζ∴ξπξ∴ξπξ∴ξπξζαζ∴ξπξ∴ξπξ∴ξπξ∴ξπξ∴ξπξ
∴ξπξζαζζαζζαζ∴ξπξ∴ξπξ∴ξπξ∴ξπξ∴ξπξζαζζαζ∴ξπξζαζζαζζαζζαζ
∴ξπξζαζζαζζαζ∴ξπξζαζζαζζαζ∴ξπξζαζζαζ∴ξπξ∴ξπξζαζ∴ξπξζαζ
∴ξπξζαζζαζζαζ∴ξπξ∴ξπξζαζ∴ξπξ∴ξπξ∴ξπξζαζ∴ξπξ∴ξπξ∴ξπξ∴ξπξ∴ξπξ
∴ξπξζαζζαζζαζ∴ξπξζαζ∴ξπξ∴ξπξ∴ξπξζαζζαζ∴ξπξζαζζαζζαζζαζ
∴ξπξ∴ξπξζαζ∴ξπξ∴ξπξ∴ξπξ∴ξπξ∴ξπξ∴ξπξζαζζαζ∴ξπξ∴ξπξζαζζαζζαζ
∴ξπξζαζζαζζαζ∴ξπξζαζ∴ξπξζαζ∴ξπξζαζζαζ∴ξπξζαζ∴ξπξ∴ξπξζαζ
∴ξπξζαζζαζ∴ξπξ∴ξπξζαζ∴ξπξ∴ξπξ∴ξπξζαζζαζ∴ξπξ∴ξπξζαζ∴ξπξζαζ
∴ξπξ∴ξπξζαζ∴ξπξ∴ξπξ∴ξπξ∴ξπξ∴ξπξ∴ξπξζαζζαζζαζ∴ξπξζαζ∴ξπξ∴ξπξ
∴ξπξζαζζαζ∴ξπξζαζ∴ξπξ∴ξπξ∴ξπξ∴ξπξζαζζαζ∴ξπξ∴ξπξζαζ∴ξπξζαζ
∴ξπξ∴ξπξζαζ∴ξπξ∴ξπξ∴ξπξ∴ξπξ∴ξπξ∴ξπξζαζζαζ∴ξπξζαζ∴ξπξ∴ξπξ∴ξπξ
∴ξπξζαζζαζζαζ∴ξπξζαζ∴ξπξζαζ∴ξπξζαζζαζ∴ξπξζαζζαζ∴ξπξζαζ
∴ξπξζαζζαζ∴ξπξ∴ξπξ∴ξπξ∴ξπξζαζ∴ξπξζαζζαζ∴ξπξζαζζαζζαζ∴ξπξ
∴ξπξ∴ξπξζαζ∴ξπξ∴ξπξ∴ξπξ∴ξπξ∴ξπξ∴ξπξζαζζαζ∴ξπξ∴ξπξ∴ξπξζαζ∴ξπξ

Coagulatio

∴ξπξζαζζαζ∵ξπξ∵ξπξζαζ∵ξπξζαζ ∵ξπξζαζζαζ∵ξπξζαζ∵ξπξ∵ξπξζαζ
∵ξπξζαζζαζ∵ξπξζαζζαζζαζ∵ξπξ ∵ξπξζαζζαζ∵ξπξ∵ξπξζαζζαζζαζ
∵ξπξ∵ξπξζαζ∵ξπξ∵ξπξ∵ξπξ∵ξπξ∵ξπξ ∵ξπξζαζζαζζαζ∵ξπξζαζ∵ξπξ∵ξπξ
∵ξπξζαζζαζ∵ξπξζαζ∵ξπξ∵ξπξ∵ξπξ ∵ξπξζαζζαζζαζ∵ξπξ∵ξπξζαζ∵ξπξ
∵ξπξζαζζαζ∵ξπξζαζζαζζαζζαζ ∵ξπξζαζζαζζαζ∵ξπξζαζ∵ξπξζαζ
∵ξπξζαζζαζ∵ξπξ∵ξπξζαζζαζζαζ ∵ξπξζαζζαζ∵ξπξζαζ∵ξπξ∵ξπξ∵ξπξ
∵ξπξ∵ξπξζαζ∵ξπξ∵ξπξ∵ξπξ∵ξπξ∵ξπξ ∵ξπξζαζζαζζαζ∵ξπξζαζ∵ξπξ∵ξπξ
∵ξπξζαζζαζ∵ξπξζαζ∵ξπξ∵ξπξ∵ξπξ ∵ξπξζαζζαζ∵ξπξ∵ξπξζαζ∵ξπξζαζ
∵ξπξ∵ξπξζαζ∵ξπξ∵ξπξ∵ξπξ∵ξπξ∵ξπξ ∵ξπξζαζζαζζαζ∵ξπξζαζζαζζαζ
∵ξπξζαζζαζ∵ξπξζαζζαζζαζζαζ ∵ξπξζαζζαζ∵ξπξ∵ξπξζαζ∵ξπξ
∵ξπξζαζζαζ∵ξπξζαζζαζ∵ξπξ∵ξπξ ∵ξπξζαζζαζ∵ξπξ∵ξπξζαζ∵ξπξ∵ξπξ
∵ξπξ∵ξπξζαζ∵ξπξζαζζαζζαζ∵ξπξ ∵ξπξ∵ξπξζαζ∵ξπξ∵ξπξ∵ξπξ∵ξπξ∵ξπξ
∵ξπξζαζ∵ξπξζαζ∵ξπξζαζ∵ξπξ∵ξπξ ∵ξπξζαζζαζ∵ξπξζαζ∵ξπξ∵ξπξ∵ξπξ
∵ξπξζαζζαζ∵ξπξ∵ξπξζαζ∵ξπξζαζ ∵ξπξζαζζαζζαζ∵ξπξ∵ξπξζαζ∵ξπξ
∵ξπξζαζζαζ∵ξπξ∵ξπξζαζ∵ξπξζαζ ∵ξπξζαζζαζ∵ξπξ∵ξπξ∵ξπξζαζ∵ξπξ
∵ξπξζαζζαζζαζζαζ∵ξπξ∵ξπξζαζ ∵ξπξ∵ξπξζαζ∵ξπξ∵ξπξ∵ξπξ∵ξπξ∵ξπξ
∵ξπξζαζζαζζαζ∵ξπξ∵ξπξζαζζαζ ∵ξπξζαζζαζ∵ξπξζαζ∵ξπξ∵ξπξ∵ξπξ
∵ξπξζαζζαζ∵ξπξ∵ξπξζαζ∵ξπξζαζ ∵ξπξ∵ξπξζαζ∵ξπξ∵ξπξ∵ξπξ∵ξπξ∵ξπξ
∵ξπξζαζζαζζαζ∵ξπξ∵ξπξ∵ξπξ∵ξπξ ∵ξπξζαζζαζ∵ξπξ∵ξπξζαζ∵ξπξζαζ
∵ξπξζαζζαζζαζ∵ξπξ∵ξπξζαζ∵ξπξ ∵ξπξζαζζαζ∵ξπξ∵ξπξζαζζαζ∵ξπξ
∵ξπξζαζζαζ∵ξπξ∵ξπξζαζ∵ξπξζαζ ∵ξπξζαζζαζ∵ξπξ∵ξπξ∵ξπξζαζζαζ
∵ξπξζαζζαζζαζ∵ξπξζαζ∵ξπξ∵ξπξ ∵ξπξζαζζαζζαζ∵ξπξ∵ξπξζαζζαζ
∵ξπξ∵ξπξζαζ∵ξπξ∵ξπξ∵ξπξ∵ξπξ∵ξπξ ∵ξπξζαζζαζ∵ξπξζαζ∵ξπξ∵ξπξ∵ξπξ
∵ξπξζαζζαζ∵ξπξ∵ξπξζαζ∵ξπξζαζ ∵ξπξζαζζαζζαζ∵ξπξ∵ξπξζαζ∵ξπξ
∵ξπξζαζζαζζαζ∵ξπξ∵ξπξζαζζαζ ∵ξπξζαζζαζ∵ξπξ∵ξπξζαζ∵ξπξζαζ
∵ξπξζαζζαζ∵ξπξζαζζαζ∵ξπξ∵ξπξ ∵ξπξζαζζαζ∵ξπξ∵ξπξζαζζαζ∵ξπξ
∵ξπξ∵ξπξζαζ∵ξπξ∵ξπξ∵ξπξ∵ξπξ∵ξπξ ∵ξπξζαζζαζ∵ξπξ∵ξπξ∵ξπξ∵ξπξζαζ
∵ξπξζαζζαζ∵ξπξ∵ξπξ∵ξπξζαζ∵ξπξ ∵ξπξζαζζαζ∵ξπξζαζζαζζαζζαζ
∵ξπξζαζζαζζαζ∵ξπξζαζζαζ∵ξπξ ∵ξπξζαζζαζ∵ξπξ∵ξπξζαζ∵ξπξζαζ
∵ξπξ∵ξπξζαζ∵ξπξ∵ξπξ∵ξπξ∵ξπξ∵ξπξ ∵ξπξζαζζαζ∵ξπξ∵ξπξ∵ξπξ∵ξπξζαζ

∴ξπξζαζζαζ∴ξπξζαζζαζζαζ∴ξπξ ∴ξπξζαζζαζ∴ξπξ∴ξπξζαζ∴ξπξ∴ξπξ
∴ξπξ∴ξπξζαζ∴ξπξ∴ξπξ∴ξπξ∴ξπξ∴ξπξ ∴ξπξζαζζαζ∴ξπξ∴ξπξ∴ξπξζαζ∴ξπξ
∴ξπξζαζζαζ∴ξπξ∴ξπξζαζ∴ξπξζαζ ∴ξπξζαζζαζ∴ξπξζαζζαζ∴ξπξ∴ξπξ
∴ξπξζαζζαζ∴ξπξζαζζαζζαζζαζ ∴ξπξζαζζαζζαζ∴ξπξζαζζαζζαζ
∴ξπξ∴ξπξζαζ∴ξπξζαζζαζ∴ξπξ∴ξπξ ∴ξπξ∴ξπξζαζ∴ξπξ∴ξπξ∴ξπξ∴ξπξ∴ξπξ
∴ξπξζαζζαζ∴ξπξ∴ξπξ∴ξπξ∴ξπξζαζ ∴ξπξζαζζαζζαζ∴ξπξζαζ∴ξπξ∴ξπξ
∴ξπξζαζζαζζαζ∴ξπξζαζ∴ξπξ∴ξπξ ∴ξπξζαζζαζ∴ξπξ∴ξπξ∴ξπξ∴ξπξζαζ

Coagulatio

∴ξπξζαζζαζ∴ξπξζαζ∴ξπξ∴ξπξζαζ∴∴ξπξζαζζαζ∴ξπξζαζζαζζαζ∴ξπξ
∴ξπξζαζζαζ∴ξπξζαζ∴ξπξ∴ξπξζαζ∴ξπξζαζζαζ∴ξπξζαζζαζζαζ∴ξπξ
∴ξπξζαζζαζ∴ξπξ∴ξπξζαζζαζζαζ∴ξπξ∴ξπξζαζ∴ξπξ∴ξπξ∴ξπξ∴ξπξ∴ξπξ
∴ξπξζαζζαζ∴ξπξ∴ξπξ∴ξπξ∴ξπξζαζ∴∴ξπξ∴ξπξζαζ∴ξπξ∴ξπξ∴ξπξ∴ξπξ∴ξπξ
∴ξπξζαζζαζ∴ξπξζαζ∴ξπξ∴ξπξ∴ξπξ∴ξπξζαζζαζ∴ξπξζαζ∴ξπξ∴ξπξζαζ
∴ξπξζαζζαζ∴ξπξ∴ξπξζαζζαζζαζ∴∴ξπξζαζζαζ∴ξπξζαζ∴ξπξ∴ξπξ∴ξπξ
∴ξπξζαζζαζ∴ξπξ∴ξπξζαζ∴ξπξζαζ∴ξπξζαζζαζζαζ∴ξπξ∴ξπξζαζ∴ξπξ
∴ξπξ∴ξπξζαζ∴ξπξ∴ξπξ∴ξπξ∴ξπξ∴ξπξ∴ξπξζαζζαζζαζ∴ξπξ∴ξπξζαζζαζ
∴ξπξζαζζαζζαζ∴ξπξζαζ∴ξπξ∴ξπξ∴ξπξζαζζαζ∴ξπξ∴ξπξ∴ξπξ∴ξπξζαζ
∴ξπξζαζζαζζαζ∴ξπξζαζ∴ξπξ∴ξπξ∴ξπξζαζζαζ∴ξπξ∴ξπξζαζ∴ξπξζαζ
∴ξπξ∴ξπξζαζ∴ξπξ∴ξπξ∴ξπξ∴ξπξ∴ξπξ∴ξπξζαζζαζ∴ξπξ∴ξπξ∴ξπξζαζ∴ξπξ
∴ξπξζαζζαζζαζζαζ∴ξπξ∴ξπξζαζ∴∴ξπξ∴ξπξζαζ∴ξπξ∴ξπξ∴ξπξ∴ξπξ∴ξπξ
∴ξπξζαζζαζ∴ξπξ∴ξπξ∴ξπξζαζ∴ξπξ∴∴ξπξζαζζαζ∴ξπξ∴ξπξζαζ∴ξπξζαζ
∴ξπξζαζζαζ∴ξπξζαζ∴ξπξ∴ξπξζαζ∴ξπξζαζζαζ∴ξπξζαζζαζζαζ∴ξπξ
∴ξπξζαζζαζ∴ξπξ∴ξπξζαζζαζζαζ∴∴ξπξ∴ξπξζαζ∴ξπξ∴ξπξ∴ξπξ∴ξπξ∴ξπξ
∴ξπξζαζζαζ∴ξπξ∴ξπξζαζζαζ∴ξπξ∴ξπξζαζζαζζαζ∴ξπξζαζ∴ξπξζαζ
∴ξπξζαζζαζ∴ξπξζαζζαζ∴ξπξ∴ξπξ∴ξπξζαζζαζ∴ξπξ∴ξπξζαζζαζ∴ξπξ
∴ξπξζαζζαζ∴ξπξζαζ∴ξπξ∴ξπξζαζ∴ξπξζαζζαζ∴ξπξζαζζαζ∴ξπξ∴ξπξ
∴ξπξζαζζαζ∴ξπξζαζζαζ∴ξπξ∴ξπξ∴ξπξζαζζαζ∴ξπξ∴ξπξζαζ∴ξπξζαζ
∴ξπξζαζζαζ∴ξπξζαζ∴ξπξ∴ξπξζαζ∴ξπξ∴ξπξζαζ∴ξπξ∴ξπξ∴ξπξ∴ξπξ∴ξπξ
∴ξπξζαζζαζ∴ξπξζαζ∴ξπξ∴ξπξζαζ∴ξπξζαζζαζ∴ξπξζαζζαζζαζ∴ξπξ
∴ξπξ∴ξπξζαζ∴ξπξ∴ξπξ∴ξπξ∴ξπξ∴ξπξ∴ξπξζαζζαζ∴ξπξ∴ξπξ∴ξπξ∴ξπξζαζ
∴ξπξζαζζαζ∴ξπξζαζζαζ∴ξπξ∴ξπξ∴ξπξζαζζαζ∴ξπξζαζζαζ∴ξπξ∴ξπξ
∴ξπξ∴ξπξζαζ∴ξπξ∴ξπξ∴ξπξ∴ξπξ∴ξπξ∴ξπξζαζζαζ∴ξπξ∴ξπξζαζ∴ξπξ∴ξπξ
∴ξπξζαζζαζ∴ξπξζαζ∴ξπξ∴ξπξζαζ∴ξπξζαζζαζ∴ξπξζαζζαζ∴ξπξζαζ
∴ξπξζαζζαζ∴ξπξ∴ξπξζαζ∴ξπξζαζ∴ξπξζαζζαζ∴ξπξζαζζαζζαζ∴ξπξ
∴ξπξζαζζαζζαζ∴ξπξ∴ξπξζαζζαζ∴ξπξζαζζαζ∴ξπξζαζ∴ξπξ∴ξπξζαζ
∴ξπξζαζζαζ∴ξπξζαζζαζζαζζαζ∴ξπξζαζζαζ∴ξπξζαζζαζζαζ∴ξπξ
∴ξπξζαζζαζζαζ∴ξπξ∴ξπξζαζζαζ∴ξπξ∴ξπξζαζ∴ξπξζαζζαζζαζ∴ξπξ
∴ξπξ∴ξπξζαζ∴ξπξ∴ξπξ∴ξπξ∴ξπξ∴ξπξ∴ξπξζαζ∴ξπξ∴ξπξζαζ∴ξπξ∴ξπξζαζ
∴ξπξζαζζαζ∴ξπξ∴ξπξζαζζαζ∴ξπξ∴ξπξ∴ξπξζαζ∴ξπξ∴ξπξ∴ξπξ∴ξπξ∴ξπξ

∵ξπξζαζζαζζαζ∵ξπξ∵ξπξζαζζαζ ∵ξπξζαζζαζ∵ξπξζαζ∵ξπξ∵ξπξ∵ξπξ
∵ξπξζαζζαζ∵ξπξ∵ξπξζαζ∵ξπξζαζ ∵ξπξ∵ξπξζαζ∵ξπξ∵ξπξ∵ξπξ∵ξπξ∵ξπξ
∵ξπξζαζζαζ∵ξπξζαζ∵ξπξ∵ξπξζαζ ∵ξπξζαζζαζζαζ∵ξπξ∵ξπξζαζζαζ
∵ξπξ∵ξπξζαζ∵ξπξ∵ξπξ∵ξπξ∵ξπξ∵ξπξ ∵ξπξζαζζαζ∵ξπξζαζζαζζαζ∵ξπξ
∵ξπξζαζζαζ∵ξπξζαζζαζζαζζαζ ∵ξπξζαζζαζζαζ∵ξπξζαζ∵ξπξ∵ξπξ
∵ξπξ∵ξπξζαζ∵ξπξ∵ξπξ∵ξπξ∵ξπξ∵ξπξ ∵ξπξζαζζαζ∵ξπξ∵ξπξζαζζαζ∵ξπξ
∵ξπξζαζζαζζαζ∵ξπξζαζ∵ξπξζαζ ∵ξπξζαζζαζ∵ξπξζαζζαζ∵ξπξ∵ξπξ
∵ξπξζαζζαζ∵ξπξ∵ξπξζαζζαζ∵ξπξ ∵ξπξζαζζαζ∵ξπξζαζ∵ξπξ∵ξπξζαζ
∵ξπξζαζζαζ∵ξπξζαζζαζ∵ξπξ∵ξπξ ∵ξπξζαζζαζ∵ξπξζαζζαζ∵ξπξ∵ξπξ
∵ξπξζαζζαζ∵ξπξ∵ξπξζαζ∵ξπξζαζ ∵ξπξζαζζαζ∵ξπξ∵ξπξζαζ∵ξπξ∵ξπξ
∵ξπξ∵ξπξζαζ∵ξπξ∵ξπξ∵ξπξ∵ξπξ∵ξπξ ∵ξπξζαζζαζ∵ξπξ∵ξπξ∵ξπξζαζ∵ξπξ
∵ξπξζαζζαζ∵ξπξζαζζαζζαζζαζ ∵ξπξζαζζαζζαζ∵ξπξζαζ∵ξπξ∵ξπξ
∵ξπξζαζζαζ∵ξπξζαζ∵ξπξ∵ξπξ∵ξπξ ∵ξπξ∵ξπξζαζ∵ξπξ∵ξπξ∵ξπξ∵ξπξ∵ξπξ
∵ξπξζαζζαζ∵ξπξ∵ξπξ∵ξπξ∵ξπξζαζ ∵ξπξζαζζαζ∵ξπξ∵ξπξ∵ξπξζαζ∵ξπξ
∵ξπξζαζζαζ∵ξπξζαζζαζζαζζαζ ∵ξπξζαζζαζζαζ∵ξπξζαζζαζ∵ξπξ
∵ξπξζαζζαζ∵ξπξ∵ξπξζαζ∵ξπξζαζ ∵ξπξ∵ξπξζαζ∵ξπξ∵ξπξ∵ξπξ∵ξπξ∵ξπξ
∵ξπξζαζζαζ∵ξπξ∵ξπξ∵ξπξ∵ξπξζαζ ∵ξπξζαζζαζ∵ξπξζαζζαζζαζ∵ξπξ
∵ξπξζαζζαζ∵ξπξ∵ξπξζαζ∵ξπξ∵ξπξ ∵ξπξ∵ξπξζαζ∵ξπξ∵ξπξ∵ξπξ∵ξπξ∵ξπξ
∵ξπξζαζζαζ∵ξπξ∵ξπξ∵ξπξζαζ∵ξπξ ∵ξπξζαζζαζ∵ξπξ∵ξπξζαζ∵ξπξζαζ
∵ξπξζαζζαζ∵ξπξζαζζαζ∵ξπξ∵ξπξ ∵ξπξζαζζαζ∵ξπξζαζζαζζαζζαζ
∵ξπξζαζζαζζαζ∵ξπξζαζζαζζαζ ∵ξπξ∵ξπξζαζ∵ξπξζαζζαζ∵ξπξ∵ξπξ
∵ξπξ∵ξπξζαζ∵ξπξ∵ξπξ∵ξπξ∵ξπξ∵ξπξ ∵ξπξζαζζαζζαζ∵ξπξ∵ξπξζαζζαζ
∵ξπξζαζζαζ∵ξπξζαζ∵ξπξ∵ξπξ∵ξπξ ∵ξπξζαζζαζ∵ξπξ∵ξπξζαζ∵ξπξζαζ
∵ξπξ∵ξπξζαζ∵ξπξ∵ξπξ∵ξπξ∵ξπξ∵ξπξ ∵ξπξζαζζαζ∵ξπξζαζ∵ξπξ∵ξπξζαζ
∵ξπξζαζζαζζαζ∵ξπξ∵ξπξζαζζαζ ∵ξπξ∵ξπξζαζ∵ξπξ∵ξπξ∵ξπξ∵ξπξ∵ξπξ
∵ξπξζαζζαζ∵ξπξζαζζαζζαζ∵ξπξ ∵ξπξζαζζαζ∵ξπξζαζζαζζαζζαζ
∵ξπξζαζζαζζαζ∵ξπξζαζ∵ξπξ∵ξπξ ∵ξπξ∵ξπξζαζ∵ξπξ∵ξπξ∵ξπξ∵ξπξ∵ξπξ
∵ξπξζαζζαζ∵ξπξ∵ξπξ∵ξπξζαζζαζ ∵ξπξζαζζαζ∵ξπξζαζζαζζαζζαζ
∵ξπξζαζζαζ∵ξπξζαζζαζ∵ξπξζαζ ∵ξπξζαζζαζζαζ∵ξπξ∵ξπξ∵ξπξ∵ξπξ
∵ξπξζαζζαζ∵ξπξζαζζαζ∵ξπξ∵ξπξ ∵ξπξζαζζαζ∵ξπξ∵ξπξζαζ∵ξπξζαζ
∵ξπξζαζζαζζαζ∵ξπξζαζ∵ξπξ∵ξπξ ∵ξπξζαζζαζ∵ξπξ∵ξπξζαζ∵ξπξζαζ

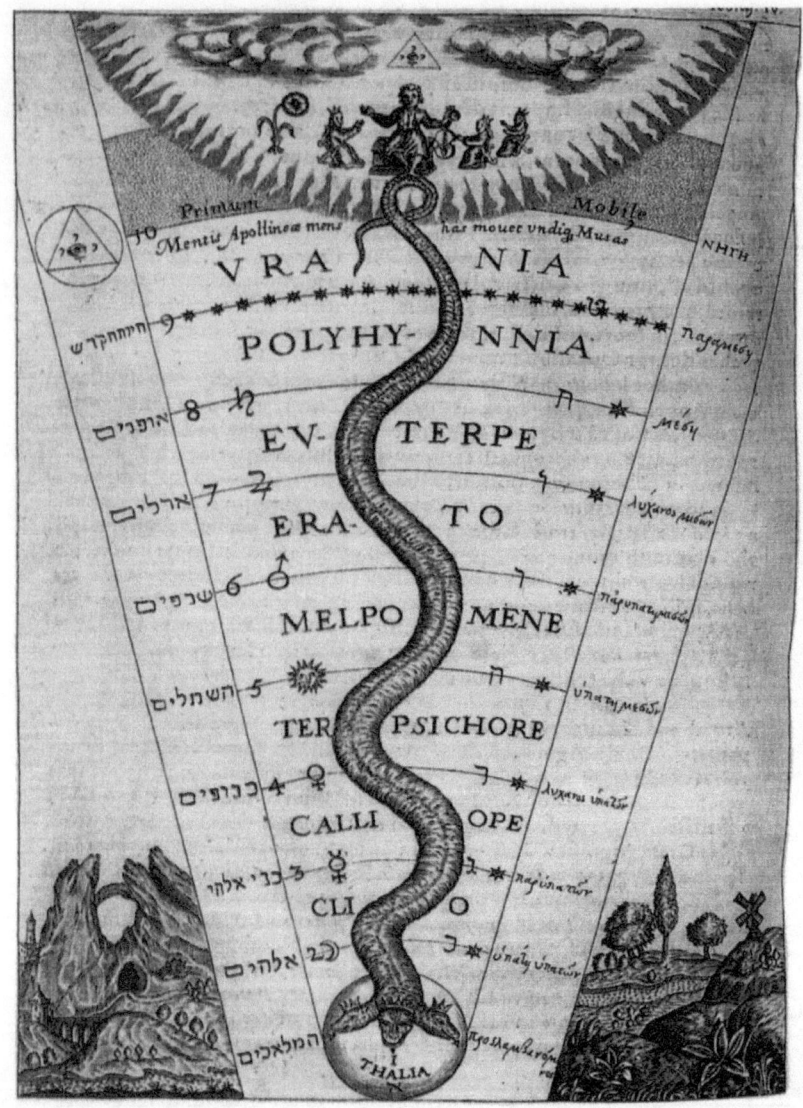

∴ξπξ∴∴ξπξζαζ∴ξπξζαζζαζζαζ∴ξπξ ∴ξπξ∴ξπξζαζ∴ξπξ∴ξπξ∴ξπξ∴ξπξ∴ξπξ
∴ξπξζαζ∴ξπξ∴ξπξ∴ξπξ∴ξπξζαζ∴ξπξ ∴ξπξζαζζαζ∴ξπξ∴ξπξζαζ∴ξπξζαζ
∴ξπξζαζζαζ∴ξπξ∴ξπξζαζζαζ∴ξπξ ∴ξπξζαζζαζ∴ξπξζαζζαζζαζζαζ
∴ξπξζαζζαζ∴ξπξ∴ξπξζαζ∴ξπξ ∴ξπξζαζζαζ∴ξπξ∴ξπξζαζ∴ξπξζαζ
∴ξπξ∴ξπξζαζ∴ξπξ∴ξπξ∴ξπξ∴ξπξ∴ξπξ ∴ξπξζαζζαζ∴ξπξ∴ξπξζαζ∴ξπξ∴ξπξ
∴ξπξζαζζαζ∴ξπξ∴ξπξζαζ∴ξπξζαζ ∴ξπξζαζζαζζαζ∴ξπξ∴ξπξζαζζαζ

∴ξπξζαζζαζ∵ξπξ∵ξπξ∵ξπξζαζζαζ∵ξπξζαζζαζ∵ξπξ∵ξπξζαζ∵ξπξζαζ
∴ξπξζαζζαζ∵ξπξζαζζαζζαζ∵ξπξ∵ξπξζαζζαζ∵ξπξ∵ξπξζαζ∵ξπξ∵ξπξ
∴ξπξζαζζαζ∵ξπξζαζ∵ξπξ∵ξπξζαζ∵ξπξζαζζαζ∵ξπξζαζζαζζαζ∵ξπξ
∴ξπξζαζζαζ∵ξπξ∵ξπξζαζζαζζαζ∵ξπξ∵ξπξζαζ∵ξπξ∵ξπξ∵ξπξ∵ξπξ
∴ξπξζαζζαζζαζ∵ξπξζαζ∵ξπξ∵ξπξ∵ξπξζαζζαζ∵ξπξζαζζαζζαζζαζ
∴ξπξ∵ξπξζαζ∵ξπξ∵ξπξ∵ξπξ∵ξπξ∵ξπξ∵ξπξζαζζαζζαζ∵ξπξζαζ∵ξπξ∵ξπξ
∴ξπξζαζζαζ∵ξπξζαζ∵ξπξ∵ξπξ∵ξπξ∵ξπξζαζζαζ∵ξπξζαζ∵ξπξ∵ξπξζαζ
∴ξπξζαζζαζζαζ∵ξπξ∵ξπξζαζζαζ∵ξπξ∵ξπξζαζ∵ξπξ∵ξπξ∵ξπξ∵ξπξ∵ξπξ
∴ξπξζαζζαζζαζ∵ξπξζαζζαζζαζ∵ξπξζαζζαζ∵ξπξζαζζαζζαζζαζ
∴ξπξζαζζαζζαζ∵ξπξ∵ξπξζαζ∵ξπξ∵ξπξζαζζαζ∵ξπξζαζζαζ∵ξπξ∵ξπξ
∴ξπξζαζζαζ∵ξπξ∵ξπξζαζ∵ξπξ∵ξπξ∵ξπξ∵ξπξζαζ∵ξπξζαζζαζ∵ξπξ∵ξπξ
∴ξπξ∵ξπξζαζ∵ξπξ∵ξπξ∵ξπξ∵ξπξ∵ξπξ∵ξπξζαζζαζζαζ∵ξπξζαζ∵ξπξ∵ξπξ
∴ξπξζαζζαζ∵ξπξζαζ∵ξπξ∵ξπξ∵ξπξ∵ξπξζαζζαζ∵ξπξ∵ξπξζαζ∵ξπξζαζ
∴ξπξ∵ξπξζαζ∵ξπξ∵ξπξ∵ξπξ∵ξπξ∵ξπξ∵ξπξζαζζαζζαζ∵ξπξ∵ξπξζαζζαζ
∴ξπξζαζζαζ∵ξπξζαζζαζζαζζαζ∵ξπξζαζζαζζαζ∵ξπξζαζ∵ξπξζαζ
∴ξπξζαζζαζ∵ξπξζαζζαζ∵ξπξ∵ξπξ∵ξπξ∵ξπξζαζ∵ξπξ∵ξπξ∵ξπξ∵ξπξ∵ξπξ
∴ξπξζαζζαζ∵ξπξζαζ∵ξπξ∵ξπξζαζ∵ξπξζαζζαζζαζ∵ξπξ∵ξπξζαζζαζ
∴ξπξ∵ξπξζαζ∵ξπξ∵ξπξ∵ξπξ∵ξπξ∵ξπξ∵ξπξζαζζαζ∵ξπξ∵ξπξζαζ∵ξπξζαζ
∴ξπξζαζζαζ∵ξπξζαζζαζ∵ξπξζαζ∵ξπξζαζζαζ∵ξπξ∵ξπξ∵ξπξ∵ξπξζαζ

Coagulatio

∴ξπξζαζζαζ∵ξπξζαζζαζζαζ∵ξπξ ∵ξπξζαζζαζ∵ξπξ∵ξπξ∵ξπξ∵ξπξζαζ
∵ξπξζαζζαζζαζ∵ξπξζαζ∵ξπξ∵ξπξ ∵ξπξζαζζαζ∵ξπξ∵ξπξζαζ∵ξπξζαζ
∵ξπξζαζζαζ∵ξπξ∵ξπξζαζ∵ξπξ∵ξπξ ∵ξπξ∵ξπξζαζ∵ξπξ∵ξπξ∵ξπξ∵ξπξ∵ξπξ
∵ξπξζαζζαζ∵ξπξ∵ξπξζαζζαζ∵ξπξ ∵ξπξζαζζαζζαζ∵ξπξ∵ξπξζαζ∵ξπξ
∵ξπξζαζζαζ∵ξπξζαζζαζζαζζαζ ∵ξπξζαζζαζ∵ξπξζαζζαζ∵ξπξζαζ
∵ξπξ∵ξπξζαζ∵ξπξ∵ξπξ∵ξπξ∵ξπξ∵ξπξ ∵ξπξζαζζαζζαζ∵ξπξζαζ∵ξπξ∵ξπξ
∵ξπξζαζζαζ∵ξπξζαζ∵ξπξ∵ξπξ∵ξπξ ∵ξπξζαζζαζ∵ξπξ∵ξπξζαζ∵ξπξζαζ
∵ξπξ∵ξπξζαζ∵ξπξ∵ξπξ∵ξπξ∵ξπξ∵ξπξ ∵ξπξζαζζαζ∵ξπξζαζζαζ∵ξπξζαζ
∵ξπξζαζζαζζαζζαζ∵ξπξ∵ξπξζαζ ∵ξπξζαζζαζζαζ∵ξπξ∵ξπξζαζζαζ
∵ξπξζαζζαζζαζ∵ξπξζαζ∵ξπξ∵ξπξ ∵ξπξζαζζαζ∵ξπξ∵ξπξζαζ∵ξπξζαζ
∵ξπξζαζζαζζαζ∵ξπξ∵ξπξζαζ∵ξπξ ∵ξπξζαζζαζζαζζαζ∵ξπξ∵ξπξζαζ
∵ξπξ∵ξπξζαζ∵ξπξ∵ξπξ∵ξπξ∵ξπξ∵ξπξ ∵ξπξζαζζαζ∵ξπξζαζζαζζαζζαζ
∵ξπξζαζζαζ∵ξπξ∵ξπξζαζζαζ∵ξπξ ∵ξπξ∵ξπξζαζ∵ξπξ∵ξπξ∵ξπξ∵ξπξ∵ξπξ
∵ξπξζαζζαζ∵ξπξζαζ∵ξπξ∵ξπξ ∵ξπξζαζζαζ∵ξπξζαζ∵ξπξ∵ξπξ∵ξπξ
∵ξπξζαζζαζ∵ξπξ∵ξπξζαζ∵ξπξζαζ ∵ξπξ∵ξπξζαζ∵ξπξ∵ξπξ∵ξπξ∵ξπξ∵ξπξ
∵ξπξζαζζαζ∵ξπξζαζ∵ξπξ∵ξπξ∵ξπξ ∵ξπξζαζζαζ∵ξπξζαζ∵ξπξ∵ξπξζαζ
∵ξπξζαζζαζ∵ξπξ∵ξπξζαζζαζζαζ ∵ξπξζαζζαζ∵ξπξζαζ∵ξπξ∵ξπξ∵ξπξ
∵ξπξζαζζαζ∵ξπξ∵ξπξζαζ∵ξπξζαζ ∵ξπξζαζζαζζαζ∵ξπξ∵ξπξζαζζαζ
∵ξπξζαζζαζζαζ∵ξπξζαζ∵ξπξ∵ξπξ ∵ξπξ∵ξπξζαζ∵ξπξ∵ξπξ∵ξπξ∵ξπξ∵ξπξ
∵ξπξζαζζαζ∵ξπξζαζζαζ∵ξπξ∵ξπξ ∵ξπξζαζζαζ∵ξπξ∵ξπξζαζ∵ξπξζαζ
∵ξπξζαζζαζζαζ∵ξπξζαζζαζ∵ξπξ ∵ξπξζαζζαζ∵ξπξ∵ξπξζαζ∵ξπξζαζ
∵ξπξζαζζαζ∵ξπξζαζζαζ∵ξπξ∵ξπξ ∵ξπξ∵ξπξζαζ∵ξπξζαζζαζζαζ∵ξπξ
∵ξπξ∵ξπξζαζ∵ξπξ∵ξπξ∵ξπξ∵ξπξ∵ξπξ ∵ξπξζαζ∵ξπξζαζ∵ξπξζαζζαζζαζ
∵ξπξζαζζαζ∵ξπξζαζ∵ξπξ∵ξπξ∵ξπξ ∵ξπξζαζζαζ∵ξπξζαζ∵ξπξ∵ξπξζαζ
∵ξπξζαζζαζ∵ξπξζαζζαζ∵ξπξ∵ξπξ ∵ξπξζαζζαζ∵ξπξ∵ξπξζαζ∵ξπξζαζ
∵ξπξ∵ξπξζαζ∵ξπξ∵ξπξ∵ξπξ∵ξπξ∵ξπξ ∵ξπξζαζζαζ∵ξπξζαζ∵ξπξ∵ξπξζαζ
∵ξπξζαζζαζ∵ξπξζαζζαζζαζ∵ξπξ ∵ξπξ∵ξπξζαζ∵ξπξ∵ξπξ∵ξπξ∵ξπξ∵ξπξ
∵ξπξζαζζαζ∵ξπξζαζ∵ξπξ∵ξπξ ∵ξπξζαζζαζ∵ξπξζαζ∵ξπξ∵ξπξ∵ξπξ
∵ξπξζαζζαζ∵ξπξζαζ∵ξπξ∵ξπξζαζ ∵ξπξζαζζαζζαζ∵ξπξ∵ξπξζαζζαζ
∵ξπξ∵ξπξζαζ∵ξπξ∵ξπξ∵ξπξ∵ξπξ∵ξπξ ∵ξπξζαζζαζζαζ∵ξπξζαζζαζζαζ
∵ξπξζαζζαζ∵ξπξζαζζαζζαζζαζ ∵ξπξζαζζαζζαζ∵ξπξ∵ξπξζαζ∵ξπξ

∴ξπξζαζζαζ∵ξπξζαζζαζ∵ξπξ∵ξπξ ∵ξπξζαζζαζ∵ξπξ∵ξπξζαζ∵ξπξ∵ξπξ
∵ξπξ∵ξπξζαζ∵ξπξ∵ξπξ∵ξπξ∵ξπξ∵ξπξ ∵ξπξζαζζαζζαζ∵ξπξ∵ξπξζαζζαζ
∵ξπξζαζζαζ∵ξπξζαζ∵ξπξ∵ξπξ∵ξπξ ∵ξπξζαζζαζ∵ξπξ∵ξπξζαζ∵ξπξζαζ
∵ξπξ∵ξπξζαζ∵ξπξ∵ξπξ∵ξπξ∵ξπξ∵ξπξ ∵ξπξζαζζαζ∵ξπξζαζ∵ξπξ∵ξπξζαζ
∵ξπξζαζζαζζαζ∵ξπξ∵ξπξζαζζαζ ∵ξπξ∵ξπξζαζ∵ξπξ∵ξπξ∵ξπξ∵ξπξ∵ξπξ
∵ξπξζαζζαζ∵ξπξ∵ξπξ∵ξπξζαζζαζ ∵ξπξζαζζαζ∵ξπξζαζζαζζαζζαζ
∵ξπξζαζζαζ∵ξπξζαζζαζ∵ξπξζαζ ∵ξπξζαζζαζζαζ∵ξπξ∵ξπξ∵ξπξ∵ξπξ
∵ξπξζαζζαζ∵ξπξζαζζαζ∵ξπξ∵ξπξ ∵ξπξζαζζαζ∵ξπξ∵ξπξζαζ∵ξπξζαζ
∵ξπξζαζζαζζαζ∵ξπξζαζ∵ξπξ∵ξπξ ∵ξπξζαζζαζ∵ξπξ∵ξπξζαζ∵ξπξζαζ
∵ξπξζαζζαζ∵ξπξ∵ξπξζαζ∵ξπξ∵ξπξ ∵ξπξ∵ξπξζαζ∵ξπξ∵ξπξ∵ξπξ∵ξπξ∵ξπξ
∵ξπξζαζζαζ∵ξπξ∵ξπξ∵ξπξζαζ ∵ξπξζαζζαζ∵ξπξζαζζαζζαζ∵ξπξ
∵ξπξζαζζαζ∵ξπξ∵ξπξζαζ∵ξπξ∵ξπξ ∵ξπξ∵ξπξζαζ∵ξπξ∵ξπξ∵ξπξ∵ξπξ∵ξπξ
∵ξπξζαζζαζ∵ξπξ∵ξπξζαζζαζ∵ξπξ ∵ξπξζαζζαζζαζ∵ξπξζαζ∵ξπξζαζ
∵ξπξζαζζαζ∵ξπξζαζζαζ∵ξπξ∵ξπξ ∵ξπξζαζζαζ∵ξπξ∵ξπξζαζζαζ∵ξπξ
∵ξπξζαζζαζ∵ξπξζαζ∵ξπξ∵ξπξζαζ ∵ξπξζαζζαζ∵ξπξζαζζαζ∵ξπξ∵ξπξ
∵ξπξζαζζαζ∵ξπξζαζζαζ∵ξπξ∵ξπξ ∵ξπξζαζζαζ∵ξπξ∵ξπξζαζ∵ξπξζαζ
∵ξπξζαζζαζ∵ξπξ∵ξπξζαζ∵ξπξ∵ξπξ ∵ξπξ∵ξπξζαζ∵ξπξ∵ξπξ∵ξπξ∵ξπξ∵ξπξ
∵ξπξζαζζαζ∵ξπξ∵ξπξ∵ξπξζαζ∵ξπξ ∵ξπξζαζζαζζαζζαζ∵ξπξ∵ξπξζαζ
∵ξπξ∵ξπξζαζ∵ξπξ∵ξπξ∵ξπξ∵ξπξ∵ξπξ ∵ξπξζαζζαζζαζ∵ξπξζαζ∵ξπξ∵ξπξ
∵ξπξζαζζαζ∵ξπξζαζ∵ξπξ∵ξπξ∵ξπξ ∵ξπξζαζζαζ∵ξπξζαζ∵ξπξ∵ξπξζαζ
∵ξπξζαζζαζ∵ξπξ∵ξπξζαζζαζ ∵ξπξ∵ξπξζαζ∵ξπξ∵ξπξ∵ξπξ∵ξπξ∵ξπξ
∵ξπξζαζζαζ∵ξπξζαζζαζ ∵ξπξζαζζαζ∵ξπξζαζζαζζαζζαζ
∵ξπξζαζζαζ∵ξπξζαζζαζ ∵ξπξζαζζαζ∵ξπξ∵ξπξζαζ∵ξπξζαζ
∵ξπξζαζζαζζαζ∵ξπξ∵ξπξζαζ∵ξπξ ∵ξπξ∵ξπξζαζ∵ξπξ∵ξπξ∵ξπξ∵ξπξ∵ξπξ
∵ξπξζαζζαζζαζ∵ξπξζαζζαζζαζ ∵ξπξζαζζαζ∵ξπξζαζζαζζαζζαζ
∵ξπξζαζζαζ∵ξπξ∵ξπξζαζ∵ξπξ ∵ξπξζαζζαζ∵ξπξζαζζαζ∵ξπξ∵ξπξ
∵ξπξζαζζαζ∵ξπξ∵ξπξζαζ∵ξπξ∵ξπξ ∵ξπξ∵ξπξζαζ∵ξπξζαζζαζζαζ∵ξπξ
∵ξπξ∵ξπξζαζ∵ξπξ∵ξπξ∵ξπξ∵ξπξ∵ξπξ
∵ξπξζαζ∵ξπξ∵ξπξ∵ξπξζαζ∵ξπξ∵ξπξ ∵ξπξζαζζαζ∵ξπξ∵ξπξζαζ∵ξπξζαζ
∵ξπξζαζζαζζαζ∵ξπξ∵ξπξ∵ξπξ∵ξπξ ∵ξπξζαζζαζ∵ξπξ∵ξπξ∵ξπξ∵ξπξζαζ
∵ξπξζαζζαζζαζ∵ξπξ∵ξπξζαζ∵ξπξ ∵ξπξζαζζαζζαζ∵ξπξζαζ∵ξπξ∵ξπξ

Coagulatio

∴ξπξζαζζαζ∴ξπξζαζ∴ξπξ∴ξπξζαζ ∴ξπξζαζζαζ∴ξπξζαζζαζζαζ∴ξπξ
∴ξπξζαζζαζ∴ξπξ∴ξπξζαζζαζζαζ ∴ξπξ∴ξπξζαζ∴ξπξ∴ξπξ∴ξπξ∴ξπξ∴ξπξ
∴ξπξζαζζαζζαζ∴ξπξζαζ∴ξπξ∴ξπξ ∴ξπξζαζζαζ∴ξπξζαζ∴ξπξ∴ξπξ∴ξπξ
∴ξπξζαζζαζ∴ξπξζαζ∴ξπξ∴ξπξζαζ ∴ξπξζαζζαζζαζ∴ξπξ∴ξπξζαζζαζ
∴ξπξ∴ξπξζαζ∴ξπξ∴ξπξ∴ξπξ∴ξπξ∴ξπξ ∴ξπξζαζζαζζαζ∴ξπξζαζζαζζαζ
∴ξπξζαζζαζ∴ξπξζαζζαζζαζζαζ ∴ξπξζαζζαζζαζ∴ξπξ∴ξπξζαζ∴ξπξ
∴ξπξζαζζαζ∴ξπξζαζζαζ∴ξπξ∴ξπξ ∴ξπξζαζζαζ∴ξπξ∴ξπξζαζ∴ξπξ∴ξπξ
∴ξπξ∴ξπξζαζ∴ξπξζαζζαζ∴ξπξ∴ξπξ ∴ξπξ∴ξπξζαζ∴ξπξ∴ξπξ∴ξπξ∴ξπξ∴ξπξ
∴ξπξζαζζαζζαζ∴ξπξ∴ξπξζαζζαζ ∴ξπξζαζζαζ∴ξπξζαζ∴ξπξ∴ξπξ∴ξπξ
∴ξπξζαζζαζ∴ξπξ∴ξπξζαζ∴ξπξζαζ ∴ξπξ∴ξπξζαζ∴ξπξ∴ξπξ∴ξπξ∴ξπξ∴ξπξ
∴ξπξζαζζαζ∴ξπξζαζ∴ξπξ∴ξπξζαζ ∴ξπξζαζζαζζαζ∴ξπξ∴ξπξζαζζαζ

∴ξπξ∴ξπξζαζ∴ξπξ∴ξπξ∴ξπξ∴ξπξ∴ξπξ ∴ξπξζαζζαζ∴ξπξ∴ξπξζαζζαζ∴ξπξ
∴ξπξζαζζαζ∴ξπξζαζ∴ξπξ∴ξπξζαζ ∴ξπξζαζζαζ∴ξπξζαζζαζ∴ξπξ∴ξπξ
∴ξπξζαζζαζ∴ξπξζαζζαζ∴ξπξ∴ξπξ ∴ξπξζαζζαζ∴ξπξ∴ξπξζαζ∴ξπξζαζ
∴ξπξζαζζαζ∴ξπξ∴ξπξζαζ∴ξπξ∴ξπξ ∴ξπξ∴ξπξζαζ∴ξπξ∴ξπξ∴ξπξ∴ξπξ∴ξπξ
∴ξπξζαζζαζζαζ∴ξπξζαζζαζζαζ ∴ξπξζαζζαζ∴ξπξζαζ∴ξπξ∴ξπξζαζ
∴ξπξζαζζαζζαζ∴ξπξζαζ∴ξπξ∴ξπξ ∴ξπξζαζζαζ∴ξπξζαζ∴ξπξ∴ξπξ∴ξπξ
∴ξπξ∴ξπξζαζ∴ξπξ∴ξπξ∴ξπξ∴ξπξ∴ξπξ ∴ξπξζαζζαζζαζ∴ξπξζαζ∴ξπξ∴ξπξ

∴ξπξζαζζαζ∴ξπξζαζ∴ξπξ∴ξπξ∴ξπξ ∴ξπξζαζζαζ∴ξπξ∴ξπξζαζ∴ξπξζαζ
∴ξπξ∴ξπξζαζ∴ξπξ∴ξπξ∴ξπξ∴ξπξ∴ξπξ ∴ξπξζαζζαζ∴ξπξ∴ξπξζαζζαζ∴ξπξ
∴ξπξζαζζαζζαζ∴ξπξζαζ∴ξπξζαζ ∴ξπξζαζζαζ∴ξπξζαζζαζ∴ξπξ∴ξπξ
∴ξπξζαζζαζ∴ξπξζαζζαζ∴ξπξ∴ξπξ ∴ξπξζαζζαζ∴ξπξζαζζαζζαζ∴ξπξ
∴ξπξζαζζαζ∴ξπξ∴ξπξζαζ∴ξπξζαζ ∴ξπξζαζζαζζαζ∴ξπξ∴ξπξζαζζαζ
∴ξπξζαζζαζζαζ∴ξπξ∴ξπξζαζζαζ ∴ξπξ∴ξπξζαζ∴ξπξ∴ξπξ∴ξπξ∴ξπξ
∴ξπξζαζζαζ∴ξπξζαζζαζζαζζαζ ∴ξπξζαζζαζ∴ξπξ∴ξπξζαζζαζ∴ξπξ
∴ξπξ∴ξπξζαζ∴ξπξ∴ξπξ∴ξπξ∴ξπξ∴ξπξ ∴ξπξζαζζαζ∴ξπξ∴ξπξ∴ξπξ∴ξπξζαζ
∴ξπξζαζζαζ∴ξπξζαζζαζ∴ξπξ∴ξπξ ∴ξπξζαζζαζ∴ξπξζαζζαζ∴ξπξ∴ξπξ
∴ξπξ∴ξπξζαζ∴ξπξ∴ξπξ∴ξπξ∴ξπξ∴ξπξ ∴ξπξζαζζαζζαζ∴ξπξζαζ∴ξπξ∴ξπξ

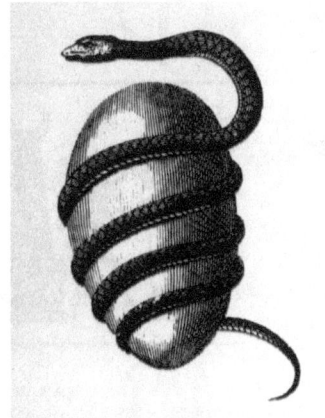

∴ξπξζαζζαζ∴ξπξζαζ∴ξπξ∴ξπξ∴ξπξ
∴ξπξζαζζαζ∴ξπξ∴ξπξζαζ∴ξπξζαζ
∴ξπξ∴ξπξζαζ∴ξπξ∴ξπξ∴ξπξ∴ξπξ∴ξπξ
∴ξπξζαζζαζζαζ∴ξπξζαζζαζζαζ
∴ξπξζαζζαζ∴ξπξζαζζαζζαζζαζ
∴ξπξζαζζαζζαζ∴ξπξ∴ξπξζαζ∴ξπξ
∴ξπξζαζζαζ∴ξπξζαζζαζ∴ξπξ∴ξπξ
∴ξπξζαζζαζ∴ξπξ∴ξπξζαζ∴ξπξ∴ξπξ
∴ξπξζαζζαζζαζ∴ξπξ∴ξπξζαζζαζ
∴ξπξ∴ξπξζαζ∴ξπξζαζζαζ∴ξπξ∴ξπξ

∴ξπξ∴ξπξζαζ∴ξπξ∴ξπξ∴ξπξ∴ξπξ∴ξπξ ∴ξπξζαζζαζζαζ∴ξπξζαζ∴ξπξ∴ξπξ
∴ξπξζαζζαζ∴ξπξζαζ∴ξπξ∴ξπξ∴ξπξ ∴ξπξζαζζαζ∴ξπξ∴ξπξζαζ∴ξπξζαζ
∴ξπξ∴ξπξζαζ∴ξπξ∴ξπξ∴ξπξ∴ξπξ∴ξπξ ∴ξπξζαζζαζζαζ∴ξπξζαζζαζζαζ
∴ξπξζαζζαζ∴ξπξζαζζαζζαζζαζ ∴ξπξζαζζαζζαζ∴ξπξ∴ξπξζαζ∴ξπξ
∴ξπξζαζζαζ∴ξπξζαζζαζ∴ξπξ∴ξπξ ∴ξπξζαζζαζ∴ξπξ∴ξπξζαζ∴ξπξ∴ξπξ
∴ξπξ∴ξπξζαζ∴ξπξ∴ξπξ∴ξπξ∴ξπξ∴ξπξ ∴ξπξζαζζαζ∴ξπξ∴ξπξ∴ξπξ∴ξπξζαζ
∴ξπξζαζζαζ∴ξπξ∴ξπξ∴ξπξζαζ∴ξπξ ∴ξπξζαζζαζ∴ξπξζαζζαζζαζζαζ
∴ξπξζαζζαζζαζ∴ξπξζαζζαζ∴ξπξ ∴ξπξζαζζαζ∴ξπξ∴ξπξζαζ∴ξπξζαζ
∴ξπξ∴ξπξζαζ∴ξπξζαζζαζ∴ξπξ∴ξπξ ∴ξπξ∴ξπξζαζ∴ξπξ∴ξπξ∴ξπξ∴ξπξ∴ξπξ
∴ξπξζαζζαζ∴ξπξ∴ξπξ∴ξπξ∴ξπξζαζ ∴ξπξζαζζαζ∴ξπξζαζζαζζαζ∴ξπξ
∴ξπξζαζζαζ∴ξπξ∴ξπξζαζ∴ξπξ∴ξπξ ∴ξπξ∴ξπξζαζ∴ξπξ∴ξπξ∴ξπξ∴ξπξ∴ξπξ

Coagulatio

∴ξπξζαζζαζζαζ∴ξπξζαζ∴ξπξ∴ξπξ ∴ξπξζαζζαζ∴ξπξζαζ∴ξπξ∴ξπξ∴ξπξ
∴ξπξζαζζαζ∴ξπξ∴ξπξζαζ∴ξπξζαζ ∴ξπξ∴ξπξζαζ∴ξπξ∴ξπξ∴ξπξ∴ξπξ∴ξπξ
∴ξπξζαζζαζ∴ξπξζαζζαζζαζ ∴ξπξζαζζαζ∴ξπξζαζζαζζαζζαζ
∴ξπξζαζζαζ∴ξπξ∴ξπξζαζ∴ξπξ ∴ξπξζαζζαζ∴ξπξζαζζαζ∴ξπξ∴ξπξ
∴ξπξζαζζαζ∴ξπξ∴ξπξζαζ∴ξπξ∴ξπξ ∴ξπξ∴ξπξζαζ∴ξπξ∴ξπξ∴ξπξ∴ξπξ∴ξπξ
∴ξπξζαζζαζ∴ξπξ∴ξπξ∴ξπξζαζ∴ξπξ ∴ξπξζαζζαζ∴ξπξ∴ξπξζαζ∴ξπξζαζ
∴ξπξζαζζαζ∴ξπξζαζζαζ∴ξπξ∴ξπξ ∴ξπξζαζζαζ∴ξπξζαζζαζζαζζαζ
∴ξπξζαζζαζζαζ∴ξπξζαζζαζζαζ ∴ξπξ∴ξπξζαζ∴ξπξζαζζαζζαζ∴ξπξ
∴ξπξ∴ξπξζαζ∴ξπξ∴ξπξ∴ξπξ∴ξπξ∴ξπξ
∴ξπξζαζ∴ξπξ∴ξπξ∴ξπξ∴ξπξ∴ξπξζαζ ∴ξπξζαζζαζζαζ∴ξπξζαζ∴ξπξ∴ξπξ
∴ξπξ∴ξπξζαζ∴ξπξ∴ξπξ∴ξπξ∴ξπξ∴ξπξ
∴ξπξζαζζαζ∴ξπξ∴ξπξζαζζαζ∴ξπξ
∴ξπξζαζζαζ∴ξπξζαζ∴ξπξ∴ξπξζαζ
∴ξπξζαζζαζζαζ∴ξπξ∴ξπξζαζ∴ξπξ
∴ξπξζαζζαζζαζ∴ξπξ∴ξπξζαζζαζ
∴ξπξζαζζαζζαζ∴ξπξζαζ∴ξπξ∴ξπξ
∴ξπξ∴ξπξζαζ∴ξπξζαζζαζ∴ξπξ∴ξπξ
∴ξπξ∴ξπξζαζ∴ξπξ∴ξπξ∴ξπξ∴ξπξ∴ξπξ
∴ξπξζαζζαζ∴ξπξ∴ξπξ∴ξπξζαζ∴ξπξ
∴ξπξζαζζαζ∴ξπξ∴ξπξζαζ∴ξπξζαζ
∴ξπξζαζζαζ∴ξπξ∴ξπξζαζζαζ∴ξπξ
∴ξπξζαζζαζ∴ξπξζαζζαζζαζζαζ
∴ξπξζαζζαζζαζ∴ξπξ∴ξπξζαζ∴ξπξ

∴ξπξζαζζαζ∴ξπξ∴ξπξζαζ∴ξπξζαζ ∴ξπξ∴ξπξζαζ∴ξπξ∴ξπξ∴ξπξ∴ξπξ∴ξπξ
∴ξπξζαζζαζ∴ξπξ∴ξπξζαζ∴ξπξ∴ξπξ ∴ξπξζαζζαζ∴ξπξ∴ξπξζαζ∴ξπξζαζ
∴ξπξζαζζαζ∴ξπξ∴ξπξζαζζαζ ∴ξπξζαζζαζ∴ξπξ∴ξπξ∴ξπξζαζζαζ
∴ξπξζαζζαζ∴ξπξ∴ξπξζαζ∴ξπξζαζ ∴ξπξζαζζαζ∴ξπξζαζζαζζαζ∴ξπξ
∴ξπξζαζζαζ∴ξπξ∴ξπξζαζ∴ξπξ∴ξπξ ∴ξπξζαζζαζ∴ξπξζαζ∴ξπξ∴ξπξζαζ
∴ξπξζαζζαζ∴ξπξζαζζαζζαζ∴ξπξ ∴ξπξζαζζαζ∴ξπξ∴ξπξζαζζαζζαζ
∴ξπξ∴ξπξζαζ∴ξπξ∴ξπξ∴ξπξ∴ξπξ∴ξπξ ∴ξπξζαζζαζζαζ∴ξπξζαζ∴ξπξ∴ξπξ
∴ξπξζαζζαζ∴ξπξζαζζαζζαζζαζ ∴ξπξ∴ξπξζαζ∴ξπξ∴ξπξ∴ξπξ∴ξπξ∴ξπξ

∴ξπξζαζζαζζαζ∴ξπξζαζ∴ξπξ∴ξπξ ∴ξπξζαζζαζ∴ξπξζαζ∴ξπξ∴ξπξ∴ξπξ
∴ξπξζαζζαζ∴ξπξζαζ∴ξπξ∴ξπξζαζ ∴ξπξζαζζαζζαζ∴ξπξ∴ξπξζαζζαζ
∴ξπξ∴ξπξζαζ∴ξπξ∴ξπξ∴ξπξ∴ξπξ∴ξπξ ∴ξπξζαζζαζζαζ∴ξπξζαζζαζζαζ
∴ξπξζαζζαζ∴ξπξζαζζαζζαζζαζ ∴ξπξζαζζαζζαζ∴ξπξ∴ξπξζαζ∴ξπξ
∴ξπξζαζζαζ∴ξπξζαζζαζ∴ξπξ∴ξπξ ∴ξπξζαζζαζ∴ξπξ∴ξπξζαζ∴ξπξ∴ξπξ
∴ξπξ∴ξπξζαζ∴ξπξζαζζαζ∴ξπξ∴ξπξ ∴ξπξ∴ξπξζαζ∴ξπξ∴ξπξ∴ξπξ∴ξπξ∴ξπξ
∴ξπξζαζζαζζαζ∴ξπξζαζ∴ξπξ∴ξπξ ∴ξπξζαζζαζ∴ξπξζαζ∴ξπξ∴ξπξ∴ξπξ
∴ξπξζαζζαζ∴ξπξ∴ξπξζαζ∴ξπξζαζ ∴ξπξ∴ξπξζαζ∴ξπξ∴ξπξ∴ξπξ∴ξπξ∴ξπξ
∴ξπξζαζζαζζαζ∴ξπξ∴ξπξζαζζαζ ∴ξπξζαζζαζ∴ξπξζαζζαζζαζζαζ
∴ξπξζαζζαζζαζ∴ξπξζαζ∴ξπξζαζ ∴ξπξζαζζαζ∴ξπξζαζζαζ∴ξπξ∴ξπξ
∴ξπξ∴ξπξζαζ∴ξπξ∴ξπξ∴ξπξ∴ξπξ∴ξπξ ∴ξπξζαζζαζ∴ξπξζαζ∴ξπξ∴ξπξζαζ
∴ξπξζαζζαζζαζ∴ξπξ∴ξπξζαζζαζ ∴ξπξ∴ξπξζαζ∴ξπξ∴ξπξ∴ξπξ∴ξπξ∴ξπξ
∴ξπξζαζζαζ∴ξπξζαζ∴ξπξ∴ξπξζαζ ∴ξπξζαζζαζ∴ξπξζαζζαζ∴ξπξζαζ

∴ξπξζαζζαζζαζ∴ξπξ∴ξπξ∴ξπξ∴ξπξ ∴ξπξζαζζαζ∴ξπξ∴ξπξζαζ∴ξπξζαζ
∴ξπξζαζζαζζαζ∴ξπξ∴ξπξζαζ∴ξπξ ∴ξπξζαζζαζ∴ξπξ∴ξπξζαζζαζ∴ξπξ
∴ξπξζαζζαζ∴ξπξ∴ξπξζαζ∴ξπξζαζ ∴ξπξζαζζαζ∴ξπξ∴ξπξ∴ξπξζαζζαζ
∴ξπξζαζζαζζαζ∴ξπξζαζ∴ξπξ∴ξπξ ∴ξπξ∴ξπξζαζζαζζαζ∴ξπξζαζζαζ
∴ξπξ∴ξπξζαζ∴ξπξ∴ξπξ∴ξπξ∴ξπξ∴ξπξ ∴ξπξζαζζαζζαζ∴ξπξ∴ξπξζαζζαζ
∴ξπξζαζζαζ∴ξπξζαζ∴ξπξ∴ξπξ∴ξπξ ∴ξπξζαζζαζ∴ξπξ∴ξπξζαζ∴ξπξζαζ
∴ξπξ∴ξπξζαζ∴ξπξ∴ξπξ∴ξπξ∴ξπξ∴ξπξ ∴ξπξζαζζαζ∴ξπξζαζ∴ξπξ∴ξπξζαζ
∴ξπξζαζζαζζαζ∴ξπξ∴ξπξζαζζαζ ∴ξπξ∴ξπξζαζ∴ξπξ∴ξπξ∴ξπξ∴ξπξ∴ξπξ
∴ξπξζαζζαζ∴ξπξζαζζαζ∴ξπξ∴ξπξ ∴ξπξζαζζαζ∴ξπξ∴ξπξ∴ξπξ∴ξπξζαζ
∴ξπξζαζζαζ∴ξπξ∴ξπξ∴ξπξζαζζαζ ∴ξπξζαζζαζ∴ξπξζαζ∴ξπξζαζζαζ

Coagulatio

∴ξπξζαζζαζ∴ξπξζαζ∴ξπξ∴ξπξζαζ∴ξπξζαζζαζ∴ξπξζαζζαζζαζ∴ξπξ
∴ξπξζαζζαζ∴ξπξ∴ξπξζαζζαζζαζ∴ξπξ∴ξπξζαζ∴ξπξ∴ξπξ∴ξπξ∴ξπξ∴ξπξ
∴ξπξζαζζαζζαζ∴ξπξ∴ξπξζαζζαζ∴ξπξζαζζαζ∴ξπξζαζζαζζαζζαζ
∴ξπξζαζζαζ∴ξπξζαζζαζ∴ξπξζαζ∴ξπξζαζζαζ∴ξπξ∴ξπξζαζ∴ξπξζαζ
∴ξπξζαζζαζζαζ∴ξπξζαζ∴ξπξ∴ξπξ∴ξπξζαζζαζ∴ξπξζαζ∴ξπξ∴ξπξ∴ξπξ
∴ξπξζαζζαζ∴ξπξζαζ∴ξπξ∴ξπξζαζ∴ξπξζαζζαζ∴ξπξζαζζαζζαζ∴ξπξ
∴ξπξζαζζαζ∴ξπξ∴ξπξζαζζαζζαζ∴ξπξ∴ξπξζαζ∴ξπξζαζζαζζαζ∴ξπξ

∴ξπξ∴ξπξζαζ∴ξπξ∴ξπξ∴ξπξ∴ξπξ∴ξπξ
∴ξπξζαζ∴ξπξ∴ξπξ∴ξπξ∴ξπξζαζ∴ξπξ∴ξπξζαζζαζζαζζαζ∴ξπξ∴ξπξζαζ
∴ξπξ∴ξπξζαζ∴ξπξ∴ξπξ∴ξπξ∴ξπξ∴ξπξ∴ξπξζαζζαζ∴ξπξ∴ξπξζαζ∴ξπξ∴ξπξ
∴ξπξζαζζαζ∴ξπξ∴ξπξζαζ∴ξπξζαζ∴ξπξζαζζαζ∴ξπξ∴ξπξζαζζαζ
∴ξπξζαζζαζ∴ξπξ∴ξπξ∴ξπξζαζζαζ∴ξπξζαζζαζ∴ξπξ∴ξπξζαζ∴ξπξζαζ
∴ξπξζαζζαζ∴ξπξζαζζαζζαζ∴ξπξ∴ξπξζαζζαζ∴ξπξ∴ξπξζαζ∴ξπξ∴ξπξ

∴ξπξζαζζαζ∴ξπξζαζ∴ξπξ∴ξπξζαζ∴ξπξζαζζαζ∴ξπξζαζζαζζαζ∴ξπξ
∴ξπξζαζζαζ∴ξπξ∴ξπξζαζζαζζαζ∴ξπξ∴ξπξζαζ∴ξπξ∴ξπξ∴ξπξ∴ξπξ∴ξπξ
∴ξπξζαζζαζζαζ∴ξπξζαζ∴ξπξ∴ξπξ∴ξπξζαζζαζ∴ξπξζαζζαζζαζζαζ
∴ξπξ∴ξπξζαζ∴ξπξ∴ξπξ∴ξπξ∴ξπξ∴ξπξ∴ξπξζαζζαζζαζ∴ξπξζαζ∴ξπξ∴ξπξ
∴ξπξζαζζαζ∴ξπξζαζ∴ξπξ∴ξπξ∴ξπξ∴ξπξζαζζαζ∴ξπξζαζ∴ξπξ∴ξπξζαζ
∴ξπξζαζζαζζαζ∴ξπξ∴ξπξζαζζαζ∴ξπξ∴ξπξζαζ∴ξπξ∴ξπξ∴ξπξ∴ξπξ∴ξπξ
∴ξπξζαζζαζζαζ∴ξπξζαζζαζζαζ∴ξπξζαζζαζ∴ξπξζαζζαζζαζζαζ
∴ξπξζαζζαζζαζ∴ξπξ∴ξπξζαζ∴ξπξ∴ξπξζαζζαζ∴ξπξζαζζαζ∴ξπξ∴ξπξ
∴ξπξζαζζαζ∴ξπξ∴ξπξζαζ∴ξπξ∴ξπξ∴ξπξ∴ξπξζαζ∴ξπξζαζζαζ∴ξπξ∴ξπξ
∴ξπξ∴ξπξζαζ∴ξπξ∴ξπξ∴ξπξ∴ξπξ∴ξπξ∴ξπξζαζζαζζαζ∴ξπξ∴ξπξζαζζαζ
∴ξπξζαζζαζ∴ξπξζαζ∴ξπξ∴ξπξ∴ξπξ∴ξπξζαζζαζ∴ξπξ∴ξπξζαζ∴ξπξζαζ
∴ξπξ∴ξπξζαζ∴ξπξ∴ξπξ∴ξπξ∴ξπξ∴ξπξ∴ξπξζαζζαζ∴ξπξζαζ∴ξπξ∴ξπξζαζ
∴ξπξζαζζαζζαζ∴ξπξ∴ξπξζαζζαζ∴ξπξ∴ξπξζαζ∴ξπξ∴ξπξ∴ξπξ∴ξπξ∴ξπξ
∴ξπξζαζζαζζαζ∴ξπξ∴ξπξ∴ξπξ∴ξπξ∴ξπξζαζζαζ∴ξπξ∴ξπξζαζ∴ξπξζαζ
∴ξπξζαζζαζζαζ∴ξπξ∴ξπξζαζ∴ξπξ∴ξπξζαζζαζ∴ξπξ∴ξπξζαζζαζ∴ξπξ
∴ξπξζαζζαζ∴ξπξ∴ξπξζαζ∴ξπξζαζ∴ξπξζαζζαζ∴ξπξ∴ξπξ∴ξπξζαζζαζ
∴ξπξζαζζαζζαζ∴ξπξζαζ∴ξπξ∴ξπξ∴ξπξζαζζαζ∴ξπξ∴ξπξζαζ∴ξπξζαζ
∴ξπξζαζζαζ∴ξπξ∴ξπξζαζ∴ξπξ∴ξπξ∴ξπξ∴ξπξζαζ∴ξπξ∴ξπξ∴ξπξ∴ξπξ∴ξπξ
∴ξπξζαζζαζ∴ξπξζαζ∴ξπξ∴ξπξζαζ∴ξπξζαζζαζ∴ξπξζαζζαζζαζ∴ξπξ
∴ξπξ∴ξπξζαζ∴ξπξ∴ξπξ∴ξπξ∴ξπξ∴ξπξ∴ξπξζαζζαζ∴ξπξ∴ξπξζαζ∴ξπξζαζ
∴ξπξζαζζαζζαζ∴ξπξζαζζαζ∴ξπξ∴ξπξζαζζαζ∴ξπξ∴ξπξζαζ∴ξπξζαζ
∴ξπξζαζζαζζαζ∴ξπξ∴ξπξζαζ∴ξπξ∴ξπξζαζζαζζαζζαζ∴ξπξ∴ξπξζαζ
∴ξπξ∴ξπξζαζ∴ξπξ∴ξπξ∴ξπξ∴ξπξ∴ξπξ∴ξπξζαζζαζ∴ξπξ∴ξπξζαζ∴ξπξ∴ξπξ
∴ξπξζαζζαζ∴ξπξζαζ∴ξπξ∴ξπξζαζ∴ξπξζαζζαζ∴ξπξζαζζαζ∴ξπξζαζ
∴ξπξζαζζαζ∴ξπξ∴ξπξζαζ∴ξπξζαζ∴ξπξζαζζαζ∴ξπξζαζζαζζαζ∴ξπξ
∴ξπξζαζζαζ∴ξπξ∴ξπξζαζζαζ∴ξπξζαζζαζ∴ξπξζαζ∴ξπξ∴ξπξζαζ
∴ξπξζαζζαζ∴ξπξζαζζαζζαζ∴ξπξζαζζαζ∴ξπξζαζζαζζαζ∴ξπξ
∴ξπξ∴ξπξζαζ∴ξπξζαζζαζζαζ∴ξπξ

6. Conjuntio

Use human Means as if there were no divine ones,
and divine as if there were no human ones.

BALTASAR GRACIAN

i *Everything now has a point,*

especially the art of making one's way in the world. There is more required nowadays to make a single wise man than formerly to make Seven Sages, and more is needed nowadays to deal with a single person than was required with a whole people in former times.

ii *Character and Intellect:*

the two poles of our capacity; one without the other is but halfway to happiness. Intellect sufficeth not, character is also needed. On the other hand, it is the fool's misfortune, to fail in obtaining the position, the employment, the neighbourhood, and the circle of friends that suit him.

iii *Keep Matters for a Time in Suspense.*

Admiration at their novelty heightens the value of your achievements, It is both useless and insipid to play with the cards on the table. If you do not declare yourself immediately, you arouse expectation, especially when the importance of your position makes you the object of general attention. Mix a little mystery with everything, and the very mystery arouses veneration. And when you explain, be not too explicit, just as you do not expose your inmost thoughts in ordinary intercourse. Cautious silence is the holy of holies of worldly wisdom. A resolution declared is never highly thought of; it only leaves room for criticism. And if it happens to fail, you are doubly unfortunate. Besides you imitate the Divine way when you cause men to wonder and watch.

iv *Knowledge and Courage*

are the elements of Greatness. They give immortality, because they are immortal. Each is as much as he knows, and the wise can do anything. A man without knowledge, a world without light. Wisdom and strength, eyes and hands. Knowledge without courage is sterile.

v *Create a Feeling of Dependence.*

Not he that adorns but he that adores makes a divinity. The wise man would rather see men needing him than thanking him. To keep them on the threshold of hope is diplomatic, to trust to their gratitude boorish; hope has a good memory, gratitude a bad one. More is to be got from dependence than from courtesy. He that has satisfied his thirst turns his back on the well, and the orange once sucked falls from the golden platter into the waste-basket. When dependence disappears, good behaviour goes with it as well as respect. Let it be one of the chief lessons of experience to keep hope alive without entirely satisfying it, by preserving it to make oneself always needed even by a patron on the throne. But let not silence be carried to excess lest you go wrong, nor let another's failing grow incurable for the sake of your own advantage.

vi *A Man at his Highest Point.*

We are not born perfect: every day we develop in our personality and in our calling till we reach the highest point of our completed being, to the full round of our accomplishments, of our excellences. This is known by the purity of our taste, the clearness of our thought, the maturity of our judgment, and the firmness of our will. Some never arrive at being complete; somewhat is always awanting: others ripen late. The complete man, wise in speech, prudent in act, is admitted to the familiar intimacy of discreet persons, is even sought for by them.

vii *Avoid Victories over Superiors.*

All victories breed hate, and that over your superior is foolish or fatal. Superiority is always detested, *à fortiori* superiority over superiority. Caution can gloss over common advantages; for example, good looks may be cloaked by careless attire. There be some that will grant you precedence in good luck or good temper, but none in good sense, least of all a prince; for good sense is a royal prerogative, any claim to that is a case of *lèse majesté*. They are princes, and wish to be so in that most princely of qualities. They will allow a man to help them but not to surpass them, and will have any advice tendered them appear like a recollection of something they have forgotten rather than as a guide to something they cannot find. The stars teach us this finesse with happy tact; though they are his children and brilliant like him, they never rival the brilliancy of the sun.

viii *To be without Passions.*

'Tis a privilege of the highest order of mind. Their very eminence redeems them from being affected by transient and low impulses. There is no higher rule than that over oneself, over one's impulses: there is the triumph of free will. While passion rules the character, no aiming at high office; the less the higher. It is the only refined way of avoiding scandals; nay, 'tis the shortest way back to good repute.

ix *Avoid the Faults of your Nation.*

Water shares the good or bad qualities of the strata through which it flows, and man those of the climate in which he is born. Some owe more than others to their native land, because there is a more favourable sky in the zenith. There is not a nation even among the most civilised that has not some fault peculiar to itself which other nations blame by way of boast or as a warning. 'Tis a triumph of cleverness to correct in oneself such national failings, or even to hide them: you get great credit for being unique among your fellows, and as it is less expected of you it is esteemed the more. There are also family failings as well as faults of position, of office or of age. If these all meet in one person and are not carefully guarded against, they make an intolerable monster.

x *Fortune and Fame.*

Where the one is fickle the other is enduring. The first for life, the second afterwards; the one against envy, the other against oblivion. Fortune is desired, at times assisted: fame is earned. The desire for fame springs from man's best part. It was and is the sister of the giants; it always goes to extremes—horrible monsters or brilliant prodigies.

xi *Cultivate those who can teach you.*

Let friendly intercourse be a school of knowledge, and culture be taught through conversation: thus you make your friends your teachers and mingle the pleasures of conversation with the advantages of instruction. Sensible persons thus enjoy alternating pleasures: they reap applause for what they say, and gain instruction from what they hear. We are always attracted to others by our own interest but in this case it is of a higher kind. Wise men frequent the houses of great noblemen not because they are temples of vanity, but as theatres of good breeding. There be gentlemen who have the credit of worldly wisdom, because they are not only themselves oracles of all nobleness by their example and their behaviour, but those who surround them form a well-bred academy of worldly wisdom of the best and noblest kind.

xii *Nature and Art:*

material and workmanship. There is no beauty unadorned and no excellence that would not become barbaric if it were not supported by artifice: this remedies the evil and improves the good. Nature scarcely ever gives us the very best; for that we must have recourse to art. Without this the best of natural dispositions is uncultured, and half is lacking to any excellence if training is absent. Every one has something unpolished without artificial training, and every kind of excellence needs some polish.

xiii *Act sometimes on Second Thoughts, sometimes on First Impulse.*

Man's life is a warfare against the malice of men. Sagacity fights with strategic changes of intention: it never does what it threatens, it aims only at escaping notice. It aims in the air with dexterity and strikes home in an unexpected direction, always seeking to conceal its game. It lets a purpose appear in order to attract the opponent's attention, but then turns round and conquers by the unexpected. But a penetrating intelligence anticipates this by watchfulness and lurks in ambush. It always understands the opposite of what the opponent wishes it to understand, and recognises every feint of guile. It lets the first impulse pass by and waits for the second, or even the third. Sagacity now rises to higher flights on seeing its artifice foreseen, and tries to deceive by truth itself, changes its game in order to change its deceit, and cheats by not cheating, and founds deception on the greatest candour. But the opposing intelligence is on guard with increased watchfulness, and discovers the darkness concealed by the light and deciphers every move, the more subtle because more simple. In this way the guile of the Python combats the far darting rays of Apollo.

xiv The Thing Itself and the Way it is done.

"Substance" is not enough: "accident"

is also required, as the scholastics say. A bad manner spoils everything, even reason and justice; a good one supplies everything, gilds a No, sweetens truth, and adds a touch of beauty to old age itself. The *how* plays a large part in affairs, a good manner steals into the affections. Fine behaviour is a joy in life, and a pleasant expression helps out of a difficulty in a remarkable way.

xv Keep Ministering Spirits.

It is a privilege of the mighty to surround themselves with the champions of intellect; these extricate them from every fear of ignorance, these worry out for them the moot points of every difficulty. 'Tis a rare greatness to make use of the wise, and far

exceeds the barbarous taste of Tigranes, who had a fancy for captive monarchs as his servants. It is a novel kind of supremacy, the best that life can offer, to have as servants by skill those who by nature are our masters. 'Tis a great thing to know, little to live: no real life without knowledge. There is remarkable cleverness in studying without study, in getting much by means of many, and through them all to become wise. Afterwards you speak in the council chamber on behalf of many, and as many sages speak through your mouth as were consulted beforehand: you thus obtain the fame of an oracle by others' toil. Such ministering spirits distil the best books and serve up the quintessence of wisdom. But he that cannot have sages in service should have them for his friends.

xvi *Knowledge and Good Intentions*

together ensure continuance of success. A fine intellect wedded to a wicked will was always an unnatural monster. A wicked will envenoms all excellences: helped by knowledge it only ruins with greater subtlety. 'Tis a miserable superiority that only results in ruin. Knowledge without sense is double folly.

xvii *Vary the Mode of Action*;

not always the same way, so as to distract attention, especially if there be a rival. Not always from first impulse; they will soon recognise the uniformity, and by anticipating, frustrate your designs. It is easy to kill a bird on the wing that flies straight: not so one that twists. Nor always act on second thoughts: they can discern the plan the second time. The enemy is on the watch, great skill is required to circumvent him. The gamester never plays the card the opponent expects, still less that which he wants.

xviii *Application and Ability*.

There is no attaining eminence without both, and where they unite there is the greatest eminence. Mediocrity obtains more with application than superiority without it. Work is the price which is paid for reputation. What costs little is little worth. Even for the highest posts it is only in some cases application that is wanting, rarely the talent. To prefer moderate success in great things than eminence in a humble post has the excuse of a generous mind, but not so to be content with humble mediocrity when you could shine among the highest. Thus nature and art are both needed, and application sets on them the seal.

xix *Arouse no Exaggerated Expectations on entering.*

It is the usual ill-luck of all celebrities not to fulfil afterwards the expectations beforehand formed of them. The real can never equal the imagined, for it is easy to form ideals but very difficult to realise them. Imagination weds Hope and gives birth to much more than things are in themselves. However great the excellences, they never suffice to fulfil expectations, and as men find themselves disappointed with their exorbitant expectations they are more ready to be disillusionised than to admire. Hope is a great falsifier of truth; let skill guard against this by ensuring that fruition exceeds desire. A few creditable attempts at the beginning are sufficient to arouse curiosity without pledging one to the final object. It is better that reality should surpass the design and is better than was thought. This rule does not apply to the wicked, for the same exaggeration is a great aid to them; they are defeated amid general applause, and what seemed at first extreme ruin comes to be thought quite bearable.

xx *A Man of the Age.*

The rarest individuals depend on their age. It is not every one that finds the age he deserves, and even when he finds it he does not always know how to utilise it. Some men have been worthy of a better century, for every species of good does not always triumph. Things have their period; even excellences are subject to fashion. The sage has one advantage: he is immortal. If *this* is not his century many others will be.

xxi *The Art of being Lucky.*

There are rules of luck: it is not all chance with the wise: it can be assisted by care. Some content themselves with placing themselves confidently at the gate of Fortune, waiting till she opens it. Others do better, and press forward and profit by their clever boldness, reaching the goddess and winning her favour on the wings of their virtue and valour. But on a true philosophy there is no other umpire than virtue and insight; for there is no luck or ill-luck except wisdom and the reverse.

xxii *A Man of Knowledge to the Point.*

Wise men arm themselves with tasteful and elegant erudition; a practical knowledge of what is going on not of a common kind but more like an expert. They possess a copious store of wise and witty sayings, and of noble deeds, and know how to employ them on fitting occasions. More is often taught by a jest than by the most serious teaching. Pat knowledge helps some more than the seven arts, be they ever so liberal.

xxiii *Be Spotless:*

the indispensable condition of perfection. Few live without some weak point, either physical or moral, which they pamper because they could easily cure it. The keenness of others often regrets to see a slight defect attaching itself to a whole assembly of elevated qualities, and yet a single cloud can hide the whole of the sun. There are likewise patches on our reputation which ill-will soon finds out and is continually noticing. The highest skill is to transform them into ornament. So Cæsar hid his natural defects with the laurel.

xxiv *Keep the Imagination under Control,*

sometimes correcting, sometimes assisting it. For it is all-important for our happiness, and even sets the reason right. It can tyrannise, and is not content with looking on, but influences and even often dominates life, causing it to be happy or burdensome according to the folly to which it leads. For it makes us either contented or discontented with ourselves. Before some it continually holds up the penalties of action, and becomes the mortifying lash of these fools. To others it promises happiness and adventure with blissful delusion. It can do all this unless the most prudent self-control keeps it in subjection.

xxv *Know how to take a Hint.*

'Twas once the art of arts to be able to discourse; now 'tis no longer sufficient. We must know how to take a hint, especially in disabusing ourselves. He cannot make himself understood who does not himself easily understand. But on the other hand there are pretended diviners of the heart and lynxes of the intentions. The very truths which concern us most can only be half spoken, but with attention we can grasp the whole meaning. When you hear anything favourable keep a tight rein on your credulity; if unfavourable, give it the spur.

xxvi *Find out each Man's Thumbscrew.*

'Tis the art of setting their wills in action. It needs more skill than resolution. You must know where to get at any one. Every volition has a special motive which varies according to taste. All men are idolaters, some of fame, others of self-interest, most of pleasure. Skill consists in knowing these idols in order to bring them into play. Knowing any man's mainspring of motive you have as it were the key to his will. Have resort to primary motors, which are not always the highest but more often the lowest part of his nature: there are more dispositions badly organised than well. First guess a man's ruling passion, appeal to it by a word, set it in motion by temptation, and you will infallibly give checkmate to his freedom of will.

xxvii *Prize Intensity more than Extent.*

Excellence resides in quality not in quantity. The best is always few and rare: much lowers value. Even among men giants are commonly the real dwarfs. Some reckon books by the thickness, as if they were written to try the brawn more than the brain. Extent alone never rises above mediocrity: it is the misfortune of universal geniuses that in attempting to be at home everywhere, are so nowhere. Intensity gives eminence, and rises to the heroic in matters sublime.

xxviii *Common in Nothing.*

First, not in taste. O great and wise, to be ill at ease when your deeds please the mob! The excesses of popular applause never satisfy the sensible. Some there are such chameleons of popularity that they find enjoyment not in the sweet savours of Apollo but in the breath of the mob. Secondly, not in intelligence. Take no pleasure in the wonder of the mob, for ignorance never gets beyond wonder. While vulgar folly wonders wisdom watches for the trick.

xxix *A Man of Rectitude*

clings to the sect of right with such tenacity of purpose that neither the passions of the mob nor the violence of the tyrant can ever cause him to transgress the bounds of right. But who shall be such a Phœnix of equity? What a scanty following has rectitude! Many praise it indeed, but—for others. Others follow it till danger threatens; then the false deny it, the politic conceal it. For it cares not if it fights with friendship, power, or even self-interest: then comes the danger of desertion. Then astute men make plausible distinctions so as not to stand in the way of their superiors or of reasons of state. But the straightforward and constant regard dissimulation as a kind of treason, and set more store on tenacity than on sagacity. Such are always to be found on the side of truth, and if they desert a party, they do not change from fickleness, but because the others have first deserted truth.

xxx *Have naught to do with Occupations of Ill-repute,*

still less with fads that bring more notoriety than repute. There are many fanciful sects, and from all the prudent man has to flee. There are bizarre tastes that always take to their heart all that wise men repudiate; they live in love with singularity. This may make them well known indeed, but more as objects of ridicule than of repute. A cautious man does not even make profession of his wisdom, still less of those matters that make their followers ridiculous. These need not be specified, for common contempt has sufficiently singled them out.

xxxi *Select the Lucky and avoid the Unlucky.*

Ill-luck is generally the penalty of folly, and there is no disease so contagious to those who share in it. Never open the door to a lesser evil, for other and greater ones invariably slink in after it. The greatest skill at cards is to know when to discard; the smallest of current trumps is worth more than the ace of trumps of the last game. When in doubt, follow the suit of the wise and prudent; sooner or later they will win the odd trick.

xxxii *Have the Reputation of being Gracious.*

'Tis the chief glory of the high and mighty to be gracious, a prerogative of kings to conquer universal goodwill. That is the great advantage of a commanding position—to be able to do more good than others. Those make friends who do friendly acts. On the other hand, there are some who lay themselves out for not being gracious, not on account of the difficulty, but from a bad disposition. In all things they are the opposite of Divine grace.

xxxiii *Know how to Withdraw.*

If it is a great lesson in life to know how to deny, it is a still greater to know how to deny oneself as regards both affairs and persons. There are extraneous occupations which eat away precious time. To be occupied in what does not concern you is worse than doing nothing. It is not enough for a careful man not to interfere with others, he must see that they do not interfere with him. One is not obliged to belong so much to all as not to belong at all to oneself. So with friends, their help should not be abused or more demanded from them than they themselves will grant. All excess is a failing, but above all in personal intercourse. A wise moderation in this best preserves the goodwill and esteem of all, for by this means that precious boon of courtesy is not gradually worn away. Thus you preserve your genius free to select the elect, and never sin against the unwritten laws of good taste.

xxxiv *Know your strongest Point—*

your pre-eminent gift; cultivate that and you will assist the rest. Every one would have excelled in something if he had known his strong point. Notice in what quality you surpass, and take charge of that. In some judgment excels, in others valour. Most do violence to their natural aptitude, and thus attain superiority in nothing. Time disillusionises us too late of what first flattered the passions.

xxv *Think over Things, most over the most Important.*

All fools come to grief from want of thought. They never see even the half of things, and as they do not observe their own loss or gain, still less do they apply any diligence to them. Some make much of what imports little and little of much, always weighing in the wrong scale. Many never lose their common sense, because they have none to lose. There are matters which should be observed with the closest attention of the mind, and thenceforth kept in its lowest depths. The wise man thinks over everything, but with a difference, most profoundly where there is some profound difficulty, and thinks that perhaps there is more in it than he thinks. Thus his comprehension extends as far as his apprehension.

xxxvi *In Acting or Refraining, weigh your Luck.*

More depends on that than on noticing your temperament. If he is a fool who at forty applies to Hippocrates for health, still more is he one who then first applies to Seneca for wisdom. It is a great piece of skill to know how to guide your luck even while waiting for it. For something is to be done with it by waiting so as to use it at the proper moment, since it has periods and offers opportunities, though one cannot calculate its path, its steps are so irregular. When you find Fortune favourable, stride boldly forward, for she favours the bold and, being a woman, the young. But if you have bad luck, keep retired so as not to redouble the influence of your unlucky star.

xxxvii *Keep a Store of Sarcasms, and know how to use them.*

This is the point of greatest tact in human intercourse. Such sarcasms are often thrown out to test men's moods, and by their means one often obtains the most subtle and penetrating touchstone of the heart. Other sarcasms are malicious, insolent, poisoned by envy or envenomed by passion, unexpected flashes which destroy at once all favour and esteem. Struck by the slightest word of this kind, many fall away from the closest intimacy with superiors or inferiors which could not be the slightest shaken by a whole conspiracy of popular insinuation or private malevolence. Other sarcasms, on the other hand, work favourably, confirming and assisting one's reputation. But the greater the skill with which they are launched, the greater the caution with which they should be received and the foresight with which they should he foreseen. For here a knowledge of the evil is in itself a means of defence, and a shot foreseen always misses its mark.

xxxviii *Leave your Luck while Winning.*

All the best players do it. A fine retreat is as good as a gallant attack. Bring your exploits under cover when there are enough, or even when there are many of them. Luck long lasting was ever suspicious; interrupted seems safer, and is even sweeter to the taste for a little infusion of bitter-sweet. The higher the heap of luck, the greater the risk of a slip, and down comes all. Fortune pays you sometimes for the intensity of her favours by the shortness of their duration. She soon tires of carrying any one long on her shoulders.

xxxix *Recognise when Things are ripe, and then enjoy them.*

The works of nature all reach a certain point of maturity; up to that they improve, after that they degenerate. Few works of art reach such a point that they cannot be improved. It is an especial privilege of good taste to enjoy everything at its ripest. Not all can do this, nor do all who can know this. There is a ripening point too for fruits of intellect; it is well to know this both for their value in use and for their value in exchange.

xl *The Goodwill of People.*

'Tis much to gain universal admiration; more, universal love. Something depends on natural disposition, more on practice: the first founds, the second then builds on that foundation. Brilliant parts suffice not, though they are presupposed; win good opinion and 'tis easy to win goodwill. Kindly acts besides are required to produce kindly feelings, doing good with both hands, good words and better deeds, loving so as to be loved. Courtesy is the politic witchery of great personages. First lay hand on deeds and then on pens; words follow swords; for there is goodwill to be won among writers, and it is eternal.

xli *Never Exaggerate.*

It is an important object of attention not to talk in superlatives, so as neither to offend against truth nor to give a mean idea of one's understanding. Exaggeration is a prodigality of the judgment which shows the narrowness of one's knowledge or one's taste. Praise arouses lively curiosity, begets desire, and if afterwards the value does not correspond to the price, as generally happens, expectation revolts against the deception, and revenges itself by under-estimating the thing recommended and the person recommending. A prudent man goes more cautiously to work, and prefers to err by omission than by commission. Extraordinary things are rare, therefore moderate ordinary valuation. Exaggeration is a branch of lying, and you lose by it the credit of good taste, which is much, and of good sense, which is more.

xlii *Born to Command.*

It is a secret force of superiority not to have to get on by artful trickery but by an inborn power of rule. All submit to it without knowing why, recognising the secret vigour of connatural authority. Such magisterial spirits are kings by merit and lions by innate privilege. By the esteem which they inspire, they hold the hearts and minds of the rest. If their other qualities permit, such men are born to be the prime motors of the state. They per-form more by a gesture than others by a long harangue.

xliii *Think with the Few and speak with the Many.*

By swimming against the stream it is impossible to remove error, easy to fall into danger; only a Socrates can undertake it. To dissent from others' views is regarded as an insult, because it is their condemnation. Disgust is doubled on account of the thing blamed and of the person who praised it. Truth is for the few, error is both common and vulgar. The wise man is not known by what he says on the house-tops, for there he speaks not with his own voice but with that of common folly, however much his inmost thoughts may gainsay it. The prudent avoid being contradicted as much as contradicting: though they have their censure ready they are not ready to publish it. Thought is free, force cannot and should not be used to it. The wise man therefore retires into silence, and if he allows himself to come out of it, he does so in the shade and before few and fit persons.

xliv *Sympathy with great Minds.*

It is an heroic quality to agree with heroes. 'Tis like a miracle of nature for mystery and for use. There is a natural kinship of hearts and minds: its effects are such that vulgar ignorance scents witchcraft. Esteem established, goodwill follows, which at times reaches affection. It persuades without words and obtains without earning. This sympathy is sometimes active, sometimes passive, both alike felicific; the more so, the more sublime. 'Tis a great art to recognise, to distinguish and to utilise this gift. No amount of energy suffices without that favour of nature.

xlv *Use, but do not abuse, Cunning.*

One ought not to delight in it, still less to boast of it. Everything artificial should be concealed, most of all cunning, which is hated. Deceit is much in use; therefore our caution has to be redoubled, but not so as to show itself, for it arouses distrust, causes much annoy, awakens revenge, and gives rise to more ills than you would imagine. To go to work with caution is of great advantage in action, and there is no greater proof of wisdom. The greatest skill in any deed consists in the sure mastery with which it is executed.

xlvi *Master your Antipathies.*

We often allow ourselves to take dislikes, and that before we know anything of a person. At times this innate yet vulgar aversion attaches Itself to eminent personalities. Good sense masters this feeling, for there is nothing more discreditable than to dislike those better than ourselves. As sympathy with great men en-nobles us, so dislike to them degrades us.

xlvii *Avoid "Affairs of Honour"*

—one of the chiefest aims of prudence. In men of great ability the extremes are kept far asunder, so that there is a long distance between them, and they always keep in the middle of their caution, so that they take time to break through it. It is easier to avoid such affairs than to come well out of them. They test our judgment; it is better to avoid them than to conquer in them. One affair of honour leads to another, and may lead to an affair of dishonour. There are men so constituted by nature or by nation that they easily enter upon such obligations. But for him that walks by the light of reason, such a matter requires long thinking over. There is more valour needed not to take up the affair than to conquer in it. When there is one fool ready for the occasion, one may excuse oneself from being the second.

xlviii *Be Thorough.*

How much depends on the person. The interior must be at least as much as the exterior. There are natures all frontage, like houses that for want of means have the portico of a palace leading to the rooms of a cottage. It is no use boring into such persons, although they bore you, for conversation flags after the first salutation. They prance through the first compliments like Sicilian barbs, but silence soon succeeds, for the flow of words soon ceases where there is no spring of thoughts. Others may be taken in by them because they themselves have but a view of the surface, but not the prudent, who look within them and find nothing there except material for scorn.

xlix *Observation and Judgment.*

A man with these rules things, not they him. He sounds at once the profoundest depths; he is a phrenologist by means of physiognomy. On seeing a person he understands him and judges of his inmost nature. From a few observations he deciphers the most hidden recesses of his nature. Keen observation, subtile insight, judicious inference: with these he discovers, notices, grasps, and comprehends everything.

l Never lose Self-respect,

or be too familiar with oneself. Let your own right feeling be the true standard of your rectitude, and owe more to the strictness of your own self-judgment than to all external sanctions. Leave off anything unseemly more from regard for your own self-respect than from fear of external authority. Pay regard to that and there is no need of Seneca's imaginary tutor.

li Know how to Choose well.

Most of life depends thereon. It needs good taste and correct judgment, for which neither intellect nor study suffices. To be choice, you must choose, and for this two things are needed: to be able to choose at all, and then to choose the best. There are many men of fecund and subtle mind, of keen judgment, of much learning, and of great observation who yet are at a loss when they come to choose. They always take the worst as if they had tried to go wrong. Thus this is one of the greatest gifts from above.

lii Never be put out.

'Tis a great aim of prudence never to be embarrassed. It is the sign of a real man. of a noble heart, for magnanimity is not easily put out. The passions are the humours of the soul, and every excess in them weakens prudence; if they overflow through the mouth, the reputation will be in danger. Let a man therefore be so much and so great a master over himself that neither in the most fortunate nor in the most adverse circumstances can anything cause his reputation injury by disturbing his self-possession, but rather enhance it by showing his superiority.

liii Diligent and Intelligent.

Diligence promptly executes what intelligence slowly excogitates. Hurry is the failing of fools; they know not the crucial point and set to work without preparation. On the other hand, the wise more often fail from procrastination; foresight begets deliberation, and remiss action often nullifies prompt judgment. Celerity is the mother of good fortune. He has done much who leaves nothing over till to-morrow. Festina lente is a royal motto.

liv Know how to show your Teeth.

Even hares can pull the mane of a dead lion. There is no joke about courage. Give way to the first and you must yield to the second, and so on till the last, and to gain your point at last costs as much trouble as would have gained much more at first. Moral courage exceeds physical; it should be like a sword kept ready for use in the scabbard of caution. It Is the shield of great place; moral cowardice lowers one more than physical. Many have had eminent qualities, yet, for want of a stout heart, they passed  inanimate lives and found a tomb in their own sloth. Wise Nature has thoughtfully combined in the bee the sweetness of its honey with the sharpness of its sting.

lv Wait.

It's a sign of a noble heart dowered with patience, never to be in a hurry, never to be in a passion. First be master over yourself if you would be master over others. You must pass through the circumference of time before arriving at the centre of opportunity. A wise reserve seasons the aims and matures the means. Time's crutch effects more than the iron club of Hercules. God Himself chasteneth not with a rod but with time. He spake a great word who said, "Time and I against any two." Fortune herself rewards waiting with the first prize.

lvi Have Presence of Mind.

The child of a happy promptitude of spirit. Owing to this vivacity and widewakeness there is no fear of danger or mischance. Many reflect much only to go wrong in the end: others attain their aim without thinking of it beforehand. There are natures of Antiperistasis who work best in an emergency. They are like monsters who succeed in all they do offhand, but fail in aught they think over. A thing occurs to them at once or never: for them there is no court of appeal. Celerity wins applause because it proves remarkable capacity; subtlety of judgment, prudence in action.

lvii Slow and Sure.

Early enough if well. Quickly done can be quickly undone. To last an eternity requires an eternity of preparation. Only excellence counts; only achievement endures. Profound intelligence is the only foundation for immortality. Worth much costs much. The precious metals are the heaviest.

lviii Adapt Yourself to your Company.

There is no need to show your ability before every one. Employ no more force than is necessary. Let there be no unnecessary expenditure either of knowledge or of power. The skilful falconer only flies enough birds to serve for the chase. If there is too much display to-day there will be nothing to show to-morrow. Always have some novelty wherewith to dazzle. To show something fresh each day keeps expectation alive and conceals the limits of capacity.

lix Finish off well.

In the house of Fortune, if you enter by the gate of pleasure you must leave by that of sorrow andvice versâ. You ought therefore to think of the finish, and attach more importance to a graceful exit than to applause on entrance. 'Tis the common lot of the unlucky to have a very fortunate outset and a very tragic end. The important point is not the vulgar applause on entrance—that comes to nearly all—but the general feeling at exit. Few in life are felt to deserve an encore. Fortune rarely accompanies any one to the door: warmly as she may welcome the coming, she speeds but coldly the parting guest.

lx A Sound Judgment.

Some are born wise, and with this natural advantage enter upon their studies, with a moiety already mastered. With age and experience their reason ripens, and thus they attain a sound judgment. They abhor everything whimsical as leading prudence astray, especially in matters of state, where certainty is so necessary, owing to the importance of the affairs involved., Such men deserve to stand by the helm of state either as pilots or as men at the wheel.

lxi To Excel in what is Excellent.

A great rarity among excellences. You cannot have a great man without something pre-eminent. Mediocrities never win applause. Eminence in some distinguished post distinguishes one from the vulgar mob and ranks us with the elect. To be distinguished in a Small post is to be great in little: the more comfort, the less glory. The highest eminence in great affairs has the royal characteristic of exciting admiration and winning goodwill.

lxii Use good Instruments.

Some would have the subtlety of their wits proven by the meanness of their instruments. 'Tis a dangerous satisfaction, and deserves a fatal punishment. The excellence of a minister never diminished the greatness of his lord. All the glory of exploits reverts to the principal actor; also all the blame. Fame only does business with principals. She does not say, "This had good, that had bad servants," but, "This was a good artist, that a bad one." Let your assistants be selected and tested therefore, for you have to trust to them for an immortality of fame.

lxiii To be the First of the Kind is an Excellence,

and to be eminent in it as well, a double one. To have the first move is a great ad-vantage when the players are equal. Many a man would have been a veritable Phœnix if he had been the first of the sort. Those who come first are the heirs of Fame; the others get only a younger brother's allowance: whatever they do, they cannot persuade the world they are anything more than parrots. The skill of prodigies may find a new path to eminence, but prudence accompanies them all the way. By the novelty of their enterprises sages write their names in the golden book of heroes. Some prefer to be first in things of minor import than second in greater exploits.

lxiv Avoid Worry.

Such prudence brings its own reward. It escapes much, and is thus the midwife of comfort and so of happiness. Neither give nor take bad news unless it can help. Some men's ears are stuffed with the sweets of flattery; others with the bitters of scandal, while some cannot live without a daily annoyance no more than Mithridates could without poison. It is no rule of life to prepare for yourself lifelong trouble in order to give a temporary enjoyment to another, however near and dear. You never ought to spoil your own chances to please another who advises and keeps out of the affair, and in all cases where to oblige another involves disobliging yourself, 'tis a standing rule that it is better he should suffer now than you afterwards and in vain.

lxv Elevated Taste.

You can train it like the intellect. Full knowledge whets desire and increases enjoyment. You may know a noble spirit by the elevation of his taste: it must be a great thing that can satisfy a great mind. Big bites for big mouths, lofty things for lofty spirits. Before their judgment the bravest tremble, the most perfect lose confidence. Things of the first importance are few; let appreciation be rare. Taste can be imparted by intercourse: great good luck to associate with the highest taste. But do not affect to be dissatisfied with everything: 'tis the extreme of folly, and more odious if from affectation than if from Quixotry. Some would have God create another world and other ideals to satisfy their fantastic imagination.

lxvi See that Things end well.

Some regard more the rigour of the game than the winning of it, but to the world the discredit of the final failure does away with any recognition of the previous care. The victor need not explain. The world does not notice the details of the measures employed;

but only the good or ill result. You lose nothing if you gain your end. A good end gilds everything, however unsatisfactory the means. Thus at times it is part of the art of life to transgress the rules of the art, if you cannot end well otherwise.

lxvii Prefer Callings "en Evidence."

Most things depend on the satisfaction of others. Esteem is to excellence what the zephyr is to flowers, the breath of life. There are some callings which gain universal esteem, while others more important are without credit. The former, pursued before the eyes of all, obtain the universal favour; the others, though they are rarer and more valuable, remain obscure and unperceived, honoured but not applauded. Among princes conquerors are the most celebrated, and therefore the kings of Aragon earned such applause as warriors, conquerors, and great men. An able man will prefer callings en evidence which all men know of and utilise, and he thus becomes immortalised by universal suffrage.

lxviii It is better to help with Intelligence than with Memory.

The more as the latter needs only recollection, the former νοῦς. Many persons omit the à proposbecause it does not occur to them; a friend's advice on such occasions may enable them to see the advantages. 'Tis one of the greatest gifts of mind to be able to offer what is needed at the moment: for want of that many things fail to be performed. Share the light of your intelligence, when you have any, and ask for it when you have it not, the first cautiously, the last anxiously. Give no more than a hint: this finesse is especially needful when it touches the interest of him whose attention you awaken. You should give but a taste at first, and then pass on to more when that is not sufficient. If he thinks of No, go in search of Yes. Therein lies the cleverness, for most things are not obtained simply because they are not attempted.

lxix *Do not give way to every common Impulse.*

He is a great man who never allows himself to be influenced by the impressions of others. Self-reflection is the school of wisdom. To know one's disposition and to allow for it, even going to the other extreme so as to find the juste milieu between nature and art. Self-knowledge is the beginning of self-improvement. There be some whose humours are so monstrous that they are always under the influence of one or other of them, and put them in place of their real inclinations. They are torn asunder by such disharmony and get involved in contradictory obligations. Such excesses not only destroy firmness of will; all power of judgment gets lost, desire and knowledge pulling in opposite directions.

lxx *Know how to Refuse.*

One ought not to give way in everything nor to everybody. To know how to refuse is therefore as important as to know how to consent. This is especially the case with men of position. All depends on the how. Some men's No is thought more of than the Yes of others: for a gilded No is more satisfactory than a dry Yes. There are some who always have No on their lips, whereby they make everything distasteful. No always comes first with them, and when sometimes they give way after all, it does them no good on account of the unpleasing herald. Your refusal need not be point-blank: let the disappointment come by degrees. Nor let the refusal be final; that would be to destroy dependence; let some spice of hope remain to soften the rejection. Let politeness compensate and fine words supply the place of deeds. Yes and No are soon said, but give much to think over.

lxxi Do not Vacillate.

Let not your actions be abnormal either from disposition or affectation. An able man is always the same in his best qualities; he gets the credit of trustworthiness. If he changes, he does so for good reason or good consideration. In matters of conduct change is hateful. There are some who are different every day; their intelligence varies, still more their will, and with this their fortune. Yesterday's white is to-day's black: to-day's No was yesterday's Yes. They always give the lie to their own credit and destroy their credit with others.

lxxii Be Resolute.

Bad execution of your designs does less harm than irresolution in forming them. Streams do less harm flowing than when dammed up. There are some men so infirm of purpose that they always require direction from others, and this not on account of any perplexity, for they judge clearly, but from sheer incapacity for action. It needs some skill to find out difficulties, but more to find a way out of them. There are others who are never in straits . their clear judgment and determined character it them for the highest callings: their intelligence tells them where to insert the thin end of the wedge, their resolution how to drive it home. They soon get through anything: as soon as they have done with one sphere of action, they are ready for another. Affianced to Fortune, they make themselves sure of success.

lxxiii Utilise Slips.

That is how smart people get out of difficulties. They extricate themselves from the most intricate labyrinth by some witty application of a bright remark. They get out of a serious contention by an airy nothing or by raising a smile. Most of the great leaders are well grounded in this art. When you have to refuse, it is often the polite way to talk of something else. Sometimes it proves the highest understanding not to understand.

lxxiv Do not be Unsociable.

The truest wild beasts live in the most populous places. To be inaccessible is the fault of those who distrust themselves, whose honours change their manners. It is no way of earning people's goodwill by being ill-tempered with them. It is a sight to see one of those unsociable monsters who make a point of being proudly impertinent. Their dependants who have the misfortune to be obliged to speak with them, enter as if prepared for a fight with a tiger armed with patience and with fear. To obtain their post these persons must have ingratiated themselves with every one, but having once obtained it they seek to indemnify themselves by disobliging all. It is a condition of their position that they should be accessible to all, yet, from pride or spleen, they are so to none. 'Tis a civil way to punish such men by letting them alone, and depriving them of opportunities of improvement by granting them no opportunity of intercourse.

lxxv Choose an Heroic Ideal;

but rather to emulate than to imitate. There are exemplars of greatness, living texts of honour. Let every one have before his mind the chief of his calling not so much to follow him as to spur himself on. Alexander wept not on account of Achilles dead and buried, but over himself, because his fame had not yet spread throughout the world. Nothing arouses ambition so much in the heart as the trumpet-clang of another's fame. The same thing that sharpens envy, nourishes a generous spirit.

lxxvi Do not always be Jesting.

Wisdom is shown in serious matters, and is more appreciated than mere wit. He that is always ready for jests is never ready for serious things. They resemble liars in that men never believe either, always expecting a lie in one, a joke in the other. One never knows when you speak with judgment, which is the same as if you had none. A continual jest soon loses all zest. Many get the repute of being witty, but thereby lose the credit of being sensible. Jest has its little hour, seriousness should have all the rest.

lxxvii Be all Things to all Men

—a discreet Proteus, learned with the learned, saintly with the sainted. It is the great art to gain every one's suffrages; their goodwill gains general agreement. Notice men's moods and adapt yourself to each, genial or serious as the case may be. Follow their lead, glossing over the changes as cunningly as possible. This is an indispensable art for dependent persons. But this savoir faire calls for great cleverness. He only will find no difficulty who has a universal genius in his knowledge and universal ingenuity in his wit.

lxxviii The Art of undertaking Things.

Fools rush in through the door; for folly is always bold. The same simplicity which robs them of all attention to precautions deprives them of all sense of shame at failure. But prudence enters with more deliberation. Its forerunners are caution and care; they advance and discover whether you can also advance without danger. Every rush forward is freed from danger by caution, while fortune some-times helps in such cases. Step cautiously where you suspect depth. Sagacity goes cautiously forward while precaution covers the ground. Nowadays there are unsuspected depths in human. intercourse, you must therefore cast the lead at every step.

lxxix *A Genial Disposition.*

If with moderation 'tis an accomplishment, not a defect. A grain of gaiety seasons all. The greatest men join in the fun at times, and it makes them liked by all. But they should always on such occasions preserve their dignity, nor go beyond the bounds of decorum. Others, again, get themselves out of difficulty quickest by a joke. For there are things you must take in fun, though others perhaps mean them in earnest. You show a sense of placability, which acts as a magnet on all hearts.

lxxx *Take care to get Information.*

We live by information, not by sight. We exist by faith in others. The ear is the area-gate of truth but the front-door of lies. The truth is generally seen, rarely heard; seldom she comes in elemental purity, especially from afar; there is always some admixture of the moods of those through whom she has passed. The passions tinge her with their colours wherever they touch her, sometimes favourably, sometimes the reverse. She always brings out the disposition, therefore receive her with caution from him that praises, with more caution from him that blames. Pay attention to the intention of the speaker; you should know beforehand on what footing he comes. Let reflection assay falsity and exaggeration.

lxxxi *Renew your Brilliance.*

'Tis the privilege of the Phœnix. Ability is wont to grow old, and with it fame. The staleness of custom weakens admiration, and a mediocrity that's new often eclipses the highest excellence grown old. Try therefore to be born again in valour, in genius, in fortune, in all. Display startling novelties, rise afresh like the sun every day. Change too the scene on which you shine, so that your loss may be felt in the old scenes of your triumph, while the novelty of your powers wins you applause in the new.

lxxxii Drain Nothing to the Dregs, neither Good nor Ill.

A sage once reduced all virtue to the golden mean. Push right to the extreme and it becomes wrong: press all the juice from an orange and it becomes bitter. Even in enjoyment never go to extremes. Thought too subtle is dull. If you milk a cow too much you draw blood, not milk.

lxxxiii Allow Yourself some venial Fault.

Some such carelessness is often the greatest recommendation of talent. For envy exercises ostracism, most envenomed when most polite, It counts it to perfection as a failing that it has no faults; for being perfect in all it condemns it in all. It becomes an Argus, all eyes for imperfection: 'tis its only consolation. Blame is like the lightning; it hits the highest. Let Homer nod now and then and affect some negligence in valour or in intellect—not in prudence—so as to disarm malevolence, or at least to prevent its bursting with its own venom. You thus leave your cloak on the horns of Envy in order to save your immortal parts.

lxxxiv Make use of your Enemies.

You should learn to seize things not by the blade, which cuts, but by the handle, which saves you from harm: especially is this the rule with the doings of your enemies. A wise man gets more use from his enemies than a fool from his friends. Their ill-will often levels mountains of difficulties which one would otherwise not face. Many have had their greatness made for them by their enemies. Flattery is more dangerous than hatred, because it covers the stains which the other causes to be wiped out. The wise will turn ill-will into a mirror more faithful than that of kindness. and remove or improve the faults referred to. Caution thrives well when rivalry and ill-will are next-door neighbours.

lxxxv Do not play Manille.

It is a fault of excellence that being so much in use it is liable to abuse. Because all covet it, all are vexed by it. It is a great misfortune to be of use to nobody; scarcely less to be of use to everybody. People who reach this stage lose by gaining, and at last bore those who desired them before. These Manilles wear away all kinds of excellence: losing the earlier esteem of the few, they obtain discredit among the vulgar. The remedy against this extreme is to moderate your brilliance. Be extraordinary in your excellence, if you like, but be ordinary in your display of it. The more light a torch gives, the more it burns away and the nearer 'tis to going out. Show yourself less and you will be rewarded by being esteemed more.

lxxxvi Prevent Scandal.

Many heads go to make the mob, and in each of them are eyes for malice to use and a tongue for detraction to wag. If a single ill report spread, it casts a blemish on your fair fame, and if it clings to you with a nickname, your reputation is in danger. Generally it is some salient defect or ridiculous trait that gives rise to the rumours. At times these are malicious additions of private envy to general distrust. For there are wicked tongues that ruin a great reputation more easily by a witty sneer than by a direct accusation. It is easy to get into bad repute, because it is easy to believe evil of any one: it is not easy to clear yourself. The wise accordingly avoid these mischances, guarding against vulgar scandal with sedulous vigilance. It is far easier to prevent than to rectify.

lxxxvii Culture and Elegance.

Man is born a barbarian, and only raises himself above the beast by culture. Culture therefore makes the man; the more a man, the higher. Thanks to it, Greece could call the rest of the world barbarians. Ignorance is very raw; nothing contributes so much to culture as knowledge. But even knowledge is coarse If without elegance. Not alone must our intelligence be elegant, but our desires, and above all our conversation. Some men are naturally elegant in internal and external qualities, in their thoughts, in their address, in their dress, which is the rind of the soul, and in their talents, which is its fruit. There are others, on the other hand, so gauche that everything about them, even their very excellences, is tarnished by an intolerable and barbaric want of neatness.

lxxxviii Let your Behaviour be Fine and Noble.

A great man ought not to be little in his behaviour. He ought never to pry too minutely into things, least of all in unpleasant matters. For though it is important to know all, it is not necessary to know all about all. One ought to act in such cases with the generosity of a gentleman, conduct worthy of a gallant man. To overlook forms a large part of the work of ruling. Most things must be left unnoticed among relatives and friends, and even among enemies. All superfluity is annoying, especially in things that annoy. To keep hovering around the object or your annoyance is a kind of mania. Generally speaking, every man behaves according to his heart and his understanding.

lxxxix Know Yourself

—in talents and capacity, in judgment and inclination. You cannot master yourself unless you know yourself. There are mirrors for the face but none for the mind. Let careful thought about yourself serve as a substitute. When the outer image is forgotten, keep the inner one to improve and perfect. Learn the force of your intellect and capacity for affairs, test the force of your courage in order to apply it, and keep your foundations secure and your head clear for everything.

---

xc The Secret of Long Life

Lead a good life. Two things bring life speedily to an end: folly and immorality. Some lose their life because they have not the intelligence to keep it, others because they have not the will. Just as virtue is its own reward, so is vice its own punishment. He who lives a fast life runs through life in a double sense. A virtuous life never dies. The firmness of the soul is communicated to the body, and a good life is long not only in intention but also in extension.

xci Never set to work at anything if you have any doubts of its Prudence.

A suspicion of failure in the mind of the doer is proof positive of it in that of the onlooker, especially if he is a rival. If in the heat of action your judgment feels scruples, it will afterwards in cool reflection condemn it as a piece of folly. Action is dangerous where prudence is in doubt: better leave such things alone. Wisdom does not trust to probabilities; it always marches in the mid-day light of reason. How can an enterprise succeed which the judgment condemns as soon as conceived? And if resolutions passed nem. con. by inner court often turn out unfortunately, what can we expect of those undertaken by a doubting reason and a vacillating judgment?

xcii Transcendant Wisdom.

I mean in everything. The first and highest rule of all deed and speech, the more necessary to be followed the higher and more numerous our posts, is: an ounce of wisdom is worth more than tons of cleverness. It is the only sure way, though it may not gain so much applause. The reputation of wisdom is the last triumph of fame. It is enough if you satisfy the wise, for their judgment is the touchstone of true success.

xciii Versatility.

A man of many excellences equals many men. By imparting his own enjoyment of life to his circle he enriches their life. Variety in excellences is the delight of life. It is a great art to profit by all that is good, and since Nature has made man in his highest development an abstract of herself, so let Art create in him a true microcosm by training his taste and intellect.

xciv Keep the extent of your Abilities unknown.

The wise man does not allow his knowledge and abilities to be sounded to the bottom, if he desires to be honoured by all. He allows you to know them but not to comprehend them. No one must know the extent of his abilities, lest he be disappointed. No one ever has an opportunity of fathoming him entirely. For guesses and doubts about the extent of his talents arouse more veneration than accurate knowledge of them, be they ever so great.

xcv Keep Expectation alive.

Keep stirring it up. Let much promise more, and great deeds herald greater. Do not rest your whole fortune on a single cast of the die. It requires great skill to moderate your forces so as to keep expectation from being dissipated.

xcvi The highest Discretion.

It is the throne of reason, the foundation of prudence: by its means success is gained at little cost. It is a gift from above, and should be prayed for as the first and best quality. 'Tis the main piece of the panoply, and so important that its absence makes a man imperfect, whereas with other qualities it is merely a question of more or less. All the actions of life depend on its application; all require its assistance, for everything needs intelligence.

Discretion consists in a natural tendency to the most rational course, combined with a liking for the surest.

xcvii Obtain and preserve a Reputation.

It is the usufruct of fame. It is expensive to obtain a reputation, for it only attaches to distinguished abilities, which are as rare as mediocrities are common. Once obtained, it is easily preserved. It confers many an obligation, but it does more. When it is owing to elevated powers or lofty spheres of action, it rises to a kind of veneration and yields a sort of majesty. But it is only a well-founded reputation that lasts permanently.

xcviii Write your Intentions in Cypher.

The passions are the gates of the soul. The most practical knowledge consists in disguising them. He that plays with cards exposed runs a risk of losing the stakes. The reserve of caution should combat the curiosity of inquirers: adopt the policy of the cuttlefish. Do not even let your tastes be known, lest others utilise them either by running counter to them or by flattering them.

xcix Reality and Appearance.

Things pass for what they seem, not for what they are. Few see inside; many take to the outside. It is not enough to be right, if right seem false and ill.

c A Man without Illusions, a wise Christian, a philosophic Courtier.

Be all these, not merely seem to be them, still less affect to be them. Philosophy is nowadays discredited, but yet it was always the chiefest concern of the wise. The art of thinking has lost all its former repute. Seneca introduced it at Rome: it went to court for some time, but now it is considered out of place there. And yet the discovery of deceit was always thought the true nourishment of a thoughtful mind, the true delight of a virtuous soul.

ci *One half of the World laughs at the other, and Fools are they all.*

Everything is good or everything is bad according to the votes they gain. What one pursues another persecutes. He is an insufferable ass that would regulate everything according to his ideas. Excellences do not depend on a single man's pleasure. So many men, so many tastes, all different. There is no defect which is not affected by some, nor need we lose heart if things please not some, for others will appreciate them. Nor need their applause turn our head, for there will surely be others to condemn. The real test of praise is the approbation of famous men and of experts in the matter. You should aim to be independent of any one vote, of any one fashion, of any one century.

cii *Be able to stomach big slices of Luck.*

In the body of wisdom not the least important organ is a big stomach, for great capacity implies great parts. Big bits of luck do not embarrass one who can digest still bigger ones. What is a surfeit for one may be hunger for another. Many are troubled as it were with weak digestion, owing to their small capacity being neither born nor trained for great employment. Their actions turn sour, and the humours that arise from their undeserved honours turn their head and they incur great risks in high place: they do not find their proper place, for luck finds no proper place in them. A man of talent therefore should show that he has more room for even greater enterprises, and above all avoid showing signs of a little heart.

viii *Let each keep up his Dignity.*

Let each deed of a man in its degree, though he be not a king, be worthy of a prince, and let his action be princely within due limits. Sublime in action, lofty in thought, in all things like a king, at least in merit if not in might. For true kingship lies in spotless rectitude, and he need not envy greatness who can serve as a model of it. Especially should those near the throne aim at true superiority, and prefer to share the true qualities of royalty rather than take parts in its mere ceremonies, yet without affecting its imperfections but sharing in its true dignity.

civ *Try your hand at Office.*

It requires varied qualities, and to know which is needed taxes attention and calls for masterly discernment. Some demand courage, others tact. Those that merely require rectitude are the easiest, the most difficult those requiring cleverness. For the former all that is necessary is character; for the latter all one's attention and zeal may not suffice. 'Tis a troublesome business to rule men, still more fools or blockheads: double sense is needed with those who have none. It is intolerable when an office engrosses a man with fixed hours and a settled routine. Those are better that leave a man free to follow his own devices, combining variety with importance, for the change refreshes the mind. The most in repute are those that have least or most distant dependence on others; the worst is that which worries us both here and hereafter.

cv *Don't be a Bore.*

The man of one business or of one topic is apt to be heavy. Brevity flatters and does better business; it gains by courtesy what it loses by curtness. Good things, when short, are twice as good. The quintessence of the matter is more effective than a whole farrago of details. It is a well-known truth that talkative folk rarely have much sense whether in dealing with the matter itself or its formal treatment. There are that serve more for stumbling-stones than centrepieces, useless lumber in every one's way. The wise avoid being bores, especially to the great, who are fully occupied: it is worse to disturb one of them than all the rest. Well said is soon said.

cvi Do not parade your Position.

To outshine in dignity is more offensive than in personal attractions. To pose as a personage is to be hated: envy is surely enough. The more you seek esteem the less you obtain it, for it depends on the opinion of others. You cannot take it, but must earn and receive it from others. Great positions require an amount of authority sufficient to make them efficient: without it they cannot be adequately filled. Preserve therefore enough dignity to carry on the duties of the office. Do not enforce respect, but try and create it. Those who insist on the dignity of their office, show they have not deserved it, and that it is too much for them. If you wish to be valued, be valued for your talents, not for anything adventitious. Even kings prefer to be honoured for their personal qualifications rather than for their station.

cvii Show no Self-satisfaction.

You must neither be discontented with yourself—and that were poor-spirited—nor self-satisfied—and that is folly. Self-satisfaction arises mostly from ignorance: it would be a happy ignorance not without its advantages if it did not injure our credit. Because a man cannot achieve the superlative perfections of others, he contents himself with any mediocre talent of his own. Distrust is wise, and even useful, either to evade mishaps or to afford consolation when they come, for a misfortune cannot surprise a man who has already feared it. Even Homer nods at times, and Alexander fell from his lofty state and out of his illusions. Things depend on many circumstances: what constitutes triumph in one set may cause a defeat in another. In the midst of all incorrigible folly remains the same with empty self-satisfaction, blossoming, flowering, and running all to seed.

cviii *The Path to Greatness is along with Others.*

Intercourse works well: manners and taste are shared: good sense and even talent grow insensibly. Let the sanguine man then make a comrade of the lymphatic, and so with the other temperaments, so that without any forcing the golden mean is obtained. It is a great art to agree with others. The alternation of contraries beautifies and sustains the world: if it can cause harmony in the physical world, still more can it do so in the moral. Adopt this policy in the choice of friends and defendants; by joining extremes the more effective middle way is found.

cix *Be not Censorious.*

There are men of gloomy character who regard everything as faulty, not from any evil motive but because it is their nature to. They condemn all: these for what they have done, those for what they will do. This indicates a nature worse than cruel, vile Indeed. They accuse with such exaggeration that they make out of motes beams wherewith to force out the eyes. They are always taskmasters who could turn a paradise into a prison; if passion intervenes they drive matters to the extreme. A noble nature, on the contrary, always knows how to find an excuse for failings, if not in the intention, at least from oversight.

cx *Do not wait till you are a Sinking Sun.*

'Tis a maxim of the wise to leave things before things leave them. One should be able to snatch a triumph at the end, just as the sun even at its brightest often retires behind a cloud so as not to be seen sinking, and to leave in doubt whether he has sunk or no.

Wisely withdraw from the chance of mishaps, lest you have to do so from the reality Do not wait till they turn you the cold shoulder and carry you to the grave, alive in feeling but dead in esteem. Wise trainers put racers to grass before they arouse derision by falling on the course. A beauty should break her mirror early, lest she do so later with open eyes.

cxi *Have Friends.*

'Tis a second existence. Every friend is good and wise for his friend: among them all everything turns to good. Every one is as others wish him; that they may wish him well, he must win their hearts and so their tongues. There is no magic like a good turn, and the way to gain friendly feelings is to do friendly acts. The most and best of us depend on others; we have to live either among friends or among enemies. Seek some one every day to be a well-wisher if not a friend; by and by after trial some of these will become intimate.

cxii *Gain Good-will.*

For thus the first and highest cause foresees and furthers the greatest objects. By gaining their good-will you gain men's good opinion. Some trust so much to merit that they neglect grace, but wise men know that Service Road without a lift from favour is a long way indeed. Good-will facilitates and supplies everything: is supposes gifts or even supplies them, as courage, zeal, knowledge, or even discretion; whereas defects it will not see because it does not search for them. It arises from some common interest, either material, as disposition, nationality, relationship, fatherland, office; or formal, which is of a higher kind of communion, in capacity, obligation, reputation, or merit. The whole difficulty is to gain good-will; to keep it is easy. It has, however, to be sought for, and, when found, to be utilised.

cxiii *In Prosperity prepare for Adversity.*

It is both wiser and easier to collect winter stores in summer. In prosperity favours are cheap and friends are many. 'Tis well therefore to keep them for more unlucky days, for adversity costs dear and has no helpers. Retain a store of friendly and obliged persons; the day may come when their price will go up. Low minds never have friends; in luck they will not recognise them: in misfortune they will not be recognised by them.

cxiv *Never Compete.*

Every competition damages the credit: our rivals seize occasion to obscure us so as to out-shine us. Few wage honourable war. Rivalry discloses faults which courtesy would hide. Many have lived in good repute while they had no rivals. The heat of conflict gives life, or even new life, to dead scandals, and digs up long-buried skeletons. Competition begins with belittling, and seeks aid wherever it can, not only where it ought. And when the weapons of abuse do not effect their purpose, as often or mostly happens, our opponents use them for revenge, and use them at least for beating away the dust of oblivion from anything to our discredit. Men of good-will are always at peace; men of good repute and dignity are men of good-will.

cxv *Get used to the Failings of your Familiars,*

as you do to ugly faces. It is indispensable if they depend on us, or we on them. There are wretched characters with whom one cannot live, nor yet without them. Therefore clever folk get used to them, as to ugly faces, so that they are not obliged to do so suddenly under the pressure of necessity. At first they arouse disgust, but gradually they lose this influence, and reflection provides for disgust or puts up with it.

cxvi *Only act with Honourable Men.*

You can trust them and they you. Their honour is the best surety of their behaviour even in misunderstandings, for they always act having regard to what they are. Hence 'tis better to have a dispute with honourable people than to have a victory over dishonourable ones. You cannot treat with the ruined, for they have no hostages for rectitude. With them there is no true friendship, and their agreements are not binding, however stringent they may appear, because they have no feeling of honour. Never have to do with such men, for if honour does not restrain a man, virtue will not, since honour is the throne of rectitude.

cxvii *Never talk of Yourself.*

You must either praise yourself, which is vain, or blame yourself, which is little-minded: it ill beseems him that speaks, and ill pleases him that hears. And if you should avoid this in ordinary conversation, how much more in official matters, and above all, in public speaking, where every appearance of unwisdom really is unwise. The same want of tact lies in speaking of a man in his presence, owing to the danger of going to one of two extremes: flattery or censure.

cxviii *Acquire the Reputation of Courtesy;*

for it is enough to make you liked. Politeness is the main ingredient of culture,—a kind of witchery that wins the regard of all as surely as discourtesy gains their disfavour and opposition; if this latter springs from pride, it is abominable; if from bad breeding, it is despicable. Better too much courtesy than too little, provided it be not the same for all, which degenerates into injustice. Between opponents it is especially due as a proof of valour. It costs little and helps much: every one is honoured who gives honour. Politeness and honour have this advantage, that they remain with him who displays them to others.

cxix *Avoid becoming Disliked.*

There is no occasion to seek dislike: it comes without seeking quickly enough. There are many who hate of their own accord without knowing the why or the how. Their ill-will outruns our readiness to please. Their ill-nature is more prone to do others harm than their cupidity is eager to gain advantage for themselves. Some manage to be on bad terms with all, because they always either produce or experience vexation of spirit. Once hate has taken root it is, like bad repute, difficult to eradicate. Wise men are feared, the malevolent are abhorred, the arrogant are regarded with disdain, buffoons with contempt, eccentrics with neglect. Therefore pay respect that you may be respected, and know that to be esteemed you must show esteem.

cxx *Live Practically.*

Even knowledge has to be in the fashion, and where it is not it is wise to affect ignorance. Thought and taste change with the times. Do not be old-fashioned in your ways of thinking, and let your taste be in the modern style. In everything the taste of the many carries the votes; for the time being one must follow it in the hope of leading it to higher things. In the adornment of the body as of the mind adapt yourself to the present, even though the past appear better. But this rule does not apply to kindness, for goodness is for all time. It is neglected nowadays and seems out of date. Truth-speaking, keeping your word, and so too good people, seem to come from the good old times: yet they are liked for all that, but in such a way that even when they all exist they are not in the fashion and are not imitated. What a misfortune for our age that it regards virtue as a stranger and vice as a matter of course! If you are wise, live as you can, if you cannot live as you would. Think more highly of what fate has given you than of what it has denied.

cxxi *Do not make a Business of what is no Business.*

As some make gossip out of everything, so others business. They always talk big, take everything in earnest, and turn it into a dispute or a secret. Troublesome things must not be taken too seriously if they can be avoided. It is preposterous to take to heart that which you should throw over your shoulders. Much that would be something has become nothing by being left alone, and what was nothing has become of consequence by being made much of. At the outset things can be easily settled, but not afterwards. Often the remedy causes the disease. 'Tis by no means the least of life's rules: to let things alone.

cxxii *Distinction in Speech and Action.*

By this you gain a position in many places and carry esteem beforehand. It shows itself in everything, in talk, in look, even in gait. It is a great victory to conquer men's hearts: it does not arise from any foolish presumption or pompous talk, but in a becoming tone of authority born of superior talent combined with true merit.

cxxiii *Avoid Affectation.*

The more merit, the less affectation, which gives a vulgar flavour to all. It is wearisome to others and troublesome to the one affected, for he becomes a martyr to care and tortures himself with attention. The most eminent merits lose most by it, for they appear proud and artificial instead of being the product of nature, and the natural is always more pleasing than the artificial. One always feels sure that the man who affects a virtue has it not. The more pains you take with a thing, the more should you conceal them, so that it may appear to arise spontaneously from your own natural character. Do not, however, in avoiding affectation fall into it by affecting to be unaffected. The sage never seems to know his own merits, for only by not noticing them can you call others' attention to them. He is twice great who has all the perfections in the opinion of all except of himself; he attains applause by two opposite paths.

cxxiv *Get Yourself missed.*

Few reach such favour with the many; if with the wise 'tis the height of happiness. When one has finished one's work, coldness is the general rule. But there are ways of earning this reward of goodwill. The sure way is to excel in your office and talents: add to this agreeable manner and you reach the point where you become necessary to your office, not your office to you. Some do honour to their post, with others 'tis the other way. It is no great gain if a poor successor makes the predecessor seem good, for this does not imply that the one is missed, but that the other is wished away.

cxxv *Do not be a Black List.*

It is a sign of having a tarnished name to concern oneself with the ill-fame of others. Some wish to hide their own stains with those of others, or at least wash them away: or they seek consolation therein—'tis the consolation of fools. They must have bad breath who form the sewers of scandal for the whole town. The more one grubs about in such matters, the more one befouls oneself. There are few without stain somewhere or other, but it is of little known people that the failings are little known. Be careful then to avoid being a registrar of faults. That is to be an abominable thing, a man that lives without a heart.

cxxvi *Folly consists not in committing Folly, but in not hiding it when committed.*

You should keep your desires sealed up, still more your defects. All go wrong sometimes, but the wise try to hide the errors, but fools boast of them. Reputation depends more on what is hidden than on what is done; if a man does not live chastely, he must live cautiously. The errors of great men are like the eclipses of the greater lights. Even in friendship it is rare to expose one's failings to one's friend. Nay, one should conceal them from oneself if one can. But here one can help with that other great rule of life: learn to forget.

cxxvii *Grace in Everything.*

'Tis the life of talents, the breath of speech, the soul of action, and the ornament of ornament. Perfections are the adornment of our nature, but this is the adornment of perfection itself. It shows itself even in the thoughts. 'Tis most a gift of nature and owes least to education; it even triumphs over training. It is more than ease, approaches the free and easy, gets over embarrassment, and adds the finishing touch to perfection. Without it beauty is lifeless, graciousness ungraceful: it surpasses valour, discretion, prudence, even majesty it-self. 'Tis a short way to dispatch and an easy escape from embarrassment.

cxxviii *Highmindedness.*

One of the principal qualifications for a gentleman, for it spurs on to all kinds of nobility. It improves the taste, ennobles the heart, elevates the mind, refines the feelings, and intensifies dignity. It raises him in whom it is found, and at times remedies the bad turns of Fortune, which only raises by striking. It can find full scope in the will when it cannot be exercised in act. Magnanimity, generosity, and all heroic qualities recognise in it their source.

cxxix *Never complain.*

To complain always brings discredit. Better be a model of self-reliance opposed to the passion of others than an object of their compassion. For it opens the way for the hearer to what we are complaining of, and to disclose one insult forms an excuse for another. By complaining of past offences we give occasion for future ones, and in seeking aid or counsel we only obtain indifference or contempt. It is much more politic to praise one man's favours, so that others may feel obliged to follow suit. To recount the favours we owe the absent is to demand similar ones from the present, and thus we sell our credit with the one to the other. The shrewd will therefore never publish to the world his failures or his defects, but only those marks of consideration which serve to keep friendship alive and enmity silent.

cxxx *Do and be seen Doing.*

Things do not pass for what they are but for what they seem. To be of use and to know how to show yourself of use, is to be twice as useful. What is not seen is as if it was not. Even the Right does not receive proper consideration if it does not seem right. The observant are far fewer in number than those who are deceived by appearances. Deceit rules the roast, and things are judged by their jackets, and many things are other than they seem. A good exterior is the best recommendation of the inner perfection.

cxxxi *Nobility of Feeling.*

There is a certain distinction of the soul, a highmindedness prompting to gallant acts, that gives an air of grace to the whole character. It is not found often, for it presupposes great magnanimity. Its chief characteristic is to speak well of an enemy, and to act even better to-wards him. It shines brightest when a chance comes of revenge: not alone does it let the occasion pass, but it improves it by using a complete victory in order to display unexpected generosity. 'Tis a fine stroke of policy, nay, the very acme of statecraft. It makes no pretence to victory, for it pretends to nothing, and while obtaining its deserts it conceals its merits.

cxxxii *Revise your Judgments.*

To appeal to an inner Court of Revision makes things safe. Especially when the course of action is not clear, you gain time either to confirm or improve your decision. It affords new grounds for strengthening or corroborating your judgment. And if it is a matter of giving, the gift is the more valued from its being evidently well considered than for being promptly bestowed: long expected is highest prized. And if you have to deny, you gain time to decide how and when to mature the No that it may be made palatable. Besides, after the first heat of desire is passed the repulse of refusal is felt less keenly in cold blood. But especially when men press for a reply is it best to defer it, for as often as not that is only a feint to disarm attention.

cxxxiii *Better Mad with the rest of the World than Wise alone.*

So say politicians. If all are so, one is no worse off than the rest, whereas solitary wisdom passes for folly. So important is it to sail with the stream. The greatest wisdom often consists in ignorance, or the pretence of it. One has to live with others, and others are mostly ignorant. "To live entirely alone one must be very like a god or quite like a wild beast," but I would turn the aphorism by saying: Better be wise with the many than a fool all alone. There be some too who seek to be original by seeking chimeras.

cxxxiv Double your Resources.

You thereby double your life. One must not depend on one thing or trust to only one resource, however pre-eminent. Everything should be kept double, especially the causes of success, of favour, or of esteem. The moon's mutability transcends everything and gives a limit to all existence, especially of things dependent on human will, the most brittle of all things. To guard against this inconstancy should be the sage's care, and for this the  chief rule of life is to keep a double store of good and useful qualities. Thus as Nature gives us in duplicate the most important of our limbs and those most exposed to risk, so Art should deal with the qualities on which we depend for success.

cxxxv Do not nourish the Spirit of Contradiction.

It only proves you foolish or peevish, and prudence should guard against this strenuously. To find difficulties in everything may prove you clever, but such wrangling writes you down a fool. Such folk make a mimic war out of the most pleasant conversation, and in this way act as enemies towards their associates rather than towards those with whom they do not consort. Grit grates most in delicacies, and so does contradiction in amusement. They are both foolish and cruel who yoke together the wild beast and the tame.

cxxxvi *Post Yourself in the Centre of Things.*

So you feel the pulse of affairs. Many lose their way either in the ramifications of useless discussion or in the brushwood of wearisome verbosity without ever realising the real matter at issue. They go over a single point a hundred times, wearying themselves and others, and yet never touch the all-important centre of affairs. This comes from a confusion of mind from which they cannot extricate themselves. They waste time and patience on matters they should leave alone, and cannot spare them afterwards for what they have left alone.

cxxxvii *The Sage should be Self-sufficing.*

He that was all in all to himself carried all with him when he carried himself. If a universal friend can represent to us Rome and the rest of the world, let a man be his own universal friend, and then he is in a position to live alone. Whom could such a man want if there is no clearer intellect or finer taste than his own? He would then depend on himself alone, which is the highest happiness and like the Supreme Being. He that can live alone resembles the brute beast in nothing, the sage in much and God in everything.

cxxxviii *The Art of letting Things alone.*

The more so the wilder the waves of public or of private life. There are hurricanes in human affairs, tempests of passion, when it is wise to retire to a harbour and ride at anchor. Remedies often make diseases worse: in such cases one has to leave them to their natural course and the moral suasion of time. It takes a wise doctor to know when not to prescribe, and at times the greater skill consists in not applying remedies. The proper way to still the storms of the vulgar is to hold your hand and let them calm down of themselves. To give way now is to conquer by and by. A fountain gets muddy with but little stirring up, and does not get clear by our meddling with it but by our leaving it alone. The best remedy for disturbances is to let them run their course, for so they quiet down.

cxxxix *Recognise unlucky Days.*

They exist: nothing goes well on them; even though the game may be changed the ill-luck remains. Two tries should be enough to tell if one is in luck to-day or not. Everything is in process of change, even the mind, and no one is always wise: chance has something to say, even how to write a good letter. All perfection turns on the time; even beauty has its hours. Even wisdom fails at times by doing too much or too little. To turn out well a thing must be done on its own day. This is why with some everything turns out ill, with others all goes well, even with less trouble. They find everything ready, their wit prompt, their presiding genius favourable, their lucky star in the ascendant. At such times one must seize the occasion and not throw away the slightest chance. But a shrewd person will not decide on the day's luck by a single piece of good or bad fortune, for the one may be only a lucky chance and the other only a slight annoyance.

cxl *Find the Good in a Thing at once.*

'Tis the advantage of good taste. The bee goes to the honey for her comb, the serpent to the gall for its venom. So with taste: some seek the good, others the ill. There is nothing that has no good in it, especially in books, as giving food for thought. But many have such a scent that amid a thousand excellences they fix upon a single defect, and single it out for blame as if they were scavengers of men's minds and hearts. So they draw up a balance sheet of defects which does more credit to their bad taste than to their intelligence. They lead a sad life, nourishing themselves on bitters and battening on garbage. They have the luckier taste who midst a thousand defects seize upon a single beauty they may have hit upon by chance.

cxli *Do not listen to Yourself.*

It is no use pleasing yourself if you do not please others, and as a rule general contempt is the punishment for self-satisfaction. The attention you pay to yourself you probably owe to others. To speak and at the same time listen to yourself cannot turn out well. If to talk to oneself when alone is folly, it must be doubly unwise to listen to oneself in the presence of others. It is a weakness of the great to talk with a recurrent "as I was saying" and "eh?" which bewilders their hearers. At every sentence they look for applause or flattery, taxing the patience of the wise. So too the pompous speak with an echo, and as their talk can only totter on with the aid of stilts, at every word they need the support of a stupid "bravo!"

cxlii *Never from Obstinacy take the Wrong Side because your Opponent has anticipated you in taking the Right One.*

You begin the fight already beaten and must soon take to flight in disgrace. With bad weapons one can never win. It was astute in the opponent to seize the better side first: it would be folly to come lagging after with the worst. Such obstinacy is more dangerous in actions than in words, for action encounters more risk than talk. 'Tis the common failing of the obstinate that they lose the true by contradicting it, and the useful by quarrelling with it. The sage never places himself on the side of passion, but espouses the cause of right, either discovering it first or improving it later. If the enemy is a fool, he will in such a case turn round to follow the opposite and worse way. Thus the only way to drive him from the better course is to take it yourself, for his folly will cause him to desert it, and his obstinacy be punished for so doing.

cxliii *Never become Paradoxical in order to avoid the Trite.*

Both extremes damage our reputation. Every undertaking which differs from the reasonable approaches foolishness. The paradox is a cheat: it wins applause at first by its novelty and piquancy, but afterwards it becomes discredited when the deceit is fore-seen and its emptiness becomes apparent. It is a species of jugglery, and in matters political would be the ruin of states. Those who cannot or dare not reach great deeds on the direct road of excellence go round by way of Paradox, admired by fools but making wise men true prophets. It argues an unbalanced judgment, and if it is not altogether based on the false, it is certainly founded on the uncertain, and risks the weightier matters of life.

cxliv *Begin with Another's to end with your Own.*

'Tis a politic means to your end. Even in heavenly matters Christian teachers lay stress on this holy cunning. It is a weighty piece of dissimulation, for the foreseen advantages serve as a lure to influence the other's will. His affair seems to be in train when it is really only leading the way for another's. One should never advance unless under cover, especially where the ground is dangerous. Likewise with persons who always say No at first, it is useful to ward off this blow, because the difficulty of conceding much more does not occur to them when your version is presented to them. This advice belongs to the rule about second thoughts [xiii], which covers the most subtle manœuvres of life.

cxlv *Do not show your wounded Finger,*

for everything will knock up against it; nor complain about it, for malice always aims where weakness can be injured. It is no use to be vexed: being the butt of the talk will only vex you the more. Ill-will searches for wounds to irritate, aims darts to try the

temper, and tries a thousand ways to sting to the quick. The wise never own to being hit, or disclose any evil, whether personal or hereditary. For even Fate sometimes likes to wound us where we are most tender. It always mortifies wounded flesh. Never therefore disclose the source of mortification or of joy, if you wish the one to cease, the other to endure.

cxlvi *Look into the Interior of Things.*

Things are generally other than they seem, and ignorance that never looks beneath the rind becomes disabused when you show the kernel. Lies always come first, dragging fools along by their irreparable vulgarity. Truth always lags last, limping along on the arm of Time. The wise therefore reserve for it the other half of that power which the common mother has wisely given in duplicate. Deceit is very superficial, and the superficial therefore easily fall into it. Prudence lives retired within its recesses, visited only by sages and wise men.

cxlvii *Do not be Inaccessible.*

None is so perfect that he does not need at times the advice of others. He is an in-corrigible ass who will never listen to any one. Even the most surpassing intellect should find a place for friendly counsel. Sovereignty itself must learn to lean. There are some that are incorrigible simply because they are inaccessible: they fall to ruin because none dares to extricate them. The highest should have the door open for friendship; it may prove the gate of help. A friend must be free to advise, and even to upbraid, without feeling embarrassed. Our satisfaction in him and our trust in his steadfast faith give him that power. One need not pay respect or give credit to every one, but in the innermost of his precaution man has a true mirror of a confidant to whom he owes the correction of his errors, and has to thank for it.

cxlviii *Have the Art of Conversation.*

That is where the real personality shows itself. No act in life requires more attention, though it be the commonest thing in life. You must either lose or gain by it. If it needs care to write a letter which is but a deliberate and written conversation, how much more the ordinary kind in which there is occasion for a prompt display of intelligence? Experts feel the pulse of the soul in the tongue, wherefore the sage said, "Speak, that I may know thee." Some hold that the art of conversation is to be without art—that it should be neat, not gaudy, like the garments. This holds good for talk between friends. But when held with persons to whom one would show respect, it should be more dignified to answer to the dignity of the person addressed. To be appropriate it should adapt itself to the mind and tone of the interlocutor. And do not be a critic of words, or you will be taken for a pedant; nor a taxgatherer of ideas, or men will avoid you, or at least sell their thoughts dear. in conversation discretion is more important than eloquence.

cxlix Know how to put off Ills on Others.

To have a shield against ill-will is a great piece of skill in a ruler. It is not the resort of incapacity, as ill-wishers imagine, but is due to the higher policy of having some one to receive the censure of the disaffected and the punishment of universal detestation. Everything cannot turn out well, nor can every one be satisfied: it is well therefore, even at the cost of our pride, to have such a scapegoat, such a target for unlucky undertakings.

cl Know to get your Price for Things.

Their intrinsic value is not sufficient; for all do not bite at the kernel or look into the interior. Most go with the crowd, and go because they see others go. It is a great stroke of art to bring things into repute; at times by praising them, for praise arouses desire at times by giving them a striking name, which is very useful for putting things at a premium, provided it is done without affectation. Again, it is generally an inducement to profess to supply only connoisseurs, for all think themselves such, and if not, the sense of want arouses the desire. Never call things easy or common: that makes them depreciated rather than made accessible. All rush after the unusual, which is more appetising both for the taste and for the intelligence.

cli Think beforehand.

To-day for to-morrow, and even for many days hence. The greatest foresight consists in determining beforehand the time of trouble. For the provident there are no mischances and for the careful no narrow escapes. We must not put off thought till we are up to the chin in mire. Mature reflection can get over the most formidable difficulty. The pillow is a silent Sibyl, and it is better to sleep on things beforehand than lie awake about them afterwards. Many act first and then think afterwards—that is, they think less of consequences than of excuses: others think neither before nor after. The whole of life should be one course of thought how not to miss the right path. Rumination and foresight enable one to determine the line of life.

clii *Never have a Companion who casts you in the Shade.*

The more he does so, the less desirable a companion he is. The more he excels in quality the more in repute: he will always play first fiddle and you second. If you get any consideration, it is only his leavings. The moon shines bright alone among the stars: when the sun rises she becomes either invisible or imperceptible. Never join one that eclipses you, but rather one who sets you in a brighter light. By this means the cunning Fabula in Martial was able to appear beautiful and brilliant, owing to the ugliness and disorder of her companions. But one should as little imperil oneself by an evil companion as pay honour to another at the cost of one's own credit. When you are on the way to fortune associate with the eminent; when arrived, with the mediocre.

cliii *Beware of entering where there is a great Gap to be filled.*

But if you do it be sure to surpass your predecessor; merely to equal him requires twice his worth. As it is a fine stroke to arrange that our successor shall cause us to be wished back, so it is policy to see that our predecessor does not eclipse us. To fill a great gap is difficult, for the past always seems best, and to equal the predecessor is not enough, since he has the right of first possession. You must therefore possess additional claims to oust the other from his hold on public opinion.

cliv *Do not Believe, or Like, lightly.*

Maturity of mind is best shown in slow belief. Lying is the usual thing; then let belief be unusual. He that is lightly led away, soon falls into contempt. At the same time there is no necessity to betray your doubts in the good faith of others, for this adds insult to discourtesy, since you make out your informant to be either deceiver or deceived. Nor is this the only evil: want of belief is the mark of the liar, who suffers from two failings: he neither believes nor is believed. Suspension of judgment is prudent in a hearer: the speaker can appeal to his original source of in-formation. There is a similar kind of imprudence in liking too easily, for lies may be told by deeds as well as in words, and this deceit is more dangerous for practical life.

clv *The Art of getting into a Passion.*

If possible, oppose vulgar importunity with prudent reflection; it will not be difficult for a really prudent man. The first step towards getting into a passion is to announce that you are in a passion. By this means you begin the conflict with command over your temper, for one has to regulate one's passion to the exact point that is necessary and no further. This is the art of arts in falling into and getting out of a rage. You should know how and when best to come to a stop: it is most difficult to halt while running at the double. It is a great proof of wisdom to remain clear-sighted during paroxysms of rage. Every excess of passion is a digression from rational conduct. But by this masterly policy reason will never be transgressed, nor pass the bounds of its own synteresis. To keep control of passion one must hold firm the reins of attention: he who can do so will be the first man "wise on horseback," and probably the last.

clvi *Select your Friends.*

Only after passing the matriculation of experience and the examination of fortune will they be graduates not alone in affection but in discernment. Though this is the most important thing in life, it is the one least cared for. Intelligence brings friends to some, chance to most. Yet a man is judged by his friends, for there was never agreement between wise men and fools. At the same time, to find pleasure in a man's society is no proof of near friendship: it may come from the pleasantness of his company more than from trust in his capacity. There are some friendships legitimate, others illicit; the latter for pleasure, the former for their fecundity of ideas and motives. Few are the friends of a man's self, most those of his circumstances. The insight of a true friend is more useful than the goodwill of others: therefore gain them by choice, not by chance. A wise friend wards off worries, a foolish one brings them about. But do not wish them too much luck, or you may lose them.

civil *Do not make Mistakes about Character.*

That is the worst and yet easiest error. Better be cheated in the price than in the quality of goods. In dealing with men, more than with other things, it is necessary to look within. To know men is different from knowing things. It is profound philosophy to sound the depths of feeling and distinguish traits of character. Men must be studied as deeply as books.

clviii *Make use of your Friends.*

This requires all the art of discretion. Some are good afar off, some when near. Many are no good at conversation but excellent as correspondents, for distance removes some failings which are unbearable in close proximity to them. Friends are for use even more than for pleasure, for they have the three qualities of the Good, or, as some say, of Being in general: unity, goodness, and truth. For a friend is all in all. Few are worthy to be good friends, and even these become fewer because men do not know how to pick them out. To keep is more important than to make friends. Select those that will wear well; if they are new at first, it is some consolation they will become old. Absolutely the best are those well salted, though they may require soaking in the testing. There is no desert like living without friends. Friendship multiplies the good of life and divides the evil. 'Tis the sole remedy against misfortune, the very ventilation of the soul.

clix *Put up with Fools.*

The wise are always impatient, for he that increases knowledge increase impatience of folly. Much knowledge is difficult to satisfy. The first great rule of life, according to Epictetus, is to put up with things: he makes that the moiety of wisdom. To put up with all the varieties of folly would need much patience. We often have to  put up with most from those on whom we most depend: a useful lesson in self-control. Out of patience comes forth peace, the priceless boon which is the happiness of the world. But let him that bath no power of patience retire within himself, though even there he will have to put up with himself.

clx *Be careful in Speaking.*

With your rivals from prudence; with others for the sake of appearance. There is always time to add a word, never to withdraw one. Talk as if you were making your will: the fewer words the less litigation. In trivial matters exercise yourself for the more weighty matters of speech. Profound secrecy has some of the lustre of the divine. He who speaks lightly soon falls or fails.

clxi *Know your pet Faults.*

The most perfect of men has them, and is either wedded to them or has illicit relations with them. They are often faults of intellect, and the greater this is, the greater they are, or at least the more conspicuous. It is not so much that their possessor does not know them: he loves them, which is a double evil: irrational affection for avoidable faults. They are spots on perfection; they displease the onlooker as much as they please the possessor. 'Tis a gallant thing to get clear of them, and so give play to one's other qualities. For all men hit upon such a failing, and on going over your qualifications they make a long stay at this blot, and blacken it as deeply as possible in order to cast your other talents into the shade.

clxii *How to triumph over Rivals and Detractors.*

It is not enough to despise them, though this is often wise: a gallant bearing is the thing. One cannot praise a man too much who speaks well of them who speak ill of him. There is no more heroic vengeance than that of talents and services which at once conquer and torment the envious. Every success is a further twist of the cord round the neck of the ill-affected, and an enemy's glory is the rival's hell. The envious die not once, but as oft as the envied wins applause. The immortality of his fame is the measure of the other's torture: the one lives in endless honour, the other in endless pain. The clarion of Fame announces immortality to the one and death to the other, the slow death of envy long drawn out.

clxiii *Never, from Sympathy with the Unfortunate, involve Yourself in his Fate.*

One man's misfortune is another man's luck, for one cannot be lucky without many being unlucky. It is a peculiarity of the unfortunate to arouse people's goodwill who desire to compensate them for the blows of fortune with their useless favour, and it happens that one who was abhorred by all in prosperity is adored by all in adversity. Vengeance on the wing is exchanged for compassion afoot. Yet 'tis to be noticed how fate shuffles the cards. There are men who always consort with the unlucky, and he that yesterday flew high and happy stands to-day miserable at their side. That argues nobility of soul, but not worldly wisdom.

clxiv *Throw Straws in the Air,*

to find how things will be received, especially those whose reception or success is doubtful. One can thus be assured of its turning out well, and an opportunity is afforded for going on in earnest or withdrawing entirely. By trying men's intentions in this way, the wise man knows on what ground he stands. This is the great rule of foresight in asking, in desiring, and in ruling.

clxv *Wage War Honourably.*

You may be obliged to wage war, but not to use poisoned arrows. Every one must needs act as he is, not as others would make him to be. Gallantry in the battle of life wins all men's praise: one should fight so as to conquer, not alone by force but by the way it is used. A mean victory brings no glory, but rather disgrace. Honour always has the upper hand. An honourable man never uses forbidden weapons, such as using a friendship that's ended for the purposes of a hatred just begun: a confidence must never be used for a vengeance. The slightest taint of treason tarnishes the good name. In men of honour the smallest trace of meanness repels: the noble and the ignoble should be miles apart. Be able to boast that if gallantry, generosity, and fidelity were lost in the world men would be able to find them again in your own breast.

clxvi *Distinguish the Man of Words from the Man of Deeds.*

Discrimination here is as important as in the case of friends, persons, and employments, which have all many varieties. Bad words even without bad deeds are bad enough: good words with bad deeds are worse. One cannot dine off words, which are wind, nor off politeness, which is but polite deceit. To catch birds with a mirror is the ideal snare. It is the vain alone who take their wages in windy words. Words should be the pledges of work, and, like pawn-tickets, have their market price. Trees that bear leaves but not fruit have usually no pith. Know them for what they are, of no use except for shade.

clxvii *Know how to take your own Part.*

In great crises there is no better companion than a bold heart, and if it becomes weak it must be strengthened from the neighbouring parts. Worries die away before a man who asserts himself. One must not surrender to misfortune, or else it would become intolerable. Many men do not help themselves in their troubles, and double their weight by not knowing how to bear them. He that knows himself knows how to strengthen his weakness, and the wise man conquers everything, even the stars in their courses.

clxviii *Do not indulge in the Eccentricities of Folly.*

Like vain, presumptuous, egotistical, untrustworthy, capricious, obstinate, fanciful, theatrical, whimsical, inquisitive, paradoxical, sectarian people and all kinds of one-sided persons: they are all monstrosities of impertinence. All deformity of mind is more obnoxious than that of the body, because it contravenes a higher beauty. Yet who can assist such a complete confusion of mind? Where self-control is wanting, there is no room for others' guidance. Instead of paying attention to other people's real derision, men of this kind blind themselves with the unfounded assumption of their imaginary applause.

clxix *Be more careful not to Miss once than to Hit a hundred times.*

No one looks at the blazing sun; all gaze when he is eclipsed. The common talk does not reckon what goes right but what goes wrong. Evil report carries farther than any applause. Many men are not known to the world till they have left it. All the exploits of a man taken together are not enough to wipe out a single small blemish. Avoid therefore falling into error, seeing that ill-will notices every error and no success.

clxx *In all Things keep Something in Reserve.*

'Tis a sure means of keeping up your importance. A man should not employ all his capacity and power at once and on every occasion. Even in knowledge there should be a rearguard, so that your resources are doubled. One must always have something to resort to when there is fear of a defeat. The reserve is of more importance than the attacking force: for it is distinguished for valour and reputation. Prudence always sets to work with assurance of safety: in this matter the piquant paradox holds good that the half is more than the whole.

clxxi *Waste not Influence.*

The great as friends are for great occasions. One should not make use of great confidence for little things: for that is to waste a favour. The sheet anchor should be reserved for the last extremity. If you use up the great for little ends what remains afterwards? Nothing is more valuable than a protector, and nothing costs more nowadays than a favour. It can make or unmake a whole world. It can even give sense and take it away. As Nature and Fame are favourable to the wise, so Luck is generally envious of them. It is therefore more important to keep the favour of the mighty than goods and chattels.

clxxii *Never contend with a Man who has nothing to Lose;*

for thereby you enter into an unequal conflict. The other enters without anxiety; having lost everything, including shame, he has no further loss to fear. He therefore re-sorts to all kinds of insolence. One should never expose a valuable reputation to so terrible a risk, lest what has cost years to gain may be lost in a moment, since a single slight may wipe out much sweat. A man of honour and responsibility has a reputation, because he has much to lose. He balances his own and the other's reputation: he only enters into the contest with the greatest caution, and then goes to work with such circumspection that he gives time to prudence to retire in time and bring his reputation under cover. For even by victory he cannot gain what he has lost by exposing himself to the chances of loss.

clxxiii *Do not be Glass in Intercourse, still less in Friendship.*

Some break very easily, and thereby show their want of consistency. They attribute to themselves imaginary offences and to others oppressive intentions. Their feelings are even more sensitive than the eye itself, and must not be touched in jest or in earnest. Motes offend them: they need not wait for beams. Those who consort with them must treat them with the greatest delicacy, have regard to their sensitiveness, and watch their demeanour, since the slightest slight arouses their annoyance. They are mostly very egoistic, slaves of their moods, for the sake of which they cast everything aside: they are the worshippers of punctilio. On the other hand, the disposition of the true lover is firm and enduring, so that it may be said that the Arrant is half adamant.

clxxiv *Do not live in a Hurry.*

To know how to separate things is to know how to enjoy them. Many finish their fortune sooner than their life: they run through pleasures without enjoying them, and would like to go back when they find they have over-leaped the mark. Postilions of life, they increase the ordinary pace of life by the hurry of their own calling. They devour more in one day than they can digest in a whole life-time; they live in advance of pleasures, eat up the years beforehand, and by their hurry get through everything too soon. Even in the search for knowledge there should be moderation, lest we learn things better left unknown. We have more days to live through than pleasures. Be slow in enjoyment, quick at work, for men see work ended with pleasure, pleasure ended with regret.

clxxv *A Solid Man.*

One who is finds no satisfaction in those that are not. 'Tis a pitiable eminence that is not well founded. Not all are men that seem to be so. Some are sources of deceit; impregnated by chimeras they give birth to impositions. Others are like them so far that they take more pleasure in a lie, because it promises much, than in the truth, because it performs little. But in the end these caprices come to a bad end, for they have no solid foundation. Only Truth can give true reputation: only reality can be of real profit. One deceit needs many others, and so the whole house is built in the air and must soon come to the ground. Unfounded things never reach old age. They promise too much to be much trusted, just as that cannot be true which proves too much.

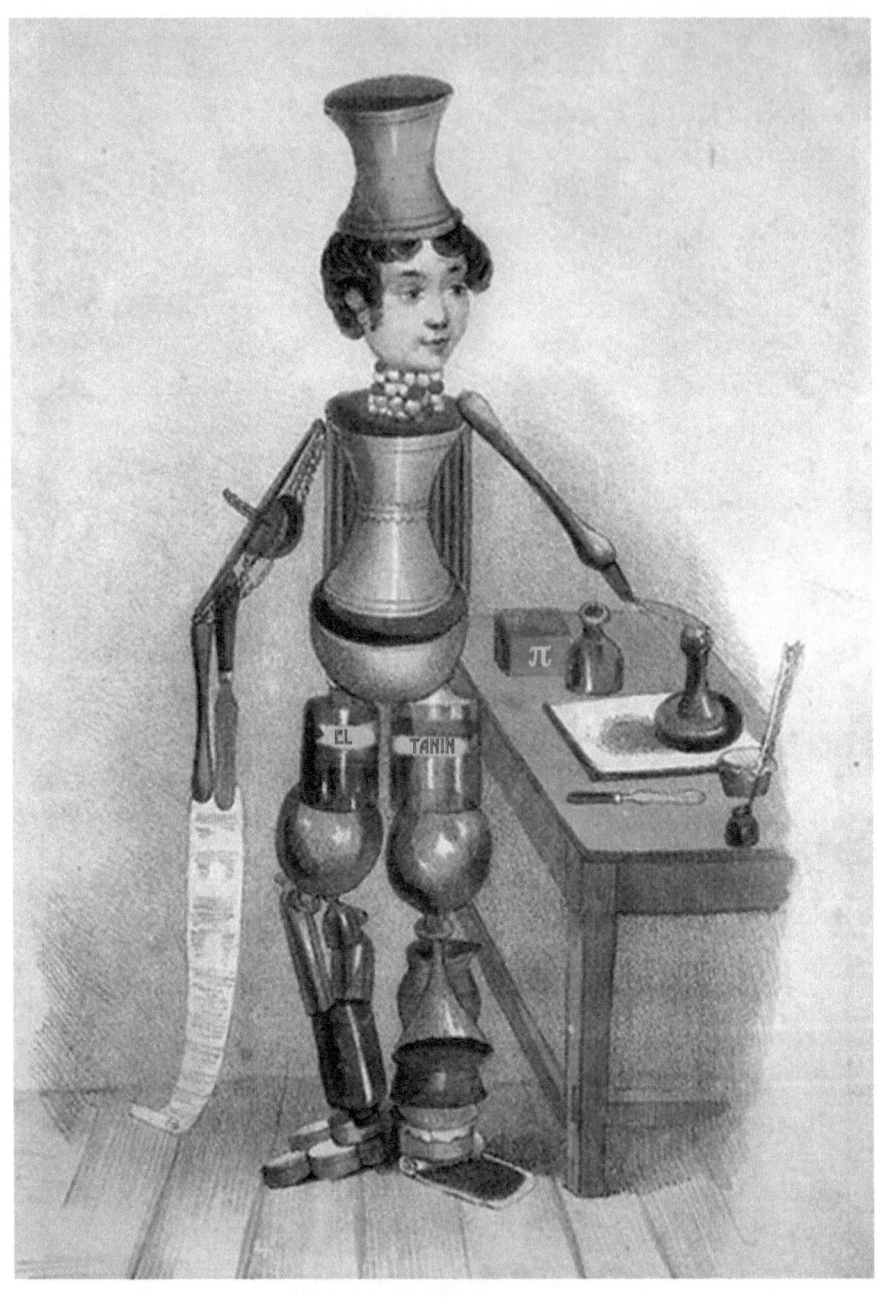

clxxvi *Have Knowledge, or know those that have Knowledge.*

Without intelligence, either one's own or another's, true life is impossible. But many do not know that they do not know, and many think they know when they know nothing. Failings of the intelligence are incorrigible, since those who do not know, do not know themselves, and cannot therefore seek what they lack. Many would be wise if they did not think themselves wise. Thus it happens that though the oracles of wisdom are rare, they are rarely used. To seek advice does not lessen greatness or argue incapacity. On the contrary, to ask advice proves you well advised. Take counsel with reason it you do not wish to court defeat.

clxxvii *Avoid Familiarities in Intercourse.*

Neither use them nor permit them. He that is familiar, loses any superiority his Influence gives him, and so loses respect. The stars keep their brilliance by not making themselves common. The Divine demands decorum. Every familiarity breeds contempt. In human affairs, the more a man shows, the less he has, for in open communication you communicate the failings that reserve might keep under cover. Familiarity is never desirable; with superiors because it is dangerous, with inferiors because it is unbecoming, least of all with the common herd, who become insolent from sheer folly: they mistake favour shown them for need felt of them. Familiarity trenches on vulgarity.

clxxviii *Trust your Heart,*

especially when it has been proved. Never deny it a hearing. It is a kind of house oracle that often foretells the most important. Many have perished because they feared their own heart, but of what use is it to fear it without finding a better remedy? Many are endowed by Nature with a heart so true that it always warns them of misfortune and wards off its effects. It is unwise to seek evils, unless you seek to conquer them.

clxxix *Reticence is the Seal of Capacity.*

A breast without a secret is an open letter. Where there is a solid foundation secrets can be kept profound: there are spacious cellars where things of moment may be hid. Reticence springs from self-control, and to control oneself in this is a true triumph. You must pay ransom to each you tell. The security of wisdom consists in temperance in the inner man. The risk that reticence runs lies in the cross-questioning of others, in the use of contradiction to worm out secrets, in the darts of irony: to avoid these the prudent become more reticent than before. What must be done need not be said, and what must be said need not be done.

clxxx *Never guide the Enemy to what he has to do.*

The fool never does what the wise judge wise, because he does not follow up the suitable means. He that is discreet follows still less a plan laid out, or even carried out, by another. One has to discuss matters from both points of view—turn it over on both sides. Judgments vary; let him that has not decided attend rather to what is possible than what is probable.

clxxxi *The Truth, but not the whole Truth.*

Nothing demands more caution than the truth: 'tis the lancet of the heart. It requires as much to tell the truth as to conceal it. A single lie destroys a whole reputation for integrity. The deceit is regarded as treason and the deceiver as a traitor, which is worse. Yet not all truths can be spoken: some for our own sake, others for the sake of others.

clxxxii *A Grain of Boldness in Everything.*

'Tis an important piece of prudence. You must moderate your opinion of others so that you may not think so high of them as to fear them. The imagination should never yield to the heart. Many appear great till you know them personally, and then dealing with them does more to disillusionise than to raise esteem. No one o'ersteps the narrow bounds of humanity: all have their weaknesses either in heart or head. Dignity gives apparent authority, which is rarely accompanied by personal power: for Fortune often redresses the height of office by the inferiority of the holder. The imagination always jumps too soon, and paints things in brighter colours than the real: it thinks things not as they are but as it wishes them to be. Attentive experience disillusionised in the past soon corrects all that. Yet if wisdom should not be timorous, neither should folly be rash. And if self-reliance helps the ignorant, how much more the brave and wise?

clxxxiii *Do not hold your Views too firmly.*

Every fool is fully convinced, and every one fully persuaded is a fool: the more erroneous his judgment the more firmly he holds it. Even in cases of obvious certainty, it is fine to yield: our reasons for holding the view cannot escape notice, our courtesy in yielding must be the more recognised. Our obstinacy loses more than our victory yields: that is not to champion truth but rather rudeness. There be some heads of iron most difficult to turn: add caprice to obstinacy and the sum is a wearisome fool. Steadfastness should be for the will, not for the mind. Yet there are exceptions where one would fail twice, owning oneself wrong both in judgment and in the execution of it.

clxxxiv *Do not be Ceremonious.*

Even in a king affectation in this was renowned for its eccentricity. To be punctilious is to be a bore, yet whole nations have this peculiarity. The garb of folly is woven out of such things. Such folk are worshippers of their own dignity, yet show how little it is justified since they fear that the least thing can destroy it. It is right to demand respect, but not to be considered a master of ceremonies. Yet it is true that a man to do without ceremonies must possess supreme qualities. Neither affect nor despise etiquette: he cannot be great who is great at such little things.

clxxxv *Never stake your Credit on a single Cast*,

for if it miscarries the damage is irreparable. It may easy happen that a man should fail once, especially at first: circumstances are not always favourable: hence they say, "Every dog has his day." Always connect your second attempt with your first: whether it succeed or fail, the first will redeem the second. Always have resort to better means and appeal to more resources. Things depend on all sorts of chances. That is why the satisfaction of success is so rare.

clxxxvi *Recognise Faults, however high placed.*

Integrity cannot mistake vice even when clothed in brocade or perchance crowned with gold, but will not be able to hide its character for all that. Slavery does not lose its vileness, however it vaunt the nobility of its lord and master. Vices may stand in high place, but are low for all that. Men can see that many a great man has great faults, yet they do not see that he is not great because of them. The example of the great is so specious that it even glosses over viciousness, till it may so affect those who flatter it that they do not notice that what they gloss over in the great they abominate in the lower classes.

clxxxvii *Do pleasant Things Yourself, unpleasant Things through Others.*

By the one course you gain goodwill, by the other you avoid hatred. A great man takes more pleasure in doing a favour than in receiving one: it is the privilege of his generous nature. One cannot easily cause pain to another without suffering pain either from sympathy or from remorse. In high place one can only work by means of rewards and punishment, so grant the first yourself, inflict the other through others. Have some one against whom the weapons of discontent, hatred, and slander may be directed. For the rage of the mob is like that of a dog: missing the cause of its pain it turns to bite the whip itself, and though this is not the real culprit, it has to pay the penalty.

clxxxviii *Be the Bearer of Praise.*

This increases our credit for good taste, since it shows that we have learnt elsewhere to know what is excellent, and hence how to prize it in the present company. It gives material for conversation and for imitation, and encourages praiseworthy exertions. We do homage besides in a very delicate way to the excellences before us. Others do the opposite; they accompany their talk with a sneer, and fancy they flatter those present by belittling the absent. This may serve them with superficial people, who do not notice how cunning it is to speak ill of every one to every one else. Many pursue the plan of valuing more highly the mediocrities of the day than the most distinguished exploits of the past. Let the cautious penetrate through these subtleties, and let him not be dismayed by the exaggerations of the one or made over-confident by the flatteries of the other; knowing that both act in the same way by different methods, adapting their talk to the company they are in.

clxxxix *Utilise Another's Wants.*

The greater his wants the greater the turn of the screw. Philosophers say privation is non-existent, statesmen say it is all-embracing, and they are right. Many make ladders to attain their ends out of wants of others. They make use of the opportunity and tantalise the appetite by pointing out the difficulty of satisfaction. The energy of desire promises more than the inertia of possession. The passion of desire increases with every increase of opposition. It is a subtle point to satisfy the desire and yet preserve the dependence.

cxc *Find Consolation in all Things.*

Even the useless may find it in being immortal. No trouble without compensation. Fools are held to be lucky, and the good-luck of the ugly is proverbial. Be worth little and you will live long: it is the cracked glass that never gets broken, but worries one with its durability. It seems that Fortune envies the great, so it equalises things by giving long life to the use-less, a short one to the important. Those who bear the burden come soon to grief, while those who are of no importance live on and on: in one case it appears so, in the other it is so. The unlucky thinks he has been for-gotten by both Death and Fortune.

cxci *Do not take Payment in Politeness*;

for it is a kind of fraud. Some do not need the herbs of Thessaly for their magic, for they can enchant fools by the grace of their salute. Theirs is the Bank of Elegance, and they pay with the wind of fine words. To promise everything is to promise nothing: promises are the pitfalls of fools. The true courtesy is performance of duty: the spurious and especially the useless is deceit. It is not respect but rather a means to power. Obeisance is paid not to the man but to his means, and compliments are offered not to the qualities that are recognised but to the advantages that are desired.

cxcii *Peaceful Life, a long Life.*

To live, let live. Peacemakers not only live: they rule life. Hear, see, and be silent. A day without dispute brings sleep without dreams. Long life and a pleasant one is life enough for two: that is the fruit of peace. He has all that makes nothing of what is nothing to him. There is no greater perversity than to take everything to heart. There is equal folly in troubling our heart about what does not concern us and in not taking to heart what does.

cxciii *Watch him that begins with Another's to end with his own.*

Watchfulness is the only guard against cunning. Be intent on his intentions. Many succeed in making others do their own affairs, and unless you possess the key to their motives you may at any moment be forced to take their chestnuts out of the fire to the damage of your own fingers.

cxciv *Have reasonable Views of Yourself and of your Affairs,*

especially in the beginning of life. Every one has a high opinion of himself, especially those who have least ground for it. Every one dreams of his good-luck and thinks himself a wonder. Hope gives rise to extravagant promises which experience does not fulfil. Such idle imaginations merely serve as a well-spring of annoyance when disillusion comes with the true reality. The wise man anticipates such errors: he may always hope for the best. but he always expects the worst, so as to receive what comes with equanimity. True, It is wise to aim high so as to hit your mark, but not so high that you miss your mission at the very beginning of life. This correction of the ideas is necessary, because before experience comes expectation is sure to soar too high. The best panacea against folly is prudence. If a man knows the true sphere of his activity and position, the can reconcile his ideals with reality.

cxcv *Know how to Appreciate.*

There is none who cannot teach somebody something, and there is none so excellent but he is excelled. To know how to make use of every one is useful knowledge. Wise men appreciate all men, for they see the good in each and know how hard it is to make anything good. Fools depreciate all men, not recognising the good and selecting the bad.

cxcvi *Know your ruling Star.*

None so helpless as not to have one; if he is unlucky, that is because he does not know it. Some stand high in the favour of princes and potentates without knowing why or wherefore, except that good luck itself has granted them favour on easy terms, merely requiring them to aid it with a little exertion. Others find favour with the wise. One man is better received by one nation than by another, or is more welcome in one city than in another. He finds more luck in one office or position than another, and all this though his qualifications are equal or even identical. Luck shuffles the cards how and when she will. Let each man know his luck as well as his talents, for on this depends whether he loses or wins. Follow your guiding star and help it without mistaking any other for it, for that would be to miss the North, though its neighbour (the polestar) calls us to it with a voice of thunder.

cxcvii *Do not carry Fools on your Back.*

He that does not know a fool when he sees him is one himself: still more he that knows him but will not keep clear of him. They are dangerous company and ruinous confidants. Even though their own caution and others' care keeps them in bounds for a time, still at length they are sure to do or to say some foolishness which is all the greater for being kept so long in stock. They cannot help another's credit who have none of their own. They are most unlucky, which is the Nemesis of fools, and they have to pay for one thing or the other. There is only one thing which is not so bad about them, and this is that though they can be of no use to the wise, they can be of much use to them as signposts or as warnings.

cxcviii *Know how to transplant Yourself.*

There are nations with whom one must cross their borders to make one's value felt, especially in great posts. Their native land is always a stepmother to great talents: envy flourishes there on its native soil, and they remember one's small beginnings rather than the greatness one has reached. A needle is appreciated that comes from one end of the world to the other, and a piece of painted glass might outvie the diamond in value if it comes from afar. Everything foreign is respected, partly because it comes from afar, partly because It is ready made and perfect. We have seen persons once the laughing-stock of their village and now the wonder of the whole world, honoured by their fellow-countrymen and by the foreigners [among whom they dwell]; by the latter because they come from afar, by the former because they are seen from afar. The statue on the altar is never reverenced by him who knew it as a trunk in the garden.

cxcix *To find a proper Place by Merit, not by Presumption.*

The true road to respect is through merit, and if industry accompany merit the path becomes shorter. Integrity alone is not sufficient, push and insistence is degrading, for things arrive by that means so besprinkled with dust that the discredit destroys reputation. The true way is the middle one, half-way between deserving a place and pushing oneself into it.

cc *Leave Something to wish for,*

so as not to be miserable from very happiness. The body must respire and the soul aspire. If one possessed all, all would be disillusion and discontent. Even in knowledge there should be always something left to know in order to arouse curiosity and excite hope. Surfeits of happiness are fatal. In giving assistance it is a piece of policy not to satisfy entirely. If there is nothing left to desire, there is everything to fear, an unhappy state of happiness. When desire dies, fear is born.

cci *They are all Fools who seem so besides half the rest.*

Folly arose with the world, and if there be any wisdom it is folly compared with the divine. But the greatest fool is he who thinks he is not one and all others are. To be wise It is not enough to seem wise, least of all to oneself. He knows who does not think that he knows, and he does not see who does not see that others see. Though all the world is full of fools, there is none that thinks himself one, or even suspects the fact.

ccii *Words and Deeds make the Perfect Man.*

One should speak well and act honourably: the one is an excellence of the head, the other of the heart, and both arise from nobility of soul. Words are the shadows of deeds; the former are feminine, the latter masculine. It is more important to be renowned than to convey renown. Speech is easy, action hard. Actions are the stuff of life, words its frippery. Eminent deeds endure, striking words pass away. Actions are the fruit of thought; if this is wise, they are effective.

cciii *Know the great Men of your Age.*

They are not many. There is one Phœnix in the whole world, one great general, one perfect orator, one true philosopher in a century, a really illustrious king in several. Mediocrities are as numerous as they are worth-less: eminent greatness is rare in every respect, since it needs complete perfection, and the higher the species the more difficult is the highest rank in it. Many have claimed the title "Great," like Cæsar and Alexander, but in vain, for without great deeds the title is a mere breath of air. There have been few Senecas, and fame records but one Apelles.

cciv *Attempt easy Tasks as if they were difficult,*
and difficult as if they were easy.

In the one case that confidence may not fall asleep, in the other that it may not be dismayed. For a thing to remain undone nothing more is needed than to think it done. On the other hand, patient industry overcomes impossibilities. Great undertakings are not to be brooded over, lest their difficulty when seen causes despair.

ccv *Know how to play the Card of Contempt.*

It is a shrewd way of getting things you want, by affecting to depreciate them: generally they are not to be had when sought for, but fall into one's hands when one is not looking for them. As all mundane things are but shadows of the things eternal, they share with shadows this quality, that they flee from him who follows them and follow him that flees from them. Contempt is besides the most subtle form of revenge. It is a fixed rule with the wise never to defend themselves with the pen. For such defence always leaves a stain, and does more to glorify one's opponent than to punish his offence. It is a trick of the worthless to stand forth as opponents of great men, so as to win notoriety by a roundabout way, which they would never do by the straight road of merit. There are many we would not have heard of if their eminent opponents had not taken notice of them. There is no revenge like oblivion, through which they are buried in the dust of their unworthiness. Audacious persons hope to make themselves eternally famous by setting fire to one of the wonders of the world and of the ages. The art of reproving scandal is to take no notice of it, to combat it damages our own case; even if credited it causes discredit, and is a source of satisfaction to our opponent, for this shadow of a stain dulls the lustre of our fame even if it cannot altogether deaden it.

ccvi *Know that there are vulgar Natures everywhere,*

even in Corinth itself, even in the highest families. Every one may try the experiment within his own gates. But there is also such a thing as vulgar opposition to vulgarity, which is worse. This special kind shares all the qualities of the common kind, just as bits of a broken glass: but this kind is still more pernicious; it speaks folly, blames impertinently, is a disciple of ignorance, a patron of folly, and past master of scandal; you need not notice what it says, still less what it thinks. It is important to know vulgarity in order to avoid it, whether it is subjective or objective. For all folly is vulgarity, and the vulgar consist of fools.

ccvii *Be Moderate.*

One has to consider the chance of a mischance. The impulses of the passions cause prudence to slip, and there is the risk of ruin. A moment of wrath or of pleasure carries you on farther than many hours of calm, and often a short diversion may put a whole life to shame. The cunning of others uses such moments of temptation to search the recesses of the mind: they use such thumbscrews as are wont to test the best caution. Moderation serves as a counterplot, especially in sudden emergencies. Much thought is needed to prevent a passion taking the bit in the teeth, and he is doubly wise who is wise on horseback. He who knows the danger may with care pursue his journey. Light as a word may appear to him who throws it out, it may import much to him that hears it and ponders on it.

ccviii *Do not die of the Fools' Disease.*

The wise generally die after they have lost their reason: fools before they have found it. To die of the fools' disease is to die of too much thought. Some die because they think and feel too much: others live because they do not think and feel: these are fools because they do not die of sorrow, the others because they do. A fool is he that dies of too much knowledge: thus some die because they are too knowing, others because they are not knowing enough. Yet though many die like fools, few die fools.

ccix *Keep Yourself free from common Follies.*

This is a special stroke of policy. They are of special power because they are general, so that many who would not be led away by any individual folly cannot escape the universal failing. Among these are to be counted the common prejudice that any one is satisfied with his fortune, however great, or unsatisfied with his intellect, however poor it is. Or again, that each, being discontented with his own lot, envies that of others; or further, that persons of to-day praise the things of yesterday, and those here the things there. Everything past seems best and everything distant is more valued. He is as great a fool that laughs at all as he that weeps at all.

ccx *Know how to play the Card of Truth.*

'Tis dangerous, yet a good man cannot avoid speaking it. But great skill is needed here: the most expert doctors of the soul pay great attention to the means of sweetening the pill of truth. For when it deals with the destroying of illusion it is the quintessence of bitterness. A pleasant manner has here an opportunity for a display of skill: with the same truth it can flatter one and fell another to the ground. Matters of to-day should be treated as if they were long past. For those who can understand a word is sufficient, and if it does not suffice, it is a case for silence. Princes must not be cured with bitter draughts; it is therefore desirable in their case to gild the pill of disillusion.

ccxi *In Heaven all is bliss:*

in Hell all misery. On earth, between the two, both one thing and the other. We stand between the two extremes, and therefore share both. Fate varies: all is not good luck nor all mischance. This world is merely zero: by itself it is of no value, but with Heaven in Front of it, it means much. Indifference at its ups and downs is prudent, nor is there any novelty for the wise. Our life gets as complicated as a comedy as it goes on, but the complications get gradually resolved: see that the curtain comes down on a good *dénoûment*.

ccxii *Keep to Yourself the final Touches of your Art.*

This is a maxim of the great masters who pride themselves on this subtlety in teaching their pupils: one must always remain superior, remain master. One must teach an art artfully. The source of knowledge need not be pointed out no more than that of giving. By this means a man preserves the respect and the dependence of others. In amusing and teaching you must keep to the rule: keep up expectation and advance in perfection. To keep a reserve is a great rule for life and for success, especially for those in high place.

ccxiii *Know how to Contradict.*

A chief means of finding things out—to embarrass others without being embarrassed. The true thumbscrew, it brings the passions into play. Tepid incredulity acts as an emetic on secrets. It is the key to a locked-up breast, and with great subtlety makes a double trial of both mind and will. A sly depreciation of another's mysterious word scents out the profoundest secrets; some sweet bait brings them into the mouth till they fall from the tongue and are caught in the net of astute deceit. By reserving your attention the other becomes less attentive, and lets his thoughts appear while otherwise his heart were inscrutable. An affected doubt is the subtlest picklock that curiosity can use to find out what it wants to know. Also in learning it is a subtle plan of the pupil to contradict the master, who thereupon takes pains to explain the truth more thoroughly and with more force, so that a moderate contradiction produces complete instruction.

ccxiv Do not turn one Blunder into two.

It is quite usual to commit four others in order to remedy one, or to excuse one piece of impertinence by still another. Folly is either related to, or identical with the family of Lies, for in both cases it needs many to support one. The worst of a bad case is having to fight it, and worse than the ill itself is not being able to conceal it. The annuity of one failing serves to support many others. A wise man may make one slip but never two, and that only in running, not while standing still.

ccxv Watch him that acts on Second Thoughts.

It is a device of business men to put the opponent off his guard before attacking him, and thus to conquer by being defeated: they dissemble their desire so as to attain it. They put themselves second so as to come out first in the final spurt. This method rarely fails if it is not noticed. Let therefore the attention never sleep when the intention is so wide awake. And if the other puts himself second so to hide his plan, put yourself first to discover it. Prudence can discern the artifices which such a man uses, and notices the pretexts he puts forward to gain his ends. He aims at one thing to get another: then he turns round smartly and fires straight at his target. It is well to know what you grant him, and at times it is desirable to give him to understand that you understand.

ccxvi *Be Expressive.*

This depends not only on the clearness but also on the vivacity of your thoughts. Some have an easy conception but a hard labour, for without clearness the children of the mind, thoughts and judgments, cannot be brought into the world. Many have a capacity like that of vessels with a large mouth and a small vent. Others again say more than they think. Resolution for the will, expression for the thought: two great gifts. Plausible minds are applauded: yet confused ones are often venerated just because they are not understood, and at times obscurity is convenient if you wish to avoid vulgarity; yet how shall the audience understand one that connects no definite idea with what he says?

ccxvii *Neither Love nor Hate, for ever*

Trust the friends of to-day as if they will be enemies to-morrow, and that of the worst kind. As this happens in reality, let it happen in your precaution. Do not put weapons in the hand for deserters from friendship to wage war with. On the other hand, leave the door of reconciliation open for enemies, and if it is also the gate of generosity so much the more safe. The vengeance of long ago is at times the torment of to-day, and the joy over the ill we have done is turned to grief, ccxviii *Never act from Obstinacy but from Knowledge.*

All obstinacy is an excrescence of the mind, a grandchild of passion which never did anything right. There are persons who make a war out of everything, real banditti of intercourse. All that they undertake must end in victory; they do not know how to get on in peace. Such men are fatal when they rule and govern, for they make government rebellion, and enemies out of those whom they ought to regard as children. They try to effect everything with strategy and treat it as the fruit of their skill. But when others have recognised their perverse humour all revolt against them and learn to overturn their chimerical plans, and they succeed in nothing but only heap up a mass of troubles, since everything serves to increase their disappointment. They have a head turned and a heart spoilt. Nothing can be done with such monsters except to flee from them, even to the Antipodes, where the savagery is easier to bear than their loathsome nature.

ccxix *Do not pass for a Hypocrite,*

though such men are indispensable nowadays. Be considered rather prudent than astute. Sincerity in behaviour pleases all, though not all can show it in their own affairs. Sincerity should not degenerate into simplicity nor sagacity into cunning. Be rather respected as wise than feared as sly. The open-hearted are loved but deceived. The great art consists in disclosing what is thought to be deceit. In the golden age simplicity flourished, in these days of iron cunning. The reputation of being a man who knows what he has to do is honourable and inspires confidence, but to be considered a hypocrite is deceptive and arouses mistrust.

ccxx *If you cannot clothe Yourself in Lionskin use Foxpelt.*

To follow the times is to lead them. He that gets what he wants never loses his reputation. Cleverness when force will not do. One way or another, the king's highway of valour or the bypath of cunning. Skill has effected more than force, and astuteness has conquered courage more often than the other way. When you cannot get a thing then is the time to despise it.

ccxxi *Do not seize Occasions to embarrass Yourself or Others.*

There are some men stumbling-blocks of good manners either for themselves or for others: they are always on the point of some stupidity. You meet with them easily and part from them uneasily. A hundred annoyances a day is nothing to them. Their humour always strokes the wrong way since they contradict all and every. They put on the judgment cap wrong side foremost and thus condemn all. Yet the greatest test of others' patience and prudence are just those who do no good and speak ill of all. There are many monsters in the wide realm of Indecorum.

ccxxii *Reserve is proof of Prudence.*

The tongue is a wild beast; once let loose it is difficult to chain. It is the pulse of the soul by which wise men judge of its health: by this pulse a careful observer feels every movement of the heart. The worst is that he who should be most reserved is the least. The sage saves himself from worries and embarrassments, and shows his mastery over himself. He goes his way carefully, a Janus for impartiality, an Argus for watchfulness. Truly Momus had better placed the eyes in the hand than the window in the breast.

ccxxiii *Be not Eccentric,*

neither from affectation nor carelessness. Many have some remarkable and individual quality leading to eccentric actions. These are more defects than excellent differences. And just as some are known for some special ugliness, so these for something repellant in their outward behaviour. Such eccentricities simply serve as trademarks through their atrocious singularity: they cause either derision or ill-will.

ccxxiv *Never take Things against the Grain,*

no matter how they come. Everything has a smooth and a seamy side, and the best weapon wounds if taken by the blade, while the enemy's spear may be our best protection if taken by the staff. Many things cause pain which would cause pleasure if you regarded their advantages. There is a favourable and an unfavourable side to everything, the cleverness consists in finding out the favourable. The same thing looks quite different in another light; look at it therefore on its best side and do not exchange good for evil. Thus it haps that many find joy, many grief, in everything. This remark is a great protection against the frowns of fortune, and a weighty rule of life for all times and all conditions.

ccxxv *Know your chief Fault.*

There lives none that has not in himself a counterbalance to his most conspicuous merit: if this be nourished by desire it may grow to be a tyrant. Commence war against it, summoning prudence as your ally, and the first thing to do is the public manifesto, for an evil once known is soon conquered, especially when the one afflicted regards it in the same light as the onlookers. To be master of oneself one should know oneself. If the chief imperfection surrender, the rest will come to an end.

ccxxvi *Take care to be Obliging.*

Most talk and act, not as they are, but as they are obliged. To persuade people of ill is easy for any, since the ill is easily credited even when at times it is incredible. The best we have depends on the opinion of others. Some are satisfied if they have right on their side, but that is not enough, for it must be assisted by energy. To oblige persons often costs little and helps much. With words you may purchase deeds. In this great house of the world there is no chamber so hid that it may not be wanted one day in the year, and then you would miss it however little is its worth. Every one speaks of a subject according to his feelings.

ccxxvii *Do not be the Slave of First Impressions.*

Some marry the very first account they hear: all others must live with them as concubines. But as a lie has swift legs, the truth with them can find no lodging. We should neither satisfy our will with the first object nor our mind with the first proposition: for that were superficial. Many are like new casks who keep the scent of the first liquor they hold, be it good or bad. If this superficiality becomes known, it becomes fatal, for it then gives opportunity for cunning mischief; the ill-minded hasten to colour the mind of the credulous. Always therefore leave room for a second hearing. Alexander always kept one ear for the other side. Wait for the second or even third edition of news. To be the slave of your impressions argues want of capacity, and is not far from being the slave of your passions.

ccxxviii *Do not be a Scandal-monger.*

Still less pass for one, for that means to be considered a slanderer. Do not be witty at the cost of others: it is easy but hateful. All men have their revenge on such an one by speaking ill of him, and as they are many and he but one, he is more likely to be overcome than they convinced. Evil should never be our pleasure, and therefore never our theme. The backbiter is always hated, and if now and then one of the great consorts with him, it is less from pleasure in his sneers than from esteem for his insight. He that speaks ill will always hear worse.

ccxxix *Plan out your Life wisely,*

not as chance will have it, but with prudence and foresight. Without amusements it is wearisome, like a long journey where there are no inns: manifold knowledge gives manifold pleasure. The first day's journey of a noble life should be passed in conversing with the dead: we live to know and to know ourselves: hence true books make us truly men. The second day should be spent with the living, seeing and noticing all the good in the world. Everything is not to be found in a single country. The Universal Father has divided His gifts, and at times has given the richest dower to the ugliest. The third day is entirely for oneself. The last felicity is to be a philosopher.

ccxxx *Open your Eyes betimes.*

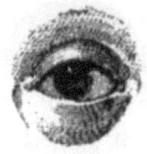
Not all that see have their eyes open, nor do all those see that look. To come up to things too late is more worry than help. Some just begin to see when there is nothing more to see: they pull their houses about their ears before they come to themselves. It is difficult to give sense to those who have no power of will, still more difficult to give energy to those who have no sense. Those who surround them play with them a game of blind man's buff, making them the butts of others, and be-cause they are hard of hearing, they do not open their eyes to see. There are often those who encourage such insensibility on which their very existence depends. Unhappy steed whose rider is blind: it will never grow sleek.

ccxxxi *Never let Things be seen half-finished.*

They can only be enjoyed when complete. All beginnings are misshapen, and this deformity sticks in the imagination. The recollection of having seen a thing imperfect disturbs our enjoyment of it when completed. To swallow something great at one gulp may disturb the judgment of the separate parts, but satisfies the taste. Till a thing is everything, it is nothing, and while it is in process of being it is still nothing. To see the tastiest dishes prepared arouses rather disgust than appetite. Let each great master take care not to let his work be seen in its embryonic stages: they might take this lesson from Dame Nature, who never brings the child to the light till it is fit to be seen.

ccxxxii *Have a Touch of the Trader.*

Life should not be all thought: there should be action as well. Very wise folk are generally easily deceived, for while they know out-of-the-way things they do not know the ordinary things of life, which are much more needful. The observation of higher things leaves them no time for things close at hand. Since they know not the very first thing they should know, and what everybody knows so well, they are either considered or thought ignorant by the superficial multitude. Let therefore the prudent take care to have something of the trader about him—enough to prevent him being deceived and so laughed at. Be a man adapted to the daily round, which if not the highest is the most necessary thing in life. Of what use is knowledge if it is not practical, and to know how to live is nowadays the true knowledge.

ccxxxiii *Let not the proffered Morsel be distasteful;*

otherwise it gives more discomfort than pleasure. Some displease when attempting to oblige, because they take no account of varieties of taste. What is flattery to one is an offence to another, and in attempting to be useful one may become insulting. It often costs more to displease a man than it would have cost to please him: you thereby lose both gift and thanks because you have lost the compass which steers for pleasure. He who knows not another's taste, knows not how to please him. Thus it haps that many insult where they mean to praise, and get soundly punished, and rightly so. Others desire to charm by their conversation, and only succeed in boring by their loquacity.

ccxxxiv *Never trust your Honour to another, unless you have his in Pledge.*

Arrange that silence is a mutual advantage; disclosure a danger to both. Where honour is at stake you must act with a partner, so that each must be careful of the other's honour for the sake of his own. Never entrust your honour to another; but if you have, let caution surpass prudence. Let the danger be in common and the risk mutual, so that your partner cannot turn king's evidence.

ccxxxv *Know how to Ask.*

With some nothing easier: with others nothing so difficult. For there are men who cannot refuse: with them no skill is required. But with others their first word at all times is No; with them great art is required, and with all the propitious moment. Surprise them when in a pleasant mood, when a repast of body or soul has just left them refreshed, if only their shrewdness has not anticipated the cunning of the applicant. The days of joy are the days of favour, for joy overflows from the inner man into the outward creation. It is no use applying when another has been refused, since the objection to a No has just been overcome. Nor is it a good time after sorrow. To oblige a person beforehand is a sure way, unless he is mean.

ccxxxvi *Make an Obligation beforehand of what would have to be a Reward afterwards.*

This is a stroke of subtle policy; to grant favours before they are deserved is a proof of being obliging. Favours thus granted beforehand have two great advantages: the promptness of the gift obliges the recipient the more strongly; and the same gift which would afterwards be merely a reward is beforehand an obligation. This is a subtle means of transforming obligations, since that which would have forced the superior to reward is changed into one that obliges the one obliged to satisfy the obligation. But this is only suitable for men who have the feeling of obligation, since with men of lower stamp the honorarium paid beforehand acts rather as a bit than as a spur.

ccxxxvii *Never share the Secrets of your Superiors.*

You may think you will share pears, but you will only share parings. Many have been ruined by being confidants: they are like sops of bread used as forks, they run the same risk of being eaten up afterwards. It is no favour in a prince to share a secret: it is only a relief. Many break the mirror that reminds them of their ugliness. We do not like seeing those who have seen us as we are: nor is he seen In a favourable light who has seen us in an unfavourable one. None ought to be too much beholden to us, least of all one of the great, unless it be for benefits done him rather than for such favours received from him. Especially dangerous are secrets entrusted to friends. He that communicates his secret to another makes himself that other's slave. With a prince this is an intolerable position which cannot last. He will desire to recover his lost liberty, and to gain it will overturn everything, including right and reason. Accordingly neither tell secrets nor listen to them.

ccxxxviii *Know what is wanting in Yourself.*

Many would have been great personages if they had not had something wanting without which they could not rise to the height of perfection. It is remarkable with some that they could be much better if they could he better in something. They do not perhaps take themselves seriously enough to do justice to their great abilities; some are wanting in geniality of disposition, a quality which their entourage soon find the want of, especially if they are in high office. Some are without organising ability, others lack moderation. In all such cases a careful man may make of habit a second nature.

ccxxxix *Do not be Captious.*

It is much more important to be sensible. To know more than is necessary blunts your weapons, for fine points generally bend or break. Common-sense truth is the surest. It is well to know but not to niggle. Lengthy comment leads to disputes. It is much better to have sound sense, which does not wander from the matter in hand.

ccxl *Make use of Folly.*

The wisest play this card at times, and there are times when the greatest wisdom lies in seeming not to be wise. You need not be unwise, but merely affect unwisdom. To be wise with fools and foolish with the wise were of little use. Speak to each in his own language. He is no fool who affects folly, but he is who suffers from it. Ingenuous folly rather than the pretended is the true foolishness, since cleverness has arrived at such a pitch. To be well liked one must dress in the skin of the simplest of animals.

ccxli *Put up with Raillery, but do not practise it.*

The first is a form of courtesy, the second may lead to embarrassment. To snarl at play has something of the beast and seems to have more. Audacious raillery is delightful: to stand it proves power. To show oneself annoyed causes the other to be annoyed. Best leave it alone; the surest way not to put on the cap that might fit. The most serious matters have arisen out of jests. Nothing requires more tact and attention. Before you begin to joke know how far the subject of your joke is able to bear it.

ccxlii *Push Advantages.*

Some put all their strength in the commencement and never carry a thing to a conclusion. They invent but never execute. These be paltering spirits. They obtain no fame, for they sustain no game to the end. Everything stops at a single stop. This arises in some from impatience, which is the failing of the Spaniard, as patience is the virtue of the Belgian. The latter bring things to an end, the former come to an end with things. They sweat away till the obstacle is surmounted, but content themselves with surmounting it: they do not know how to push the victory home. They prove that they can but will not: but this proves always that they cannot, or have no stability. If the undertaking is good, why not finish it? If it is bad, why undertake it? Strike down your quarry, if you are wise; be not content to flush it.

ccxliii *Do not be too much of a Dove.*

Alternate the cunning of the serpent with the candour of the dove. Nothing is easier than to deceive an honest man. He believes in much who lies in naught; who does no deceit, has much confidence. To be deceived is not always due to stupidity, it may arise from sheer goodness. There are two sets of men who can guard themselves from injury: those who have experienced it at their own cost, and those who have observed it at the cost of others. Prudence should use as much suspicion as subtlety uses snares, and none need be so good as to enable others to do him ill. Combine in yourself the dove and the serpent, not as a monster but as a prodigy.

ccxliv *Create a feeling of Obligation.*

Some transform favours received into favours bestowed, and seem, or let it be thought, that they are doing a favour when receiving one. There are some so astute that they get honour by asking, and buy their own advantage with applause from others. They manage matters so cleverly that they seem to be doing others a service when receiving one from them. They transpose the order of obligation with extraordinary skill, or at least render it doubtful who has obliged whom. They buy the best by praising it, and make a flattering honour out of the pleasure they express. They oblige by their courtesy, and thus make men beholden for what they themselves should be beholden. In this way they conjugate "to oblige" in the active instead of in the passive voice, thereby proving themselves better politicians than grammarians. This is a subtle piece of *finesse*; a still greater is to perceive it, and to retaliate on such fools' bargains by paying in their own coin, and so coming by your own again.

ccxlv *Original and out-of-the-way Views*

are signs of superior ability. We do not think much of a man who never contradicts us that is no sign he loves us, but rather that he loves himself. Do not be deceived by flattery, and thereby have to pay for it: rather condemn it. Besides you may take credit for being censured by some, especially if they are those of whom the good speak ill. On the contrary, it should disturb us if our affairs please every one, for that is a sign that they are of little worth. Perfection is for the few.

ccxlvi *Never offer Satisfaction unless it is demanded.*

And if they do demand it, it is a kind of crime to give more than necessary. To excuse oneself before there is occasion is to accuse oneself. To draw blood in full health gives the hint to ill-will. An excuse unexpected arouses suspicion from its slumbers. Nor need a shrewd person show himself aware of another's suspicion, which is equivalent to seeking out offence. He had best disarm distrust by the integrity of his conduct.

ccxlvii *Know a little more, live a little less.*

Some say the opposite. To be at ease is better than to be at business. Nothing really belongs to us but time, which even he has who has nothing else. It is equally unfortunate to waste your precious life in mechanical tasks or in a profusion of important work. Do not heap up occupation and thereby envy: otherwise you complicate life and exhaust your mind. Some wish to apply the same principle to knowledge, but unless one knows one does not truly live.

ccxlviii *Do not go with the last Speaker.*

There are persons who go by the latest edition, and thereby go to irrational extremes. Their feelings and desires are of wax: the last comer stamps them with his seal and obliterates all previous impressions. These never gain anything, for they lose everything so soon. Every one dyes them with his own colour. They are of no use as confidants; they remain children their whole life. Owing to this instability of feeling and volition, they halt along cripples in will and thought, and totter from one side of the road to the other.

ccxlix Never begin Life with what should end it.

Many take their amusement at the beginning, putting off anxiety to the end; but the essential should come first and accessories afterwards if there is room. Others wish to triumph before they have fought. Others again begin with learning things of little consequence and leave studies that would bring them fame and gain to the end of life. Another is just about to make his fortune when he disappears from the scene. Method is essential for knowledge and for life.

ccl When to change the Conversation.

When they talk scandal. With some all goes contrariwise: their No is Yes, and their Yes, No. If they speak ill of a thing it is the highest praise. For what they want for them-selves they depreciate to others. To praise a thing is not always to speak well of it, for some, to avoid praising what's good, praise what's bad, and nothing is good for him for whom nothing is bad.

ccli Use human Means as if there were no divine ones, and divine as if there were no human ones.

A masterly rule: it needs no comment.

cclii Neither belong entirely to Yourself nor entirely to Others.

Both are mean forms of tyranny. To desire to be all for oneself is the same as desiring to have all for oneself. Such persons will not yield a jot or lose a tittle of their comfort. They are rarely beholden, lean on their own luck, and their crutch generally breaks. It is convenient at times to belong to others, that others may belong to us. And he that holds public office is no more nor less than a public slave, or let a man give up both berth and burthen, as the old woman said to Hadrian. On the other hand, others are all for others, which is folly, that always flies to extremes, in this case in a most unfortunate manner. No day, no hour, is their own, but they have so much too much of others that they may be called the slaves of all. This applies even to knowledge, where a man may know everything for others and nothing for himself. A shrewd man knows that others when they seek him do not seek *him*, but their advantage in him and by him.

ccliii Do not Explain overmuch.

Most men do not esteem what they understand, and venerate what they do not see. To be valued things should cost dear: what is not understood becomes overrated. You have to appear wiser and more prudent than he requires with whom you deal, if you desire to give him a high opinion of you: yet in this there should be moderation and no excess. And though with sensible people common sense holds its own, with most men a little elaboration is necessary. Give them no time for blame: occupy them with understanding your drift. Many praise a thing without being able to tell why, if asked. The reason is that they venerate the unknown as a mystery, and praise it because they hear it praised.

ccliv *Never despise an Evil, however small,*

for they never come alone: they are linked together like pieces of good fortune. Fortune and misfortune generally go to find their fellows. Hence all avoid the unlucky and associate with the fortunate. Even the doves with all their innocence resort to the whitest walls. Everything fails with the unfortunate—himself, his words, and his luck. Do not wake Misfortune when she sleeps. One slip is a little thing: yet some fatal loss may follow it till you do not know where it will end. For just as no happiness is perfect, so no ill-luck is complete. Patience serves with what comes from above; prudence with that from below.

cclv *Do Good a little at a time, but often.*

One should never give beyond the possibility of return. Who gives much does not give but sells. Nor drain gratitude to the dregs, for when the recipient sees all return is impossible he breaks off correspondence. With many persons it is not necessary to do more than overburden them with favours to lose them altogether: they cannot repay you, and so they retire, preferring rather to be enemies than perpetual debtors. The idol never wishes to see before him the sculptor who shaped him, nor does the benefited wish to see his benefactor always before his eyes. There is a great subtlety in giving what costs little yet is much desired, so that it is esteemed the more.

cclvi *Go armed against Discourtesy,*

and against perfidy, presumption, and all other kinds of folly. There is much of it in the world, and prudence lies in avoiding a meeting with it. Arm yourself each day before the mirror of attention with the weapons of defence. Thus you will beat down the attacks of folly. Be prepared for the occasion, and do not expose your reputation to vulgar contingencies. Armed with prudence, a man cannot be disarmed by impertinence. The road of human intercourse is difficult, for it is full of ruts which may jolt our credit. Best to take a byway, taking Ulysses as a model of shrewdness. Feigned misunderstanding is of great value in such matters. Aided by politeness it helps us over all, and is often the only way out of difficulties.

cclvii *Never let Matters come to a Rupture,*

for our reputation always comes injured out of the encounter. Every one may be of importance as an enemy if not as a friend. Few can do us good, almost any can do us harm. In Jove's bosom itself even his eagle never nestles securely from the day he has quarrelled with a beetle. Hidden foes use the paw of the declared enemy to stir up the fire, and meanwhile they lie in ambush for such an occasion. Friends provoked become the bitterest of enemies. They cover their own failings with the faults of others. Every one speaks as things seem to him, and things seem as he wishes them to appear. All blame us at the beginning for want of foresight, at the end for lack of patience, at all times for imprudence. If, however, a breach is inevitable, let it be rather excused as a slackening of friendship than by an outburst of wrath: here is a good application of the saying about a good retreat.

cclviii *Find out some one to share your Troubles.*

You will never be all alone, even in dangers, nor bear all the burden of hate. Some think by their high position to carry off the whole glory of success, and have to bear the whole humiliation of defeat. In this way they have none to excuse them, none to share the blame. Neither fate nor the mob are so bold against two. Hence the wise physician, if he has failed to cure, looks out for some one who, under the name of a consultation, may help him carry out, the corpse. Share weight and woe, for misfortune falls with double force on him that stands alone.

cclix *Anticipate Injuries and turn them into Favours.*

It is wiser to avoid than to revenge them. It is an uncommon piece of shrewdness to change a rival into a confidant, or transform into guards of honour  those who were aiming attacks at us. It helps much to know how to oblige, for he leaves no time for injuries that fills it up with gratitude. That is true *savoir faire* to turn anxieties into pleasures. Try and make a confidential relation out of ill-will itself.

cclx *We belong to none and none to us, entirely.*

Neither relationship nor friendship nor the most intimate connection is sufficient to effect this. To give one's whole confidence is quite different from giving one's regard. The closest intimacy has its exceptions, without which the laws of friendship would be broken. The friend always keeps one secret to himself, and even the son always hides something from his father. Some things are kept from one that are **revealed** to another and *vice versâ*. In this way one reveals all and conceals all, by making a distinction among the persons with whom we are connected.

cclxi *Do not follow up a Folly.*

Many make an obligation out of a blunder, and because they have entered the wrong path think it proves their strength of character to go on in it. Within they regret their error, while outwardly they excuse it. At the beginning of their mistake they were regarded as inattentive, in the end as fools. Neither an unconsidered promise nor a mistaken resolution are really binding. Yet some continue in their folly and prefer to be constant fools.

cclxii *Be able to Forget.*

It is more a matter of luck than of skill. The things we remember best are those better for-gotten. Memory is not only unruly, leaving us in the lurch when most needed, but stupid as well, putting its nose into places where it is not wanted. In painful things it is active, but neglectful in recalling the pleasurable. Very often the only remedy for the ill is to forget it, and all we forget is the remedy. Nevertheless one should cultivate good habits of memory, for it is capable of making existence a Paradise or an Inferno. The happy are an exception who enjoy innocently their simple happiness.

cclxiii *Many things of Taste one should not possess oneself.*

One enjoys them better if another's than if one's own. The owner has the good of them the first day, for all the rest of the time they are for others. You take a double enjoyment in other men's property, being without fear of spoiling it and with the pleasure of novelty. Everything tastes better for having been without it: even water from another's well tastes like nectar. Possession not alone hinders enjoyment: it increases annoyance whether you lend or keep. You gain nothing except keeping things for or from others, and by this means gain more enemies than friends.

cclxiv *Have no careless Days.*

Fate loves to play tricks, and will heap up chances to catch us unawares. Our intelligence, prudence, and courage, even our beauty, must always be ready for trial. For their day of careless trust will be that of their discredit. Care always fails just when it was most wanted. It is thoughtlessness that trips us up into destruction. Accordingly it is a piece of military strategy to put perfection to its trial when unprepared. The days of parade are known and are allowed to pass by, but the day is chosen when least expected so as to put valour to the severest test.

cclxv *Set those under you difficult Task,*

Many have proved themselves able at once when they had to deal with a difficulty, just as fear of drowning makes a swimmer of a man, In this way many have discovered their own courage, knowledge, or tact, which but for the opportunity would have been for ever buried beneath their want of enterprise. Dangers are the occasions to create a name for oneself; and if a noble mind sees honour at stake, he will do the work of thousands. Queen Isabella the Catholic knew well this rule of life, as well as all the others, and to a shrewd favour of this kind from her the Great Captain won his fame, and many others earned an undying name. By this great art she made great men.

cclxvi *Do not become Bad from sheer Goodness.*

That is, by never getting into a temper. Such men without feeling are scarcely to be considered men. It does not always arise from laziness, but from sheer inability. To feel strongly on occasion is something personal: birds soon mock at the mawkin. It is a sign of good taste to combine bitter and sweet. All sweets is diet for children and fools. It is very bad to sink into such insensibility out of very goodness.

cclxvii Silken Words, sugared Manners.

Arrows pierce the body, insults the soul. Sweet pastry perfumes the breath. It is a great art in life to know how to sell wind. Most things are paid for in words, and by them you can remove impossibilities. Thus we deal in air, and a royal breath can produce courage and power. Always have your mouth full of sugar to sweeten your words, so that even your ill-wishers enjoy them. To please one must be peaceful.

cclxviii The Wise do at once what the Fool does at last.

Both do the same thing; the only difference lies in the time they do it: the one at the right time, the other at the wrong. Who starts out with his mind topsyturvy will so continue till the end. He catches by the foot what he ought to knock on the head, he turns right into left, and in all his acts is but a child. There is only one way to get him in the right way, and that is to force him to do what he might have done of his own accord. The wise man, on the other hand, sees at once what must be done sooner or later, so he does it willingly and gains honour thereby.

cclxix Make use of the Novelty of your Position;

for men are valued while they are new. Novelty pleases all because it is uncommon, taste is refreshed, and a brand new mediocrity is thought more of than accustomed excellence.

Ability wears away by use and becomes old. However, know that the glory of novelty is short-lived: after four days respect is gone. Accordingly, learn to utilise the first fruits of appreciation, and seize during the rapid passage of applause all that can be put to use. For once the heat of novelty over, the passion cools and the appreciation of novelty is exchanged for satiety at the customary: believe that all has its season, which soon passes.

cclxx *Do not condemn alone that which pleases all.*

There must be something good in a thing that pleases so many; even if it cannot be explained it is certainly enjoyed. Singularity is always hated, and, when in the wrong, laughed at. You simply destroy respect for your taste rather than do harm to the object of your blame, and are left alone, you and your bad taste. If you cannot find the good in a thing, hide your incapacity and do not damn it straightway. As a general rule bad taste springs from want of knowledge. What all say, is so, or will be so.

cclxxi *In every Occupation if you know little stick to the safest.*

If you are not respected as subtle, you will be regarded as sure. On the other hand, a man well trained can plunge in and act as he pleases. To know little and yet seek danger is nothing else than to seek ruin. In such a case take stand on the right hand, for what is done cannot be undone. Let little knowledge keep to the king's highway, and in every case, knowing or unknowing, security is shrewder than singularity.

cclxxii *Sell Things by the Tariff of Courtesy.*

You oblige people most that way. The bid of an interested buyer will never equal the return gift of an honourable recipient of a favour. Courtesy does not really make presents, but really lays men under obligation, and generosity is the great obligation. To a right-minded man nothing costs more dear that what is given him: you sell it him twice and for two prices: one for the value, one for the politeness. At the same time it is true that with vulgar souls generosity is gibberish, for they do not understand the language of good breeding.

cclxxiii *Comprehend their Dispositions with whom you deal,*

so as to know their intentions. Cause known, effect known, beforehand in the disposition and after in the motive. The melancholy man always foresees misfortunes, the backbiter scandals; having no conception of the good, evil offers itself to them. A man moved by passion always speaks of things differently from what they are; it is his passion speaks, not his reason. Thus each speaks as his feeling or his humour prompts him, and all far from the truth. Learn how to decipher faces and spell out the soul in the features. If a man laughs always, set him down as foolish; if never, as false. Beware of the gossip: he is either a babbler or a spy. Expect little good from the misshapen: they generally take revenge on Nature, and do little honour to her, as she has done little to them. Beauty and folly generally go hand in hand.

cclxxiv *Be Attractive.*

magnet of your pleasant qualities more to obtain goodwill than good deeds, but apply it to all. Merit is not enough unless supported by grace, which is the sole thing that gives general acceptance, and the most practical means of rule over others. To be in vogue is a matter of luck, yet it can be encouraged by skill, for art can best take root on a soil favoured by nature. There goodwill grows and develops into universal favour.

cclxxv *Join in the Game as far as Decency permits.*

Do not always pose and be a bore: this is a maxim for gallant bearing. You may yield a touch of dignity to gain the general good-will: you may now and then go where most go, yet not beyond the bounds of decorum. He who makes a fool of himself in public will not be regarded as discreet in private life. One may lose more on a day of pleasure than has been gained during a whole life of labour. Still you must not always keep away: to be singular is to condemn all others. Still less act the prude—leave that to its appropriate sex: even religious prudery is ridiculous. Nothing so becomes a man as to be a man: a woman may affect a manly bearing as an excellence, but not *vice versâ.*

cclxxvi *Know how to renew your Character,*

with the help both of Nature and of Art, Every seven years the disposition changes, they say. Let it be a change for the better and for the nobler in your taste. After the first seven comes reason, with each succeeding lustre let a new excellence be added.

Observe this change so as to aid it, and hope also for betterment in others. Hence it arises that many change their behaviour when they change their position or their occupation. At times the change is not noticed till it reaches the height of maturity. At twenty Man is a Peacock, at thirty a Lion, at forty a Camel, at fifty a Serpent, at sixty a Dog, at seventy an Ape, at eighty nothing at all.

cclxxvii *Display yourself.*

'Tis the illumination of talents: for each there comes an appropriate moment; use it, for not every day comes a triumph. There are some dashing men who make much show with a little, a whole exhibition with much. If ability to display them is joined to versatile gifts, they are regarded as miraculous. There are whole nations given to display: the Spanish people take the highest rank in this. Light was the first thing to cause Creation to shine forth. Display fills up much, supplies much, and gives a second existence to things, especially when combined with real excellence. Heaven that grants perfection, provides also the means of display; for one without the other were abortive. Skill is however needed for display. Even excellence depends on circumstances and is not always opportune. Ostentation is out of place when it is out of time. More than any other quality it should be free of any affectation. This is its rock of offence, for it then borders on vanity and so on contempt: it must be moderate to avoid being vulgar, and any excess is despised by the wise. At times it consists in a sort of mute eloquence, a careless display of excellence, for a wise concealment is often the most effective boast, since the very withdrawal from view piques curiosity to the highest. 'Tis a fine subtlety too not to display one's excellence all at one time, but to grant stolen glances at it, more and more as time goes on. Each exploit should be the pledge of a greater, and applause at the first should only die away in expectation of its sequel.

cclxxviii *Avoid Notoriety in all Things.*

Even excellences become defects if they become notorious. Notoriety arises from singularity, which is always blamed: he that is singular is left severely alone. Even beauty is discredited by coxcombry, which offends by the very notice it attracts. Still more does this apply to discreditable singularities. Yet among the wicked there are some that seek to be known for seeking novelties in vice so as to attain to the fame of infamy. Even in matters of the intellect want of moderation may degenerate into loquacity.

cclxxix *Do not contradict the Contradicter.*

You have to distinguish whether the contra-diction comes from cunning or from vulgarity. It is not always obstinacy, but may be artfulness. Notice this: for in the first case one may get into difficulties, in the other into danger. Caution is never more needed than against spies. There is no such countercheck to the picklock of the mind as to leave the key of caution in the lock.

cclxxx *Be Trustworthy.*

Honourable dealing is at an end: trusts are denied: few keep their word: the greater the service, the poorer the reward: that is the way with all the world nowadays. There are whole nations inclined to false dealing: with some treachery has always to be feared, with others breach of promise, with others deceit. Yet this bad behaviour of others should rather be a warning to us than an example. The fear is that the sight of such unworthy behaviour should override our integrity. But a man of honour should never forget what he is because he sees what others are.

cclxxxi *Find Favour with Men of Sense.*

The tepid Yes of a remarkable man is worth more than all the applause of the vulgar: you cannot make a meal off the smoke of chaff. The wise speak with understanding and their praise gives permanent satisfaction. The sage Antigonus reduced the theatre of his fame to Zeus alone, and Plato called Aristotle his whole school. Some strive to fill their stomach albeit only with the breath of the mob. Even monarchs have need of authors, and fear their pens more than ugly women the painter's pencil.

cclxxxii *Make use of Absence to make yourself more esteemed or valued.*

If the accustomed presence diminishes fame, absence augments it. One that is regarded as a lion in his absence may be laughed at when present as the ridiculous result of the parturition of the mountains. Talents get soiled by use, for it is easier to see the exterior rind than the kernel of greatness it encloses. Imagination reaches farther than sight, and disillusion, which ordinarily comes through the ears, also goes out through the ears. He keeps his fame that keeps himself in the centre of public opinion. Even the Phoenix uses its retirement for new adornment and turns absence into desire.

cclxxxiii *Have the Gift of Discovery.*

It is a proof of the highest genius, yet when was genius without a touch of madness? If discovery be a gift of genius, choice of means is a mark of sound sense. Discovery comes by special grace and very

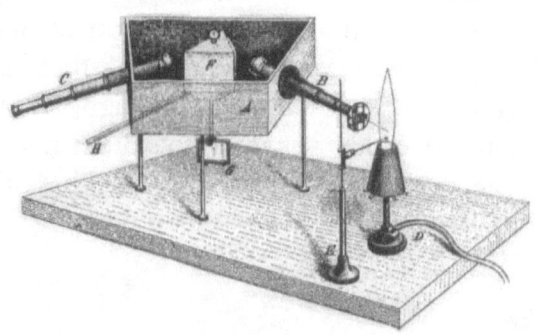

seldom. For many can follow up a thing when found, but to find it first is the gift of the few, and those the first in excellence and in age. Novelty flatters, and if successful gives the possessor double credit. In matters of judgment novelties are dangerous because leading to paradox, in matters of genius they deserve all praise. Yet both equally deserve applause if successful.

cclxxxiv *Do not be Importunate,*

and so you will not be slighted. Respect yourself if you would have others respect you. Be sooner sparing than lavish with your presence. You will thus become desired and so well received. Never come unasked and only go when sent for. If **you** undertake a thing of your own accord you get all the blame if it fails, none of the thanks If it succeeds. The importunate is always the butt of blame; and because he thrusts himself in without shame he is thrust out with it.

cclxxxv *Never die of another's Ill-luck.*

Notice those who stick in the mud, and observe how they call others to their aid so as to console themselves with a companion in misfortune. They seek some one to help them to bear misfortune, and often those who turned the cold shoulder on them in prosperity give them now a helping hand. There is great caution needed in helping the drowning without danger to oneself.

cclxxxvi *Do not become responsible for all or for every one,*

otherwise you become a slave and the slave of all. Some are born more fortunate than others: they are born to do good as others to receive it. Freedom is more precious than any gifts for which you may be tempted to give it up. Lay less stress on making many dependent on you than on keeping yourself independent of any. The sole advantage of power is that you can do more good. Above all do not regard responsibility as a favour, for generally it is another's plan to make one dependent on him.

cclxxxvii *Never act in a Passion.*

If you do, all is lost. You cannot act for yourself if you are not yourself, and passion always drives out reason. In such cases inter-pose a prudent go-between who can only be prudent if he keeps cool. That is why lookers-on see most of the game, because they keep cool. As soon as you notice that you are losing your temper beat a wise retreat. For no sooner is the blood up than it is spilt, and in a few moments occasion may be given for many days' repentance for oneself and complaints of the other party.

cclxxxviii *Live for the Moment.*

Our acts and thoughts and all must be determined by circumstances. Will when you may, for time and tide wait for no man. Do not live by certain fixed rules, except those that relate to the cardinal virtues. Nor let your will subscribe fixed conditions, for you may have to drink the water to-morrow which you cast away to-day. There be some so absurdly paradoxical that they expect all the circumstances of an action should bend to their eccentric whims and not *vice versâ*. The wise man knows that the very polestar of prudence lies in steering by the wind.

cclxxxix *Nothing depreciates a Man more than to show he is a Man like other Men.*

The day he is seen to be very human he ceases to be thought divine. Frivolity is the exact opposite of reputation. And as the reserved are held to be more than men, so the frivolous are held to be less. No failing causes such failure of respect. For frivolity is the exact opposite of solid seriousness. A man of levity cannot be a man of weight even when he is old, and age should oblige him to be prudent. Although this blemish is so common it is none the less despised.

ccxc *'Tis a piece of good Fortune to combine Men's Love and Respect.*

Generally one dare not be liked if one would be respected. Love is more sensitive than hate. Love and honour do not go well together. So that one should aim neither to be much feared nor much loved. Love introduces confidence, and the further this advances, the more respect recedes. Prefer to be loved with respect rather than with passion, for that is a love suitable for many.

ccxci *Know how to Test.*

The care of the wise must guard against the snare of the wicked. Great judgment is needed to test that of another. It is more important to know the characteristics and properties of persons than those of vegetables and minerals. It is indeed one of the shrewdest things in life. You can tell metals by their ring and men by their voice. Words are proof of integrity, deeds still more. Here one requires extraordinary care, deep observation, subtle discernment, and judicious decision.

ccxcii *Let your personal Qualities surpass those of your Office,*

Let it not be the other way about. How-ever high the post, the person should be higher. An extensive capacity expands and dilates more and more as his office becomes higher. On the other hand, the narrow-minded will easily lose heart and come to grief with diminished responsibilities and reputation. The great Augustus thought more of being a great man than a great prince. Here a lofty mind finds fit place, and well-grounded confidence finds its opportunity.

ccxciii *Maturity.*

It is shown in the costume, still more in the customs. Material weight is the sign of a precious metal; moral, of a precious man. Maturity gives finish to his capacity and arouses respect. A composed bearing in a man forms a *façade* to his soul. It does not consist in the insensibility of fools, as frivolity would have it, but in a calm tone of authority. With men of this kind sentences are orations and acts are deeds. Maturity finishes a man off, for each is so far a complete man according as he possesses maturity. On ceasing to be a child a man begins to gain seriousness and authority.

ccxciv *Be moderate in your Views.*

Every one holds views according to his interest, and imagines he has abundant grounds for them. For with most men judgment has to give way to inclination. It may occur that two may meet with exactly opposite views and yet each thinks to have reason on his side, yet reason is always true to itself and never has two faces. In such a difficulty a prudent man will go to work with care, for his decision of his opponent's view may cast doubt on his own. Place yourself in such a case in the other man's place and then investigate the reasons for his opinion. You will not then condemn him or justify yourself in such a confusing way.

ccxcv *Do not affect what you have not effected.*

Many claim exploits without the slightest claim. 'With the greatest coolness they make a mystery of all. Chameleons of applause they afford others a surfeit of laughter. Vanity is always objectionable, here it is despicable. These ants of honour go crawling about filching scraps of exploits. The greater your exploits the less you need affect them: content yourself with doing, leave the talking to others. Give away your deeds but do not sell them. And do not hire venal pens to write down praises in the mud, to the derision of the knowing ones. Aspire rather to be a hero than merely to appear one.

ccxcvi Noble Qualities.

Noble qualities make noblemen: a single one of them is worth more than a multitude of mediocre ones. There was once a man who made all his belongings, even his household utensils, as great as possible. How much more ought a great man see that the qualities of his soul are as great as possible. In God all is eternal and infinite, so in a hero everything should be great and majestic, so that all his deeds, nay, all his words, should he pervaded by a transcendent majesty.

ccxcvii *Always act as if your Acts were seen.*

He must see all round who sees that men see him or will see him. He knows that walls have ears and that ill deeds rebound back. Even when alone he acts as if the eyes of the whole world were upon him. For as he knows that sooner or later all will be known, so he considers those to be present as witnesses who must afterwards hear of the deed. He that wished the whole world might always see him did not mind that his neighbours could see him over their walls.

ccxcviii *Three Things go to a Prodigy.*

They are the choicest gifts of Heaven's prodigality—a fertile genius, a profound intellect, a pleasant and refined taste. To think well is good, to think right is better: 'tis the understanding of the good. It will not do for the judgment to reside in the backbone: it would be of more trouble than use. To think aright is the fruit of a reasonable nature. At twenty the will rules; at thirty the intellect; at forty the judgment. There are minds that shine in the dark like the eyes of the lynx, and are most clear where there is most darkness. Others are more adapted for the occasion: they always hit on that which suits the emergency: such a quality produces much and good; a sort of fecund felicity. In the meantime good taste seasons the whole of life.

ccxcix *Leave off Hungry.*

One ought to remove even the bowl of nectar from the lips. Demand is the measure of value. Even with regard to bodily thirst it is a mark of good taste to slake but not to quench it. Little and good is twice good. The second time comes a great falling off. Surfeit of pleasure was ever dangerous and brings down the ill-will of the Highest Powers. The only way to please is to revive the appetite by the hunger that is left. If you must excite desire, better do it by the impatience of want than by the repletion of enjoyment. Happiness earned gives double joy.

ccc In one word, be a Saint.

So is all said at once. Virtue is the link of all perfections, the centre of all the felicities. She it is that makes a man prudent, discreet, sagacious, cautious, wise, courageous, thoughtful, trustworthy, happy, honoured, truthful, and a universal Hero. Three HHH's make a man happy—Health, Holiness, and a Headpiece. Virtue is the sun of the microcosm, and has for hemisphere a good conscience. She is so beautiful that she finds favour with both God and man. Nothing is lovable but virtue, nothing detestable but vice. Virtue alone is serious, all else is but jest. A man's capacity and greatness are to be measured by his virtue and not by his fortune. She alone is all-sufficient. She makes men lovable in life, memorable after death.

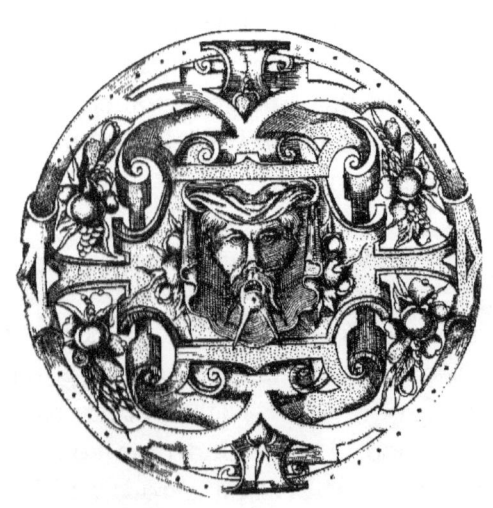

Afterword

The universal medicine for the Soul is the Supreme Reason and Absolute Justice; for the mind, mathematical and practical Truth; for the body, the Quintessence, a combination of light and gold.

ALBERT PIKE, 33°

In preparing this work, we have been equally Authors and Compilers; since we have extracted quite half its contents from the works of the best writers and most philosophic or eloquent thinkers. Perhaps it would have been better and more acceptable if we had extracted more and written less.

Still, perhaps half of it is our own; and, in incorporating here the thoughts and words of others, we have continually changed and added to the language, often intermingling, in the same sentences, our own words with theirs. It not being intended for the world at large, we have felt at liberty to make, from all accessible sources, a Compendium of Guidance, to re-mould sentences, change and add to words and phrases, combine them with our own, and use them as if they *were* our own, to be dealt with at your pleasure and so availed of as to make the whole most valuable for the purposes intended. We claim, therefore, little of the merit of authorship, and do not care to distinguish our own from that which we have taken form other sources, being quite willing that every portion of the book, in turn, may be regarded as borrowed from some old and better writer.

It is up to our readers to borrow what they would for themselves.

Field Notes

Field Notes

Field Notes

Field Notes

Field Notes

Field Notes

Field Notes